Diving into the back, Bolan yelled, "Go, go, go!"

Liao hit the gas, and the truck leaped forward. "They'll never catch us now!" he shouted.

Bolan slumped against the tailgate. His leg twitched, and he felt his phone vibrating. He dug it out and answered. "We're—"

Tokaido's voice screamed in his ear. "Missile! They've locked-on an antitank missile!"

"Stop! Right now!" Bolan yelled as he shoved the phone into his pocket and grabbed the machine gun with his other hand.

The truck skidded to a halt and, as Liao turned to him, Bolan yelled, "Incoming missile—get out now!"

Liao scrabbled at the door handle and got it open as Bolan hit the ground. He made sure Liao was racing from the truck before running himself.

Bolan saw the bright flash of a missile launch and shouted, "Hit the dirt!" as he threw himself forward.

Two seconds later, the world exploded.

DON PENDLETON'S MACK BOLAN®

LETHAL RISK

A GOLD EAGLE BOOK FROM

WORLDWIDE®

TORONTO • NEW YORK • LONDON
AMSTERDAM • PARIS • SYDNEY • HAMBURG
STOCKHOLM • ATHENS • TOKYO • MILAN
MADRID • WARSAW • BUDAPEST • AUCKLAND

Recycling programs
for this product may
not exist in your area.

First edition September 2015

ISBN-13: 978-0-373-61579-7

Special thanks and acknowledgment to
Travis Morgan for his contribution to this work.

Lethal Risk

Printed in U.S.A.

A leader is best when people barely know he exists. When his work is done, his aim fulfilled, they will say: we did it ourselves.

—Lao Tzu

A single person can change the course of history, and when one of these people needs help, I'll move heaven and earth to make it happen—and go through anyone who stands in my way.

—Mack Bolan

PROLOGUE

Edward Carstairs couldn't stop drumming his fingers on the worsted wool of his navy blue dress slacks. Barely containing his impatient sigh, he peered through the thick, gray smog at the bumper-to-bumper traffic inching along the eight-lane superhighway. Although there was still an hour before sunset, the cloud of pollution lent a hazy, unreal appearance to the world outside.

We'll never get there at this rate, he worried. "How long now?" he asked his driver in flawless Mandarin.

"Ten, fifteen minutes," the man replied.

Rolling his eyes, Carstairs ran a hand through his thinning brown hair. It was the exact same answer he'd gotten the last three times he'd asked—inflection and all—over the past forty-five minutes.

He took a deep breath, tasting the pervasive, acrid odor of Beijing's polluted air, and stared out the window, pondering what the successful completion of this assignment could mean to his career.

Carstairs had only been in China for eight weeks, and was still figuring things out at the US Embassy. So far the capital city had been a constant swirl of contradictions, delightful one day, maddening the next. But when a coded message had arrived from Washington, DC, instructing his superior to send a car and an escort with a stated "low profile" to pick up a family from an exclusive address in a gated community and bring them back to the embassy, Ambassador Balcius had picked Edward to carry out the task.

"It should be a simple pickup," he'd said. "No one knows you're coming, and the neighborhood is fairly close to your home. Your background and recent arrival make you perfect for the job, as no one has gotten a bead on you yet—at least, as far as we know. I'm sorry I can't give you more information other than the minimum need-to-know, just know that this assignment has repercussions far beyond its seeming mundanity. Above all, be careful—the government here has its hand in everything. Take nothing for granted, and above all, trust no one."

His superior's words ran through Carstairs's mind again and he patted his right pocket, feeling the small tube of metal there. If he was caught carrying it, or even worse, using it, it would be a diplomatic incident at the least, and get him expelled from the country and possibly even end his career at the worst.

But Edward Carstairs was well prepared to handle just about anything that might happen; three years in the US Army had seen to that. He would have gone into Ranger School but for the accident that had blown out his knee; however, his ASVAB score had allowed him to move to intelligence. After his four-year hitch was up, his flawless command of Mandarin made him a top recruit of the State Department, and Carstairs soon found himself swimming in the murky waters of international diplomacy on the other side of the world.

With a lurch, the traffic knot untangled itself and as quickly as they'd been blocked, the nondescript sedan sped up and took the next exit to the neighborhood and the address Carstairs was heading to. As they left the jam-packed main streets behind and entered the rarified neighborhood, his breathing quickened. He already knew that this was more than just a simple pickup—whoever he was going to collect was important to the United States, which meant there could be trouble before the night was over.

His sedan motored down wide, empty streets with homes built like Italian villas on either side. He stared, eyebrows raised, at the Western-style grounds that made the neighborhood even more surreal. To buy a house out here took *real* money, even considering China's artificially inflated economy. Whatever was going on, it was bigger than anything in which Carstairs had previously been involved.

In a few minutes the car stopped in front of a more modest, Tudor-influenced house several blocks inside the neighborhood. His driver pointed to the home. "This is address."

Carstairs looked up from his smartphone, which had confirmed his driver's words, and down the block. There was no one else in sight. His car was the only one here. "Keep the engine running. I'll be back with three other people very soon."

His driver nodded and grunted a response. Edward slipped his paper mask over his nose and mouth, then stepped out into the night air.

It was a little easier to breathe out here. Glancing up he was surprised to be able to barely make out the night sky amid the smog and light pollution. Carstairs trotted up the flagstone-inlaid walk to the large, double front doors made of some sort of exotic wood he didn't recognize, complete with a small, inset door for seeing who was outside. Scanning the area one last time, he noticed there were no lights on inside as he raised his fist and knocked on the door. There was no answer at first and Carstairs was just about to knock again when the viewing portal cracked open. A woman's eyes stared at him.

"Good evening, Mrs. Liao," Edward began, "My name is Edward Carstairs, and I am from the United States Embassy—"

He had only gotten to "United" when the portal closed and he heard locks being opened on the other side. The door cracked open just wide enough for him to enter, and a woman's hand shot out, grabbed his arm and pulled him inside.

Before he could react, Carstairs found himself standing in an opulent vestibule. The floor was white marble, and an unlit, massive, blackened-iron candelabrum hung overhead. The woman who had yanked him inside was also wearing a breathing mask, and dressed all in subdued gray and black. She was younger than he expected, somewhere around thirty years old, and clutched a dark green leather Hermès satchel purse, her only apparent nod to fashion. Two children stood in the doorway, a girl of about ten years old and a boy about eight, both wearing backpacks. The boy stared at him silently. The girl had her nose buried in some kind of portable game console.

"You are American," she said. "From the embassy?" The second sentence was practically a statement, with the barest upward inflection at the end to hint at uncertainty.

Carstairs nodded. "Yes, I've been sent to get you and your family and to take you back to our compound." He looked over the children's heads into what appeared to be a richly appointed dining room.

"Where is your husband?"

"He is—not home."

The pause in her words told him more than she could have possibly known. *He* was most likely the real target, but the United States was securing his family so the Chinese couldn't get to them and use them as leverage. "Are you ready to go?"

She nodded then turned to check her children. "Zhou, put that away. I need you to pay attention to me now." To Carstairs's surprise, the girl tucked her game into her backpack and regarded her mother and him steadily.

"All right, here's what's going to happen." Turning to the portal, Carstairs cracked it open enough to see up and down the block. His car, idling at the curb, was still the only one outside. "I'll go out first. You give me three steps, then take the children's hands and follow me. If anything happens, get them inside the car. The driver will take you to the embassy. Understand?" She nodded tightly. "All right, let's go."

Slipping his right hand into his pocket as he opened the door, Carstairs swept his practiced gaze left then right as he strode confidently outside and down the walk. Even while sending a brief, coded text to the embassy telling them he'd made the pickup, every sense was on overwatch, searching their surroundings for the slightest hint of a threat. Carstairs was aware of the woman and her children two steps behind him as they walked toward the idling car. Five steps away, four, three—

Headlights bloomed down the street as a large sedan with government plates rounded the corner and headed toward them.

"Keep moving," he said as he stood at the rear of the car, shielding her and the kids with his body. "Get inside."

Mrs. Liao did exactly that, efficiently shuttling her two children into the backseat, then sliding in after them. The sedan pulled to a stop in front of Carstairs's vehicle, and a man got out of the passenger's side. He was dressed in a simple black suit with a white shirt and black tie, and screamed government intelligence to the American. Not local police—probably someone from the Ministry of State Security.

Carstairs casually slipped his hand out of his pocket and held it at his side, fingers loosely curled to conceal what he was holding.

The man had no doubt spotted the diplomatic plates on the embassy car—and Carstairs knew that if they wanted Liao's family that badly, the plates wouldn't mean dick. Even so, he tried feigning innocence; it was possible, although improbable, that these guys had spotted the diplomatic plates and were just out for an evening shakedown.

"Can I help you?" he asked as the man walked up to him.

The man didn't answer for long seconds, his gaze raking the sedan as a tendril of smoke curled up from his crooked butt. Carstairs waited patiently, already aware that the men knew who he was and why he was there. "You are from the US Embassy." He didn't even try to make it a question.

"Yes."

"What are you doing in this neighborhood at this hour?"

Carstairs had had more than enough time to come up with a plausible cover story for this trip—as long as his accuser didn't know what was really going on. The problem was that in China, even one wrong word could be misconstrued as an insult, or even worse, evidence of something improper or illegal occurring. "I'm helping a friend of mine—Mr. Liao. He asked me to look in on his family while he's away. We're going to dinner." It was about as simple as he could make it, and reasonably plausible. The fact that he was an American might raise an eyebrow or two, but usually the weight of his being with the embassy silenced any questions.

Not, however, this time.

The man shook his head curtly. "These three are wanted for questioning by the Ministry of State Security. They will have to come with us." He turned to the car door even as Carstairs interposed himself between the man and the vehicle.

"I'm afraid that I cannot allow you to do that, sir. These people are now in a United States Embassy vehicle, and as such, are under the protection of my country."

It was a major gamble Carstairs was trying, and he knew it. He'd seen the "diplomatic protection" gambit used in a movie when he was a child, and he knew that US Navy ships were considered sovereign territory, but he wasn't aware of any official laws rendering a car to be defined as sovereign US territory. However, he was determined to play as many cards as he could before resorting to any kind of violence.

His words actually stopped the man for a moment and he regarded Carstairs with a quizzical expression. "Do not make this into trouble for yourself and your country. Surrender the three people inside to me and go home." He pushed back his rumpled coat to reveal a matte-black pistol Carstairs didn't recognize on his hip.

The novice diplomat sighed and turned to the car door. "Very well. However, I want your name and identification number, as my superiors—" Instead of reaching for the door, however, he whirled and sprayed the man in the face with his pocket pepper spray canister. The man stumbled away, coughing and clutching his face with both hands, unable to even think about drawing his gun.

Carstairs yanked open the front passenger door and got in as the driver's side door of the MSS car opened.

"Go! Get us out of here!" He turned to the woman and children in the backseat. "Get down and stay down!"

The driver put his car in Reverse and backed down the street as Carstairs turned back in time to see the MSS driver with his pistol out and aimed at them. He hunched in his seat as the flat cracks of the firing pistol were heard over the racing car engine. The front windshield starred as a bullet hit it, but it didn't penetrate, ricocheting off into the night.

Carstairs's driver backed onto a side street and slammed the car to a stop, then put it into gear and rocketed them forward as he turned toward the highway. Carstairs glanced behind them to see the headlights of the MSS sedan in the distance, gaining rapidly.

If we can just make the highway, we can probably lose them... But even as the thought materialized, the sedan caught up with them, looming even larger in their rear windshield. Underneath it huddled Mrs. Liao and her children, all staring at him with wide, frightened eyes. Carstairs noted that they all had their seat belts on, which was good, since the possibility of an accident was high now.

The sedan rammed them from behind, making the embassy car shake and lurch forward. The Chinese sedan accelerated, pulling alongside the car on Carstairs's side. Now, unfortunately, the driver could shoot at them if he wished, but instead he jerked his steering wheel sharply, slamming his car into theirs and making his driver fight for control.

"Ram him back!" Carstairs ordered. His driver slowed a bit, allowing the MSS car to pull ahead. But just when Carstairs thought the enemy car was going to cut them off, his driver flicked the wheel, sending their car into the other's rear quarter panel. The expertly executed pit maneuver made the MSS car skid and swerve wildly out of control. It crossed in front of Carstairs's car, close enough that he could see the driver's furious face as he struggled to avoid crashing. Then they were past, and his car was accelerating up the entrance ramp to merge with the busy but flowing evening traffic.

Still breathing hard, Carstairs checked behind them for any signs of pursuit, but no battered black sedan came flying up from an off-ramp after them. He took a deep breath, aware that his pounding heartbeat was starting to slow, and checked on Mrs. Liao and her children. They all seemed to be all right, although the boy had tears running down his face, even though he had never made a sound.

"It's all right. We're taking you back to the US Embassy, where you'll be safe—" Even as he said that, Edward felt the car swerve suddenly. He turned to find them taking an unfamiliar off-ramp.

"Where are we going?" he asked.

"Accident ahead. Taking detour," his driver answered.

Carstairs blinked at that answer, even as he pulled out his smartphone. A hand covering it made him look up in surprise.

"Do not use. Ministry agents track you through it," the driver said.

"Oh. Okay. Just get us back to the embassy as quickly as possible."

"Yes, of course."

But as they drove on, Carstairs's instincts alerted him that something was wrong. He glanced at the driver, who navigated the cramped side streets with ease. There was nothing outwardly remarkable about him—just another Chinese national who had gotten a job driving for one of the many embassies in Beijing, a highly prized position in the city. And yet... Carstairs began reviewing the events of the evening.

He hadn't seemed surprised by the two men at Liao's house, he thought. However, as the ambassador had said, the government had its hand in most everything here, so perhaps it just wasn't that surprising to see them following a US Embassy car with diplomatic plates.

But what about that pit maneuver? That was more uncommon, as was the way he had handled the chase in general.

Glancing at the man again, Carstairs was surprised to see part of a tattoo, consisting of Chinese characters, on his forearm. "That's a nice tattoo. What does it mean?"

His driver glanced down, then sidelong at the American before replying. "'Loyalty to the nation.'"

His words sent a chill through Carstairs. While that could have been any loyal young Chinese's man's symbol of dedication to his country, he knew that particular tattoo had special meaning for those in the Chinese military.

The phrase had become famous since the twelfth century when a Chinese army general named Yue Fei had quit his post and returned home, only to be scolded by his mother for leaving his post and abandoning his duty to his country. According to legend, she had tattooed that exact same phrase on his back, and he had returned to duty, becoming one of China's most celebrated warriors.

To this day, many lifelong military recruits, especially among the younger generations, got the same tattoo as a symbol of their fidelity to the military and the People's Liberation Army in particular. Carstairs had become aware of it during his studies of Chinese military history.

Shit, he's military intelligence!

Carstairs slid his hand around the pepper spray again and waited for the opportunity to strike. He had one shot at surprising the man, who was probably equally trained in hand-to-hand combat as he was, maybe better.

Ahead, a small traffic jam made the driver slow the vehicle as a motorcycle rickshaw had collided with a panel truck. The accident blocked the entire street and traffic was at a standstill. The moment the car pulled to a stop, Carstairs made his move.

Flipping up the safety cover, he brought the container out of his pocket and blasted the driver in the face. But instead of screaming and trying to protect himself, the Chinese man shoved his arm up, deflecting the tear gas spray into the roof. Quicker than Carstairs could react, he brought his left arm over, grabbed the wrist of Carstairs's canister-holding hand and twisted it toward the windshield. The chemical was having some effect—his eyes were red and watering, and his nose was dripping, as well—but the man didn't seem incapacitated in the least.

He's had chemical desensitizing, Carstairs realized before a fist streaked toward his face. The blow was off balance and startled him more than doing any real damage. His head bounced off the door window, and he managed to throw his left arm up to block the second punch coming his way.

The pain in his wrist was increasing, but Carstairs

managed to turn the canister toward the man's face and blast him again. Although the chemicals didn't faze him, the buffeting spray did make him instinctively turn his face away, which was what Carstairs had wanted.

Plucking the canister out of his pinned hand, he smashed it into the driver's face, feeling the man's cheekbone break with a palpable *snap*. Carstairs didn't let up; driving the end of the plastic-and-metal device into the side of the man's face, ignoring his weakening attempts to fend him off.

Finally, when the driver was bloody and semiconscious, and no longer an immediate threat, Carstairs reached across, opened the driver's door and shoved him into the street.

Sliding into the driver's seat and trying not to cough at the lingering wisps of gas, he put the car in Reverse and began backing up to the nearest intersection. Fortunately there was no one behind him.

"What was all that? Why did you do that to him?" Mrs. Liao asked.

"He was Chinese military," Carstairs said between coughs. "Whatever your husband has done, a lot of people want him really bad—"

As he said that, they reached the intersection and were immediately flooded with bright white floodlights. Carstairs had just enough time to look over when the car was broadsided by a huge truck. The impact sent them flying across the intersection and into the side street, where the car landed on its roof.

Flung around by the crash, Carstairs found himself lying on the ceiling of the overturned car, a heavy tightness compressing his chest. He tasted blood. One eye was swelling shut and a dull pain bloomed in his ribs. Even so, he knew he had to get Mrs. Liao and her children out and away before more soldiers came. He tried to move, but found himself pinned by the seat. He looked around for his phone but couldn't see it nearby.

Footsteps crunched on the shattered glass from the window and Carstairs looked out to see a pair of wing tips standing next to the wrecked sedan.

Sets of combat boots appeared next to the shoes and a face leaned down to look in at him in surprise. "The American is still alive."

"Kill him and collect the others," came a curt reply. "Make it look like the car accident did it."

The man looking in on him produced a pistol and turned it around so he was holding it by the barrel. Trapped and unable to move, Edward Carstairs watched as, without a word, the Chinese soldier began crawling toward him, pistol held at the ready to bash his skull in.

CHAPTER ONE

"Well, it just goes to show that you can always trust the State Department to take what should be a simple extraction job and screw up the entire thing."

Mission controller Barbara Price stared at Hal Brognola, director of the Sensitive Operations Group, based at Stony Man Farm, for a long moment before shaking her head. "Coming down a bit hard on State, aren't you, Hal? It's one thing to dodge the local police, or even the ministry. It's another thing to go up against the Chinese military—"

The gruff man sitting across from her snatched the chewed-to-death cigar from his mouth and used it like a big, brown exclamation point as he interrupted her. "Whenever an officer of the United States government is performing his duty in what is perceived as a foreign environment, which by nature should be considered potentially hostile, all necessary precautions must be taken to ensure his safety as well as the safety of those he comes into contact with."

Brognola stuck the remains of the unlit cigar back into a corner of his mouth. "Above all, the embassy should not send out just one man to collect the family of the biggest potential defector since Tretyakov! Now it's turned into the largest screwup since Wang Lijun!"

"The hero police chief of Chonqing City, who was

also investigated for the organ transplant facility he founded—"

"Organ transplant facility, my ass," Brognola interrupted again. "Those butchers are harvesting the insides of political prisoners like the Falun Gong and selling them to the highest bidder. They conveniently get rid of their 'protestors' once and for all, and make a tidy profit to boot. Wang tried to buy his way into the US with a trove of documents implicating several high-ranking Chinese officials. Supposedly, although we were never able to confirm this, those documents were instrumental in taking down power politician Bo Xilai. And when State gets the chance to pull in someone who'd make Wang's knowledge look like peanuts, they bungle the whole thing from the start. Now he's in the wind *and* nobody knows where the family went! Balcius will be lucky to keep his job after all this. Not to mention we have to go in and somehow clean up this unholy mess."

"Well, we're good at that," Price reminded him.

"I know, I know. But Striker's going to have to stay so far under the radar on this one he might as well tunnel into Beijing. We can't afford to let this spiral into an international incident. We're just lucky the Chinese also want to keep this as quiet as we do. The black eye on relations between the two countries would take years to fade."

Price looked down at her tablet, hiding a smile. She didn't blame Brognola for his irascible attitude. As the Farm's liaison to the President and a head honcho at the Justice Department, the big Fed had to wade into the alphabet soup that was Washington, DC, on a daily basis to try to glean whatever useful intel he could from the multitude of often-bickering departments on the Hill.

"What's Striker's ETA?"

"We sent him the Priority One message—" Price consulted her watch "—nine minutes ago. I'm sure Cowboy and he are double-timing it back." She referred to John "Cowboy" Kissinger, the Farm's premier weaponsmith.

As if in confirmation of her statement, her tablet pinged with a message from Akira Tokaido, a top hacker and member of the Farm's cyber team.

Striker inbound. Coming your way in 10 seconds.

"He's on his way here right now," she confirmed, making sure her presentation was ready.

They both looked up as Mack Bolan, aka the Executioner, strode into the War Room carrying a ceramic mug. "Barbara. Hal," he said, greeting each of them with a nod.

As he slid into a high-backed leather chair, Bolan blew on the mug of steaming coffee and sipped it cautiously, grimacing as he swallowed. "Just when I thought I was used to Bear's brew, he changes it up on me." He glanced at Brognola with a raised eyebrow. "Sure you don't want a cup, Hal? It'll take the edge off."

"Bear" was Aaron Kurtzman, who was as good with making Stony Man's computers do everything but sit up and dance as he was bad at brewing remotely drinkable coffee.

"Yeah, that and ten years off my life." Brognola had already pulled out the other indispensable aid he was never without, a roll of antacid tablets, and thumbed a pair into his mouth. "Keep that damn cup as far away from me as possible. The smell's bad enough. I'd hate to have to actually drink it."

Despite the potentially top-secret materials they were about to discuss, Price watched the two men sparring with an internal grin. Between them, Bolan and Brognola had carried the fight for justice and freedom to all four corners of the globe, and knew each other better than any person alive. Even she wasn't privy to all parts of their relationship, which was fine by her. Some things were best left alone.

"Barbara, why don't you fill Striker in on the mess we've found ourselves in, courtesy of those jackasses over at State?"

Barely resisting rolling her eyes, Price exchanged an it's-gonna-be-one-of-those-days glances with Bolan as she started her program deck.

On the large flat-screen monitor at the end of the room, a man's face appeared in a candid shot taken as he was walking down a busy street. He was Chinese, dressed in an expensive suit, and had the look of some-one who appeared at ease on the surface but carrying a heavy internal load.

"Three months ago, a midlevel employee at our US Embassy in Beijing was approached by a man claim-ing to work at the highest levels of the Chinese govern-ment," Price began. "He wanted to defect to the United States with his family, and was willing to provide a vast amount of information on everything China is involved in, from their military plans for the rest of South Asia and beyond, to top-secret economic programs being ex-ecuted around the world."

Bolan frowned. "Almost seems too good to be true. Who is he?"

"Zhang Liao. A career politician, his family's made its fortune at the top of the Chinese government for the past four generations," Price replied. "The Liao family has showed a particular aptitude for reading the political winds and shifting with them. No member has ever been caught in a scandal or punished as part of a change in the government. They even survived the incident in Tiananmen Square with their reputation intact, when most of the rest of the government suffered from the fallout."

"So why the sudden change of heart?" Bolan asked.

"Liao said that he feared the course the current government was taking would lead inexorably to war, whether that be with Taiwan, or any of a half-dozen other countries, over the Spratly Islands, or the recent dustup with Vietnam over territorial waters, or even Japan, which has been flexing its military muscle recently, most likely to avoid the appearance of weakness. He even brought up the possibility of a military plan that could eventually bring in the other superpowers. He didn't divulge any more details, but said he could provide proof that China was taking steps to expand its influence and power over the other countries in the region and beyond."

"No kidding." Brognola grunted. "The buildup of the Chinese military on the Indian border has the Indians alternately rattling sabers one minute while selling them trade goods the next. And the Chinese are practically buying Africa wholesale as it is, pouring billions into power grid and other infrastructure projects and dams in the interior. Those poor nations who think they're getting a great deal right now don't understand the bill that will come due afterward. The Chinese are masters of the long game—they don't do anything without factoring in the ramifications years from now."

While Bolan listened to Brognola, his eyes hadn't left the picture of Liao's face. "I assume standard verification and cross-referencing protocols were followed?"

"To the letter. Everything he starting feeding us to prove his bona-fides checked out," Price said. "He gave us advance intel on troop movements for a buildup near Tibet pending a new crackdown on independence seekers there, and was also able to give us their previously unseen action plan for Taiwan, which involves them taking control of the country within the next decade."

"Not much of a surprise there," Bolan replied. "Any half-decent analyst could sift what we already know and come up with the same conclusion."

"Yeah, but predicting's one thing. Proof is something else entirely," Brognola said. "This guy could give us enough intel to blunt or at least slow the intended Chi-Com advance across Asia for the next couple of decades."

The corner of Bolan's mouth quirked up at the old reference to the Chinese Communist Party. "Okay, so where is he?"

"He's missing," Price stated. "Although State claims they followed every protocol and procedure by the book—" Price couldn't resist glancing at Brognola to see if he was going to chime in, but he held his peace "—the scheduled attempt to take him into US custody and begin the asylum process never got started. He was supposed to lose any government watchers and enter our embassy secretly three days ago. He never showed."

"Are we sure that State didn't just get cold feet again, like they did with Wang Lijun?" Bolan asked. "As I recall, the US turned down his asylum request because the government didn't want to embarrass the Chinese so close to their VP's visit to the States. Isn't it possible this is along those same lines, and now State's just covering its ass?"

"I could go along with that, if what I'm about to tell you hadn't happened two nights ago," Brognola said around his unlit cigar. "With typical State ham-fistedness, they sent one guy out to pick up his family."

An American face appeared on the screen with vitals listed next to it. "Edward Carstairs. Good man, ex-Army, smart as hell, 99th percentile on his AFQT, but new to the region," the big Fed continued. "The suits thought he'd be perfect, since he wasn't known to anyone there yet. He made the pickup of Liao's family—the embassy got a verified text from his phone, and also traced it to Liao's home address two nights ago, but they never made it back."

Price brought up the next slide, showing a totaled sedan that had been T-boned with a vengeance. "The official story is that the car was in an accident—which fits at first glance. Except the usual driver of the car was missing and hasn't been seen anywhere since. Carstairs's body was the only one found at the scene, although hairs and fiber samples showed there were at least two other people in the car with him."

Bolan's gaze had narrowed at the news. "How did he die?"

"Our embassy sent out a press release stating that he died in a car accident," Price replied. "Forensic autopsy showed he suffered multiple blunt force traumas to the head, causing a cerebral edema that ultimately killed him." She paused for a moment before continuing. "Bruises on his hands and arms showed that he attempted to defend himself during the assault."

"The bastards beat him to death," Bolan said.

"I'm afraid so," Price confirmed. "The whereabouts of Liao's family is currently unknown."

"And what are we supposed to do about it?"

"Officially, nothing, of course—even for us," Brognola

said then took a deep breath. "Unofficially, the President wants one man to go in, locate Liao's family *and* him *and* get them all out of the country."

"One person?"

Brognola nodded. "That's right. But wait, it gets better. Although the White House has classified Liao a Priority One target, I've been ordered not to give you any backup or even support while you're in-country. The potential risk of trace-back to assets in the US, or to any in-place assets is deemed too high, so you'll be completely on your own. No extraction if the op gets blown and no aid if you get caught. I raised as much holy hell as I could, but the Man is holding firm.

"You have to be false flagged, in case you're caught, so the blowback will be aimed at another country. Given your knowledge of the language, I think we'll have to go Russian, maybe even Georgian. An operative tasked with getting to Liao before the US does."

Bolan snorted. "That cover won't hold up to a sneeze. There's no way the Georgians would be able to penetrate Chinese intelligence that deeply. Assuming that we're going forward, we'd best make this come straight down from Moscow. At the very least, if it did get exposed, it might make the President feel a little more paranoid about his neighbor to the east, and vice versa."

"Of course, you're going to do your damnedest not to get caught."

"As always," Bolan replied. "Besides, I've heard enough about Chinese prisons that I have no desire to see what one looks like up close." He watched as Price and Brognola exchanged glances. "What?"

"Well, regardless of whether you want to or not, you're heading into a Chinese prison anyway." The mission controller flipped to another slide. "We've located Liao—inside Qincheng Prison."

Bolan stared at the overhead satellite view of the prison built with cooperation from the Soviets during the 1950s. "Well, at least they won't suspect anyone trying to break into the place."

"Yes, that may be your only advantage," Price said. "Bear and Akira are working up an infiltration plan as we speak. They'll work this mission exclusively."

"Well, then, there isn't much else to say, is there?"

Bolan put both hands on the table and started to rise, but caught Brognola's troubled look. "If you chomp that cigar any harder, Hal, you'll end up eating half of it. What's on your mind?"

To her surprise, Price saw something very rare—a hesitant reply from Hal Brognola. "Striker, you can always refuse this mission. We've done a lot over the years, you and me. Pounded a lot of ground, kicked in a lot of doors."

"And did a lot of good along the way, too," Bolan reminded him.

The big Fed nodded. "I know, I know. And normally, I'd be the first person backing you wherever you needed to go to complete the mission. I get it, and I get the risks you and the others take every time you're in the field. But this one…" He spread his hands helplessly. "I just have a bad feeling about it. You're sticking your head right into the dragon's maw, and all by your lonesome, too. Shit, I don't even think the embassy can help you if you get in a jam over there. You can say no."

"Hal, you know I wouldn't refuse a mission the President thinks is important. And if the intelligence this man can deliver gives us the edge in dealing with the Chinese

—and can prevent them from starting a war in the region—then it's worth the risk," Bolan replied. "I've executed enough missions with minimal equipment going in before. Besides, it's Beijing. I'm sure there's a thriving black market that will supply me with everything I need at only modestly exorbitant prices."

"Be that as it may, Striker, this whole thing is starting to stink to me. We should consider the possibility that this is a trap, that this Liao could be a double-agent dangled in front of the US in the hope of catching us in the act."

"Hal—" Bolan regarded the big Fed soberly for a moment "—I go into just about every foreign country thinking someone's gunning for me, because usually someone is. But the day I let that stop me from doing what we think is right is the day I hang it up for good."

"All right, I've said my piece." Brognola turned to Price. "Do you have anything to add?"

The Farm's mission controller cleared her throat. "Given the potential difficulties of you not having access to your usual assets in the field, I've taken the liberty of working up a mission profile that would at least have you working with someone over there that could ease your way. He would have to travel as a tourist and rendezvous with you in the city itself—"

"If you're going to say John Trent's name, forget it," Bolan interrupted her. "He almost got killed in one of Stony Man's ops. I'm not saying he wouldn't help, but it's pretty clear to me that the President would pitch a fit if he even got a whiff of a civilian being involved. It wouldn't matter anyway. This one's too big for John, and that's not a slight. It's going to have to be me—and me alone—going in."

Price grinned as part of Brognola's tortured cigar hit the conference table.

"Don't worry, Hal. I'll be back before you know it. The good news in all this is that they have no idea I'm coming. If Liao is already in custody, they probably think the matter's over already. You'd be surprised at how much I can get done in those circumstances. Just make sure that cover jacket is airtight. The last thing we need is anyone in China getting even a hint that there's a US operative in their midst."

Price slid a flash drive across the table to him. "This contains all of the data that Bear and Akira have been able to find so far. It's a thirteen-hour flight from DC to Moscow, where you'll officially launch from, so hopefully they'll be able to ascertain where Liao's family is being held in that time. Do you have any questions?"

"Just one," the Executioner replied. "When do I leave?"

CHAPTER TWO

Zhang Liao's eyes fluttered open and he blinked at the soft white light shining down on him from the ceiling.

Turning his face away from the glow, he licked his dry lips and tried to swallow through a parched throat. His mouth also tasted sour and fuzzy, as though he'd been asleep for a long time. His head was pounding and slow, too, as if he'd just tied several on at the bar before going home. Liao didn't drink, however—a rarity among Chinese. He preferred to keep his mind sharp to navigate the intricate corridors of power and deals within deals he had been trained to handle since he was a teenager.

So, if he hadn't had anything to drink…what had happened to him? The last thing he remembered was leaving his office for what would have been the last time…

The embassy!

He was supposed to be going to the US Embassy to defect, but something had happened on the way… He had been jostled by a stranger, and that was the last thing he could remember.

Reaching up to touch his forehead as he tried to recall what had happened to him, Liao got another surprise upon seeing his bare arm, which was usually dressed in an English-cut, button-down Oxford shirt. His eyes widened in surprise when he looked down to realize he was now dressed in a paper-thin hospital gown.

His gaze traveled the rest of the room, taking in the metal-framed hospital bed he was laying on, the sterile, bare walls surrounding him, the door that appeared to lead to a small washroom, the safety-wired glass window with drawn curtains, and the security-locked, handleless door that was keeping him from leaving. Instinctively he sucked in a breath of the slightly metallic-tasting air as he realized that wherever he was, he was a prisoner.

He looked down to the left at a cheap pressboard nightstand next to his bed, and right, where a wheeled tray sat with what looked like a call button on it. With cold fear starting to swirl in the pit of his stomach, Liao tested his legs and found that they worked just fine. Swinging them over the side, he got up, steadied himself as a wave of dizziness crashed over him, and walked to the washroom.

Everything in here was either stainless steel—like the toilet and sink, which were both bolted to the wall—or plastic, like the water cup, which was so flimsy it couldn't be used for anything other than its intended purpose. Liao drank two cups of flat, warm water, and washed his mouth out with another cupful. He splashed some water on his face, feeling somewhat refreshed at the wet sensation, then dried himself with the small rough-cotton cloth sitting on the side of the sink.

With nothing left to do, he returned to the bed and sat. Spotting the window again, he got up and walked over to it, moving the blinds aside just enough to peek out.

As he'd feared, it didn't show the outdoors. Instead it looked out onto a drab hallway, where men and women in drab-colored scrubs bustled back and forth down the corridor. One additional thing that he knew most hospitals didn't have: the armed guard standing outside his door.

What is this place? he wondered. *Where am I?*

Just then the door clicked and swung inward, making him scoot back toward the bed. A man in a doctor's white coat and dark maroon scrubs walked in, followed by the armed guard he had seen outside his room. The doctor, carrying a computer tablet under his arm, was probably a decade younger than him, his black hair already receding from his forehead buzzed short so he didn't have to worry about it. The guard was even younger, maybe midtwenties and, from what Liao could see, in excellent physical shape. He was also well armed, with a holstered black pistol on the belt at his waist and a stubby submachine gun hanging from a strap over his shoulder. He stood stiffly just inside the door and never took his eyes off Liao.

"Mr. Liao, so good to see you awake!" the doctor said in Cantonese, forcing Liao to focus on him. "I hope you have been comfortable during your stay."

Liao frowned at the man's seemingly easy manner. "Who are you? Where am I? What is going on here?" He rose from the bed as he asked the last question, making the guard step forward.

Without turning, the doctor raised his hand, gesturing for the guard stop in his tracks.

His expression sobered and he motioned for Liao to sit.

"Very well. You wish answers, and there is no reason to keep them from you. I am Dr. Chen Xu, head of surgery here at the Guaw Li transplant facility. You are Zhang Liao, a government employee turned traitor and attempted defector. Instead of holding a trial, which could prove very embarrassing to the government, they have delivered you to me."

"What?" Liao's heart sank. "There must be some mistake," he said, his brow creasing in confusion.

The doctor smiled. "Oh, no. If you are brought here, then there was a very good reason. But do not worry about trying to contact anyone. This facility has been built over the past decade at great cost and secrecy, to avoid public embarrassments like what has happened with other facilities of the same type."

"And what is to happen now?" Liao asked, even though he had a terrifying feeling he knew the answer.

Xu consulted his tablet, flicking through screens with his finger. "Well, we still have to run a few tests to get a sense of just how healthy you are—your blood work came back with excellent results, by the way." He looked down at Liao and all trace of human warmth or compassion was gone from his demeanor. "And once those are completed to our satisfaction, we will sedate you and harvest as many of your internal organs as possible."

Liao stared at the doctor for a long moment. He'd heard what the man said, but it was as if his brain refused to comprehend the words. His mouth opened and closed as he struggled to come to terms with what was going on. "But…you can't…what about my family?"

Xu checked his watch, as casually as if making sure he wasn't running behind in his appointments. "By now, they are no doubt in the hands of the Ministry of State Security. But do not worry, Mr. Liao, you will provide a far greater service to your country and its people in death than you ever did in life."

He turned and began walking to the door, temporarily blocking the guard's view of the prisoner.

Blind, unreasoning rage suddenly filled Liao. If what the doctor had said was true—if his family was captured, and him slated to die, with no one possibly knowing where he was and what had happened to him—then he might as well take at least one of them with him.

Liao launched himself off the bed at the doctor's back. He leaped on the doctor and bore him to the floor, his clutching fingers seeking the other man's neck. If he could just get his hands around the smug bastard's throat—

Blinding white stars exploded in his vision and Liao blinked them away, only to find himself lying on the floor, clutching his head. The guard stood over him, his pistol aimed at his face.

"Stop! Do not fire!" Xu said as he picked himself up and straightened his disheveled lab coat. "I do not hold your actions against you, Mr. Liao. In your circumstances, I cannot be sure I would not have reacted in much the same way to this news. I am sure that, given a choice, you would not have wanted it to end this way. However, sometimes we do not have a choice in what happens to us.

"Double the guard on this room, and no one is to attend to him alone," the doctor said to the guard as he left.

Pistol still aimed at Liao's face, the guard slowly walked backward to the door and exited, leaving the man bruised, sore and very much alone.

For the next several hours all he did was lie on the floor and weep softly.

CHAPTER THREE

Forty-one hours after the briefing at Stony Man Farm, Mack Bolan sat in the back of a fifty-year-old, olive-drab military truck among a load of crated, bright green melons as it jounced along narrow mountain roads toward the outskirts of Beijing.

Unlike most insertions, this one had been much more difficult. There had to be absolutely no trace back to any US military involvement, which scratched most of the usual methods, such as a HALO drop into the boonies. There was no way the United States was going to risk sending an aircraft into Chinese airspace—it would most likely bring their air force and army down on him.

A commercial flight had been out of the question, as well. Even with an airtight cover, once he began moving through Beijing, any police attention would quickly trace him back to his entry into the country. Even if he had taken a trip through Europe, they would have backtracked him to the United States.

In the end Bolan had hopped on a commercial airliner to Moscow, changed his identity there and then caught a local flight to Irkutsk International Airport, in the middle of Russia. From there, he had taken a dizzying array of transportation modes—including a two-hundred-mile cab ride and a six-hour stretch in the back of a horse-drawn wagon—before reaching Beijing. He'd crossed

Mongolia entirely; every time his Russian passport had seen him through.

Bolan had been careful to keep any answers to questions short and to the point. He didn't have a native Russian accent, and didn't want to give any customs officers a reason to suspect he was anything more than he was pretending to be: an ordinary Russian businessman traveling to the east.

It wasn't the most perfect—or direct—plan, but it had gotten him here. Stiff from the many hours of sitting on things from a too short metal bench seat to a wooden wagon bed, he took a moment to stretch, careful not to dislodge any of the harvest surrounding him. Running on about ten hours of sleep total, he was still feeling pretty decent.

Bolan took a deep breath, feeling oddly naked at the moment and even more oddly free. The President had been so paranoid that he hadn't allowed him any of his usual devices to maintain contact with Stony Man. Since he was in one of the largest cities on Earth, he would have to purchase off-the-shelf items to use for communication. What he did have, in a concealed belt around his waist, was Chinese yuan, and plenty of them. Buying most of his gear wouldn't be a problem. Using it to find four needles in a gigantic haystack containing more than twenty-two million pieces of hay—*that* was going to be a problem.

And then, springing them out of wherever they were being held—another problem. Nothing exactly insurmountable, but definitely a challenge. And one Bolan was absolutely up for.

In fact, he felt as disconnected to the rest of the world as possible at the moment, a ghost floating through landscapes and small towns and villages, with no primary base of operations, no backup…and little to no options if he was captured. It was a strangely heady feeling, relying primarily on his skills and wits to sustain him.

The truck slowed and a fist thumped against the back of the cab. That was the driver's signal—relayed through guessing and pantomime—for Bolan to climb up on top of the old 4x4, as they would be coming to a checkpoint soon. When the driver had stopped for Bolan, who had been walking at the side of the road after hitching a ride with three half-stoned college students on a driving tour through Asia, he'd blinked at Bolan's attempt to tell his story—a stuck traveler trying to get to Beijing—and paid far more attention to the fistful of money Bolan had held out. He had scrutinized the Executioner carefully, then nodded as he fired off another burst of incomprehensible Mandarin. After a few minutes Bolan had gathered that he wasn't supposed to have any passengers, so he would have to climb on top when the time came, which was now.

The soldier stood, careful to balance himself against the rocking truck, and headed to the open back. As he did, he wondered idly where the farmer had gotten hold of a battered and patched deuce-and-a-half.

Probably cut a deal with someone unloading surplus military hardware after Vietnam, he thought. Climbing onto the tailgate, he steadied himself against the side for a moment, then reached up and grabbed the flapping canvas roof. He pulled himself up and threw a leg over, then rolled on top, careful to situate himself between two of the metal framing ribs that gave the covering its shape. Lying down would also conceal him from any guards on the ground. Pulling out a knockoff Chicago Cubs baseball cap, he jammed it onto his head, counting on the brim to help conceal his face from security cameras.

The canvas was sun-faded and worn, but held his weight without difficulty. The truck lumbered on for a few more miles, with Bolan enjoying the spring sunlight after almost two days of being cooped up in cramped airplane seats and huddled on narrow benches. He was hungry, too—the last time he'd eaten was about twelve hours ago—and looked forward to getting a bite once they reached the city proper.

As they got closer to Beijing, Bolan noticed the smell first—a thick, acrid odor indicating they had reached the edge of the pollution zone around the city. The surrounding landscape was beginning to change from the foothills that had slowly fallen away from the mountains to the north to long sections of plains interspersed with rolling hills. Signs of habitation were becoming more common as well, with small clusters of single-room homes next to gardens or fields.

The farmer had let Bolan know that he'd be stopping on the outskirts of the city, far from its center. Given how sprawling Beijing was, Bolan knew he was at least an hour from the main city, perhaps two or more. He hoped he'd be able to find a ride into the neighborhood he needed to reach. A Caucasian hitchhiking along the road would definitely attract the wrong kind of attention.

With a grinding of worn gears and a belch of black smoke as the farmer downshifted, the truck began slowing. Bolan risked lifting his head just enough to see what they were approaching. He caught the glimpse of a large, metal-roofed, open pavilion that stretched across the entire highway, with a narrow, long building on one side. It was manned not by the standard police, but by what looked like camouflage-clad soldiers carrying assault rifles.

Damn! Bolan dropped back down, wondering if somehow the military was already on to him. The reams of data Kurtzman and Tokaido had provided had said nothing about the military manning city checkpoints.

The truck was about two hundred yards from the checkpoint and pulling into a line. Bolan gauged the height of the roof as he kept an eye on vehicles being inspected before they were allowed to move ahead. He couldn't get caught here, before his mission had even really started.

His hope that they were doing a cursory inspection was dashed when a panel truck's roof and underbody was checked with mirrors on poles. The next few minutes passed agonizingly slowly. There were only two positives to the situation. The first was that the soldiers seemed inclined to stay under the shade of the metal roof. The second was that most cars were content to pass the large truck and move through one of the other faster-moving lanes. Bolan divided his attention between the guards ahead and the traffic behind him. It wouldn't do to be spotted by several civilians on their way to work.

By now the roofed structure loomed large in his vision; they would be driving under it in the next few minutes. Bolan wondered if the old farmer was sweating as much as he was at the moment, and what he would say if they detected the stowaway atop his vehicle. He wasn't going to let that happen if he could avoid it, however.

He saw cameras mounted at the corners of the building and cursed. They appeared to be aimed below him, but he couldn't be sure. *Maybe I should have stayed inside with the melons,* he thought, although the odds of escaping detection there were nonexistent—the guards were doing a thorough job of checking larger vehicles.

By now he was only a few yards away from the roof, which had at least a three-foot gap between the truck's roof and the bottom of the building's roof. He was going to have to jump up and swing himself onto it as fast as he could. Any slip-up or hesitation and his mission would be over before it ever really began.

Rising to his hands and knees, Bolan positioned his feet on the nearest metal strut and cast a glance behind him to make sure that no one was watching the truck roof. Five yards…four…three…two… Now!

In one fluid movement he exploded up in a perfectly timed leap. Catching the edge of the roof, he kicked his leg over, rolled onto it and over toward the center. The entire action had taken maybe two seconds.

When he was a few yards in, Bolan flattened himself against the hot metal and listened for any shouts of alarm or honking horns. When he heard no alerts that he had been detected, he rose to a crouch and carefully crept to the other side, listening for the deuce-and-a-half's diesel engine, laboring at idle underneath him.

The truck inspection seemed to take forever, and Bolan kept glanced back, expecting a shout as a uniformed soldier popped up to arrest him. No one came, however, and eventually he heard the truck's gears grind as it lurched into motion. Now came the second problem —getting back onto its roof without attracting attention. Ideally, the guards would be facing the incoming traffic, and the other drivers would be more concerned with the soldiers than watching for the unusual sight of a man dropping from the pavilion roof onto an ancient military truck.

The old vehicle pulled out from under the roof and Bolan jumped as soon as he saw the cargo roof. He landed with a bounce, and tried to keep himself as flat as possible, splaying his body as the truck drove away from the checkpoint.

That was too close of an escape, and way too far from my objective, he thought as the skyscrapers of Beijing gradually became visible through the haze of pollution. I'm going to have to disembark and find less conspicuous transportation.

He began looking for a good spot to get off the truck and head into the suburbs.

CHAPTER FOUR

"Jesus H..." Hal Brognola tilted his head back and let the breath he'd been holding out in a long, steady stream. "Nearly scratched the whole op before it even started. That would have been embarrassing as hell."

Just because the US government had forbidden Stony Man from assisting its man on the ground didn't mean they weren't going to keep an eye on him. Using a network of satellites orbiting the globe, the Farm could pinpoint Bolan's exact location within a five-minute window. The satellite imagery was so crystal clear that they could read magazine print over someone's shoulder if they had to.

Stony Man Farm had some of the most advanced technology in the world, including specialized computers used to advance weapons the likes of which the US military could only dream about, and yet all of that was worthless because of the parameters of their current mission.

Brognola and Price were standing in the Computer Room behind Aaron Kurtzman and Akira Tokaido, members of Stony Man's top-notch cyber team. Kurtzman, a burly, bearded man confined to a wheelchair, had a no-nonsense attitude that could rival Brognola's on a bad day. Tokaido was a laid-back twenty-something Japanese American who lived and breathed the twenty-first-century computing systems he worked with. They could do things with a computer that Price and Brognola could only dream about. But right now, they couldn't do the one thing the mission controller desperately wanted to happen—somehow reach out through the monitors and wireless signals and burst transmissions to help Mack Bolan.

That was one of the worst things about being the mission controller: having to sit there, safe and sound, in a comfortable room in the United States and watch good men risk their lives fighting against the very worst kind of evil, whether it be terrorists, dictators or even the countless spying eyes of an entire nation's government, as was happening right in front of her.

And the worst part was that if something went wrong, there wasn't much Price could do about it. Sure, she could bring in reinforcements—usually—but that didn't take away the agony of waiting and wondering if they were going to come out alive this time.

And the mingled anticipation and dread of knowing that the next time, they might not. While Price was an expert at weighing the risks and rewards of any given mission, the fact remained that although she didn't look as if she was ever reacting to any of the various Stony Man operations around the world, the truth was that they always affected her, from the moment they began until the moment they ended.

But she was a professional, and the men who undertook missions for Stony Man were counting on her to do her job, which she took a lot of pride in doing very well. And she would be damned if she let them down even once—even if she had been specifically ordered not to assist.

Right now her lips were pressed tightly together and her arms folded across her chest as she watched Bolan evade the armed guards at the city checkpoint. "And why didn't we know about these increased security measures?"

Tokaido brought up a two-week-old news article on his thirty-five-inch monitor. "Because there are no accompanying pictures with the data. The article simply stated that specially trained police officers had been assigned to the checkpoints around Beijing. We had no idea they were sending the equivalent of Chinese SWAT team members to stand around and check cars."

Price nodded, although she would have made someone's head roll if this had been a critical mistake. It sounded as though there simply hadn't been a reason to follow up on a relatively innocuous bit of intel. Once again, she was reminded of the hazards of accepting things at face value, particularly when an item in question was on the other side of the world.

"This is flat-out ridiculous, Hal," she said. "There must be something more we can do from here."

As she spoke, Price noticed Kurtzman and Tokaido exchange a swift glance before returning their attentions to their stations.

"And that would be what?" Brognola popped two antacid tablets. "I can't even joke about packing someone inside his suitcase, because he didn't take one. When I say our hands are tied, our hands are tied."

The two cyber wizards glanced at each other again and Price sighed. "What? If either one of you has anything pertinent to add to this conversation, now's the time."

Tokaido swept back his long hair before replying.

"Well, China is one of the most heavily surveilled nations on Earth—"

"Yeah, behind only the US and maybe England," Kurtzman added.

"Regardless, it is technically feasible to hack their systems and search for a particular face or build. It would even be possible to track said target's movements throughout the city, allowing us to keep an eye on his movements and interactions."

"Great, so we can see him get caught by the MSS or the military. There must be something more we can give him from here," Price said. "Chinese hackers are battering at our firewalls every day. Surely you guys can do more than just get us a look through some cameras?"

Again the two men exchanged glances, then Kurtzman pushed his wheelchair back from his station and turned to face her. "Are you sure you want to continue down this path, Barb? We all know what the orders from Washington stated. So, what *exactly* would you like us to do?"

Price stared at the bearded computer genius for a few seconds, evaluating him and his question. It sounded as though he was trying to get her to drop it, but he was regarding her with a frank, open stare. She was pretty sure she knew what he was asking, but she had to kick the decision upstairs—in this case, to the man in the rumpled shirt standing next to her, before she could find out.

"Hal?"

He regarded her with a gimlet stare. "You're the mission controller, Barb. How do you want to proceed?"

"We're already providing data assistance as the situation develops. I want Bear and Akira to provide whatever mission-critical assistance they can to Striker without being detected." She waited to see if either Brognola or

Kurtzman had picked up on the discrepancy in the two sentences.

"Given the mission parameters, are we providing standard electronic antidetection?" Kurtzman asked. He was referring to the standard erasure that happened during stealth and infiltration missions, where the Stony Man cyber team removed all evidence that their operatives had been on site—altering vehicle logs, looping or deleting surveillance camera footage, deleting fingerprints on file or mug shots where necessary.

That was the lifeline Price needed. She grabbed it. "Yes, especially on this mission. Of course, you both will need to balance that aspect of this op with the mission-critical assistance."

Kurtzman nodded, the hint of a smile playing around his lips. "Of course we will."

Brognola held his gaze on Price a few seconds longer, then swiveled his head to look at Kurtzman and Tokaido. "You both heard the lady."

The computer genius nodded once. "Understood. Now, if you'll both excuse us—" he wheeled around to face his glowing bank of monitors "—we have work to do."

"You will, of course, update us on the mission's status as appropriate?" the big Fed asked.

"Of course. We always do," Kurtzman replied without looking at him.

"Come on, let's leave them to their work." Price turned and headed toward the door, pausing there to make sure he was following her.

Outside, Brognola made sure to close the door to the Computer Room before turning to her. "Did what I think just happened in there happen?"

"That depends. And if you'd prefer to not get an answer you may not like, I'd suggest you not ask the question leading to it."

"Barbara, you know I'm not against bending the rules when I think the circumstances warrant it."

"And I can't think of a better time for that to happen than right now," she replied. "Aaron gave me the opening I needed to direct them to assist Striker without blowback. He also just gave us plausible deniability if we ever needed it."

"You realize that if either of those two get caught sneaking around China's computers, by the book we'd be forced to hang them out to dry, right?"

Price nodded. "Yes. But I don't see that happening. First, Aaron and Akira are unmatched when it comes to breaking into enemy computer systems, no matter what country. And second, there is no way in hell I would let either of those two men go down as having done something perceived as illegal on my watch. I'll fight for them every step of the way, if it ever comes to that."

"Good, then we're on the same page in that regard." The big Fed glanced at the closed door a few feet away. "Not that I don't appreciate what the guys are doing, but they didn't have to go all cloak-and-dagger on us."

"That's what I love about this team, Hal. Everyone helps in the way they think is best." Price smiled. "Come on. I'll make us some decent coffee in the farmhouse. It'll help distract me until the next update."

"Agreed." Brognola fell into step beside her as they headed down the hall. "You worried about Striker out there?"

"Yes," was all she said.

Every time he leaves…

CHAPTER FIVE

Who knew it'd be so damn hard to find a car outside Beijing?

Bolan had put a couple of miles between himself and the checkpoint, staying off the main roads and avoiding anyone he saw coming his way. More than once that had necessitated ducking into the lightly wooded area near the smaller road he was traveling. One time he'd had to drop to his stomach in some tall grass as a trio of giggling girls dressed in what looked like school uniforms walked by a few yards away.

But the farther he got from the countryside, the closer he got to the more populated suburbs—and the harder it was to locate a suitable vehicle to steal. In the country, the only vehicles available were tractors and bicycles. In this area it wasn't that there weren't any around, it was just that vehicles were all under lock and key, kept in some kind of building, whether that was a cinder-block garage or a makeshift shack of tin panels.

While Bolan wasn't worried about breaking into a place to steal a car, he wanted to be as inconspicuous as possible about it. It was hard enough being a six-foot-three-inch man in a country where the average height was five-seven. Add that he was a Caucasian, and it meant that any sighting of him doing anything illegal would be the kind of thing that would definitely stick in the minds of the locals.

The countryside had grown quiet again and Bolan resumed his approach toward a cluster of houses in the near distance. With luck, he could find something here to take him into the city.

The houses were simple, one-story structures with white walls and red-tiled roofs. A moped was parked outside the front doors of several homes. Keeping his head down and his cap brim low on his face, Bolan surreptitiously checked the driveways and lawns of each house as he passed.

A door slamming made him tense and he ducked behind a tree while casting around for the source of the noise. On the next block, a man in a short-sleeved shirt and black tie, and carrying a briefcase, trotted out of the largest house in the area—it had a small second story on it—and headed for his car, a medium-size, well-used sedan. Bolan looked closer and saw that the trunk was ajar, held shut by a length of white cord. Wherever the man was headed, it had to be somewhere more populated, where Bolan could acquire better transportation.

A shout sounded from the doorway and he looked back to see a heavily pregnant woman in a house coat holding what looked like a sheaf of papers in her hand. The man ran back to the doorway and snatched the papers, getting into a brief discussion with his wife, Bolan surmised. But his attention wasn't entirely focused on them—he was moving toward the car.

The lightly forested grassy area he was creeping through ended in a small green hedge that led almost up to the back end of the sedan. With the couple still talking about something, the soldier crept along the hedge to the trunk, reaching it as the couple's voices got louder. The rope securing the broken trunk was tied in a simple square knot. Bolan untied it in a few seconds. Now came the tricky part—opening it wide enough to get inside without attracting the couple's attention. He carefully eased it open just enough for him to squeeze inside, folding himself around the small, bald spare tire and thanking the Universe that this guy didn't keep his trunk full of crap.

Bolan had just gotten the trunk lid back down when he heard approaching footsteps crunch on the gravel driveway. Clenching one hand into a fist—just in case he had to subdue the guy—Bolan waited for the car to start moving, wondering if the man noticed that the back end of his car was a couple inches lower now. The car door opened then closed, and after a few seconds, Bolan felt the car begin to move underneath him.

He kept hold of the rope so he could keep the trunk from opening, yet still give himself enough of a space to view the outside. His initial suspicion had been correct—they seemed to be heading deeper into the city. Crammed like a sardine into the dusty, smelly compartment, this was by far the worst accommodation Bolan had found on his trip so far. The car had definitely seen better days, and once it accelerating to about thirty miles per hour, the rattling over the washboard road jarred his spine and ribs unmercifully. But he was making a lot better time, and wherever they ended up, it had to be a place with more possibilities than what he'd seen so far.

As long as he doesn't get a flat tire, I'll be fine, he thought as the car rattled and swayed onto a major arterial highway, giving Bolan hope that he would be able to find what he needed near the driver's final destination.

An hour later the car creaked to a stop on a narrow side road. The driver spent a few minutes wedging his car in among rows of similar sedans, then got out and walked down the street toward whatever office building he worked in. Bolan gave him five more minutes—in case he forgot something in his car—then eased the trunk open and looked around.

He found himself in what looked like an anonymous business section on the outskirts of the city. The streets were lined with small shops selling everything from knockoff clothes to electronics. Pulling his cap low, Bolan checked his cash and hit the first electronics store he found.

Four stores, forty-five minutes, a lot of pointing and around fifty thousand yuan later, Bolan was set electronically, with four cheap smartphones, three small tablets, several items of clothing and a backpack to carry everything. The phones were burners; he would use each one for a day, then destroy it. The tablets were along the same lines. Changing access accounts would be a pain, but it definitely beat spending time in a Chinese prison for cyber espionage.

Finding the nearest cyber café, he got a cup of black tea and sat in an isolated corner to set up a phone and a tablet and log on to the internet. Despite being knockoffs, both devices worked well. Using an innocuous local provider and webmail account, Bolan sent a brief message confirming his safe arrival to an address that would send the message bouncing around the world until it arrived at a secure server outside the United States that could be accessed by the Stony Man team. Then he leaned back, sipped his weak tea and waited.

Seven minutes later a reply came, along with an encrypted data file. Bolan downloaded it, making sure he could save it to the tablet's hard drive, then turned off his internet connection. Only then did he open the file.

Still aware that the local government could trace his downloads if they somehow got on his trail, Bolan opened the file only long enough to commit the information to memory, then trashed the data, overwriting it several times, hoping that nothing could be recovered. Once finished, he got up and headed outside to find a car, since he had to travel about five miles south-southwest in the next two hours to pick up a package.

Normally he would simply take a taxi to his destination. However, since his destination was in a disreputable part of town, Bolan didn't want a driver to remember the foreigner he or she had dropped off in the area.

A light rain started to fall as he walked around looking for a suitable vehicle, something relatively small but able to carry a good deal, like a hatchback or a small truck. After casing several overcrowded parking lots, he happened on a small parking lot hidden by a high brick wall.

Inside were several small- and medium-size trucks, all several years old, including a few pickups that were exactly what he needed. Casting a quick glance around, Bolan strolled inside and up to the door to the nearest one. Three quick movements later, the door was open and he slipped behind the wheel.

The next part was trickier, but he'd hot-wired more cars than he could remember. In under a minute Bolan had the truck running was easing it onto the clogged street, where he immediately slowed to a crawl. He checked the time on his smartphone. An hour and a half remained before his meeting.

I just might make it in time, he thought as he leaned on the horn.

CHAPTER SIX

Baozhai Liao had found both success and difficulty in her relatively young life. But facing the man sitting across from her now was one of the most terrifying things she had ever done.

She had grown up on the far outskirts of Beijing, near enough to see the towering skyscrapers in the distance, yet far enough to realize at a very young age that if she ever wanted to get closer to them, she would need to find a way to do so by herself.

Growing up, her parents had been of little help. Her father was a small, local merchant, barely making ends meet by buying and selling whatever he could, and drinking up whatever profit he brought home. Her mother kept their tiny house, scrimping and saving to put food on the table and dreaming of the day when her husband would someday make a deal that would make them all rich. Baozhai slept in a cramped attic every night and dreamed of getting out of there as soon as she could.

But when the means to that end arrived, it wasn't through any sort of brilliant business deal of her father's. Several years earlier, the local government had come through one day and announced that their neighborhood was being rezoned for apartments and that all of the inhabitants had to move. However, they would receive compensation.

When they heard the amount—forty thousand yuan—the teenage Baozhai had felt something shift inside her. Before that day she had been a loyal family member, trying to do whatever she could to help her parents survive. But when she heard about the yuan her family would soon receive, she realized that the opportunity she had been waiting for had finally come.

Once the payment had been transferred to their bank, the next morning she had forged a withdrawal slip and her father's signature and withdrew ten thousand yuan from the account. The bank teller didn't even look at her twice, as they were all used to Huan's daughter making deposits and withdrawals for her father.

But Baozhai didn't take the money back home. Instead she had walked into the city, nervously clutching the worn satchel filled with bills, ready to make her own way.

She found a cheap room in the basement of a four-story apartment building, and hid the rest of her money, not trusting banks. Then she began looking for a job, and soon found one in a local restaurant. And it was there her luck turned again.

Baozhai's mother had always doted on her only child, contrary to most Chinese families, which preferred sons. In particular, she had said that her daughter's beauty could rival that of a princess. Well, apparently the man who stopped in for lunch one day thought so as well, for he gave her his card and told her to come by his office on her next day off. The company name on the card was for one of the largest modeling agencies in China.

Two days later Baozhai, wearing the best clothes she could buy in her neighborhood and made up as well as she knew how, walked into the offices of Dao International Models Management and handed the card to the well-coiffed woman at the front desk. Five minutes later she was sitting in a chair in Mr. Peng's office, watching him watch her. He had her speak, then asked her to rise and walk across the room. Baozhai didn't know what exactly he was looking for, but he apparently liked what he saw for he signed her to a contract and she started modeling two days later.

The next few years had passed in a blur of trips around the world, lavish parties, and meeting and mingling with the rich and famous from across China and beyond. Baozhai soaked up every bit of it and transformed herself from a meek, shy, lower-class girl into a sleek, polished model whose face made men desire her and woman envious.

To her, the funniest part was that she didn't think she was all that attractive. The makeup artists and stylists performed miracles, transforming her from what she considered to be a plain girl into the graceful-looking, stylish woman who could sell cars, perfume or jewels with equal ease. But when the shoot was over and she wiped her face clean, the person staring back at her from the mirror was the everyday, ordinary Baozhai.

Everything had been going along perfectly—she had even arranged to repay her parents the ten thousand yuan "loan"—when tragedy struck. During a party to launch a new Chinese vodka, the company CEO had gotten very drunk and tried forcing her to have sex with him. Baozhai wouldn't have any of it and had pushed him away—so hard that he had fallen into a glass table and severely injured himself.

The blowback was swift and severe. Neither company wanted the incident to become public, so they swept it under the rug and shunted aside any witnesses. Unfor-

tunately that included Baozhai. Mr. Peng had retired by
then, and the new head of the agency had been busy putting his own stamp on their lineup. The incident with
Baozhai had given him the perfect excuse to fire her and,
to ensure that she wouldn't talk about why, he blackballed
her among all the major modeling agencies.

Baozhai went from being the toast of the town to having nothing again. Locked out of her company penthouse,
her Lexus taken back by the company, she was able to
recover and use the funds she had saved to check into the
Four Seasons while she figured out what her next steps
were going to be.

And that was where she had met Zhang Liao.

Baozhai was far too worldly, or perhaps jaded, to believe in love at first sight, especially since she had seen
other friends of hers in the modeling world get used,
abused and discarded by men and women as often as the
changing of the seasons. It was why she had avoided any
sort of romantic entanglements during her modeling career, even though it brought accusations of being cold, a
lesbian or just not "with it."

But with Zhang, it was different. Divorced from the
persona she had inhabited for years, Baozhai was free
to be herself around him, unguarded, or perhaps less
guarded. She knew his family—there was hardly anyone
in Beijing who didn't—and yet he was polite, friendly
and approachable. They had first bumped into each other
at the front desk, then again in the elevator. When their
paths crossed at the restaurant that evening, Zhang in-
sisted that it had to be fate and invited her to join him
for dinner. Five minutes after sitting down, she realized
why they were so good together—they were both from
similar, isolating worlds, surrounded by sycophants and

yes-men, and always not entirely sure whom to trust and whom to watch out for.

By the end of their superb meal, when he asked to see her again, Baozhai didn't have to think about her answer.

She kept her previous life concealed for the first few months of their relationship—entertainment and politics were often a dangerous combination, and there was also the mystery of her sudden disappearance from the fashion world. She had vanished so cleanly that the media had no idea where she had gone. The tabloids spread rumors and pored over every "clue" they discovered. For her part, Baozhai read the international papers and laughed when she learned what had "happened" to her that day—she had gotten gender reassignment surgery, and was now working as "Bao" in men's modeling; she had gotten hooked on drugs and resorted to pornography.

When she had revealed her former life, Zhang had smiled and said he'd already been aware of it—her background had been assiduously researched before their second date—and he simply figured she would tell him about it when she was ready. It was at that moment, with his trust in her revealed so easily and honestly, that Baozhai realized she was in love with him.

Their relationship progressed rapidly after that, and eight months after they first met, they were married, with their first child soon following. When Baozhai had gotten pregnant with their second, she had been concerned, but Zhang had told her not to worry. "There are rules for the majority of Chinese families, and there are rules for the rest of us," he'd said with a smile. "But not the same rules for both." True to his word, they hadn't ever been bothered once by the government regarding their two children.

Zhang's fortunes had seemed to continue climbing ever upward; trusted by people both inside and outside the bureaucracy, he ascended the political ranks with ease. But the higher he went, the more troubled he became. He grew more and more stressed, even drinking in the evening when he came home. He was always unfailingly kind and polite to his wife and children, and never raised his voice or laid a hand on them in any way. But he just as firmly refused to discuss what was causing him so much distress, despite Baozhai's efforts to get him to confide in her.

It had all come to a head one night a few weeks earlier, when Zhang had finally spoken to her after the children were asleep. He told Baozhai enough to make her fearful for their safety; even though Zhang had assured her that she and their children were safe. But she knew better. Even in her world, she had seen men and women disappear after they had said the wrong thing, talked to the wrong person. Zhang thought his family connections would save him, that his lineage's long, distinguished record of service to the nation would save him. But she knew he was wrong.

She had tried to warn him, tried to make plans to get out of the country. But by then it was too late. And when the man from the US Embassy had shown up at her door for her and their children, she'd known that even if the United States somehow managed to get her and her children out of the country, their life was over as she knew it.

Since the brave American's—Carstairs was his name, she made a point of remembering—sacrifice for them had all come to naught, her next priority was to somehow protect her children. Baozhai was desperate to know where her husband was, but a colder, more rational part of her had pushed him to the back of her mind, simply because she had absolutely no idea where he was right now, but she did know where her children were.

That was how the men who questioned her every day were trying to break her—by limiting her interactions with her children. They only allowed her to see one at a time and only for about an hour each day. Baozhai could already see the toll this was taking on Zhou, her daughter, and Cheng, her son. Both quiet, polite children, Zhou was now spending hours each day playing that maddening game, and becoming more insolent and resistant during their time together, while Cheng was withdrawing further inside himself. If something didn't change soon, she feared the emotional damage would have long-term repercussions—

"Mrs. Liao?"

The question jolted her back to the present, and the man sitting casually across from her. Despite herself, Baozhai was impressed with him. He was either military or had served, but hid it well enough to fool the average observer. Not so her—she had participated in far too many government parties to not recognize the type.

"I'm sorry, could you repeat the question?"

He smiled. That was also his problem; he looked too damn affable. In her experience there were only two types of government people: humorless elder leaders or young men who thought they could change the world. Both could be easily corrupted, with the right leverage. This one didn't fit into either stereotype.

He was handsome—not movie-star handsome, but an honest, regular face. He wore his hair short and neat—not buzzed, like many military personnel, but short enough. She figured he got it cut every other week. He was dressed well, not well enough to be on the take, but his suit was only a year out of date and his shoes were relatively new.

It was his eyes. His warm, inviting, brown eyes that were his most dangerous weapons. The majority of government men she had met often used their stares as a weapon, to intimidate, menace, demand. He had never raised his voice to her, never threatened her, never shouted. He just asked his questions in the same steady, inviting tone, and stared at her with those eyes that made her want to believe that he wanted to help her, that if she could just say the right things, just tell him what he wanted to know, then all of this messy business would go away and she and her children would be free to leave.

There were just two problems with that scenario.

"What can you tell me about your husband's subversive activities with the Americans?"

First, other than the vague conversation they'd had had that one evening, she had absolutely no idea of the details of what her husband had been doing with the US Embassy. Any answer she would give would have been a lie, because Zhang hadn't wanted to tell her—for her own protection. That omission was what was now keeping her here. Trapping her here.

But, of course, if she had known the truth, it wouldn't have helped, either. Once she told them what she knew, she would be either sent to prison or killed. There was no way out of this, not for her.

Not for her children.

And yet, Baozhai clung to some faint yet slowly dying hope that she could find some way to protect her children. She understood that it was very likely that her own life was forfeit, but she would gladly sacrifice herself if her children wouldn't suffer because of what their father had done.

But how could she make that happen? What could she possibly offer this genial, smiling man that could guarantee her children's lives?

Baozhai sat straighter in the wing-backed chair and flashed her best smile—the one she'd honed on hostile reporters—on her interrogator. "I wish very much to help you, Major, but I am afraid that I cannot tell you what I do not know. My husband was very secretive about his business, and never discussed it at home."

That part was mostly true—Chinese men rarely discussed their business at home. While it wouldn't gain her any real sympathy, she could hope for pity, perhaps?

The major nodded, his smile slipping a bit. "That may be, but tell me, how did you come to be in a United States Embassy car, with an American attaché escorting you to what I can only assume was their embassy?"

Well, she had to try. Baozhai licked her lips and smoothed an imaginary wrinkle out of her slacks. "I am not exactly sure why that happened myself. I had received a call from my husband earlier that evening saying to meet him at a restaurant in the vicinity." She named a place near the American building. "Since my husband's work had him associating with the Americans, we often went there for dinner. I didn't think anything of it when he sent a car for us, as he planned to meet us there. It was only when we were detained outside our house that I feared something was wrong."

"Yes, let's talk about that, if you don't mind." The man shifted in his chair, still mostly radiating calm and openness. "You claim that two men from the Ministry of State Security attempted to take you into custody, and that this—Mr. Carstairs—fended them off, injuring one in the process, and then ordered his driver to leave the scene, is that right?"

Baozhai nodded, trying to stay ahead of the major long enough to weave some kind of plausible story. So far, she wasn't coming up with anything besides her usual answers—an in-the-dark housewife caught up in larger events that she didn't understand.

"And all the while, you had absolutely no idea as to why representatives of the Chinese government would be looking to take you and your children into custody?"

Baozhai crossed her legs to try to stop them from shaking. "I...can only assume that they were sent for my family's protection."

"Yet you did not go with them when ordered, but stayed with Mr. Carstairs."

"I could not hear exactly what was said between the two men. I just saw them together, then the American did something to the other man, making him shout and move away, and he got into our car. The rest of what happened is in my statement." Although regrettable, Baozhai thanked her lucky stars that the American had been killed in the accident, so he wouldn't disprove her story. She had heard enough about the prisons of her homeland to know they would have gotten the truth out of him in short order.

Realizing that she, too, had nothing to lose, she decided to try being a bit more assertive. "Begging your pardon, but we have already gone over all of this several times in the past few days. I have not gotten the chance to see my children yet today. I would like to see them now."

He snapped shut the manila folder he had been reading from and tucked it under his arm. "Rewards are granted for positive results, Mrs. Liao. Since we have not accomplished any positive results today, I am afraid that I cannot allow that. Perhaps you should think very carefully about what you had seen or discussed with your husband, and when I come tomorrow to ask these questions again, you will be more forthcoming with your answers."

With that, he rose and walked out of the room, leaving Baozhai alone again.

CHAPTER SEVEN

"Blood pressure one-seventeen over seventy-five. You're doing quite well, Mr. Liao, although your pressure has been creeping up over the past few days."

Liao nodded blandly. "I can't imagine why," he deadpanned. If it hadn't been for the circumstances, he would have thought he was in a normal hospital, undergoing a battery of tests in preparation for a normal procedure or operation. Everything fit—the efficient nurses, the bland yet nourishing hospital food, the scheduled checks by the doctors. If only the end result hadn't been the termination of his life, he would have considered himself to be receiving very good care overall. However, there was that looming end result.

He had spent the first two or three days—he had to estimate, since there was no clock in his room—in a deep depression. He ate little, didn't talk to anyone and just stayed in his bed for most of the day. He was depressed, it was true, but after the first twelve or fifteen hours, he had been primarily faking the symptoms to gain some time to think.

That in itself had been difficult. At first his thoughts had been consumed with where his family was and how they were doing. He dared not ask, for fear of being told the worst—at this point, he figured it was simply better that he not know.

To distract himself from that, he tried to come up with an escape plan, which proved to be extremely difficult. The guards were very professional in executing their duties. No one was ever allowed in his room by themselves, and the guard was always standing by the door, too far to reach, overpower him and seize his weapon, which Liao wasn't even sure he knew how to use. Also, he'd learned that the main room was watched through closed-circuit television, and most likely his bathroom as well, making preparing any sort of device—not that he could come up with one—or plan unseen pretty much impossible. The one time he had inadvertently walked into the blind spot under where he thought the camera was, a pair of guards had appeared in his room within sixty seconds. The only way they could have known what was going on was because someone watching him had told them.

The other option, taking a hostage, probably wouldn't get him anywhere, either. Although the guards *probably* wouldn't actually kill a nurse or a doctor, he couldn't assume that they didn't have a shoot-escapees-on-sight policy. Besides, he didn't have anything to make a weapon out of, so taking a hostage was out of the question. The tray, cup and utensils for his meals were all soft plastic, sturdy enough to use, but useless for fashioning into any sort of weapon. They were also counted before and after he ate, and Liao was certain that anything missing would be found—one way or another. He supposed he could try to fashion some kind of strangling cord out of his bedsheet, but again there was the problem of being watched. The single ventilation shaft high on the wall was bolted shut; it was too small for him to squeeze through anyway. There simply was no remotely feasible way to escape.

Therefore, with no way out, and his family most likely lost to him, Liao grew resigned to his fate. Well, not entirely. While he might not have been able to escape it, he realized that he could circumvent the reason they were keeping him here in the first place. All he had to do was to figure out a way to injure himself so that his organs would be unusable.

They may kill me, he thought while lying in bed one evening, but they damn sure aren't going to profit from my body!

There only remained the question of how. A hunger strike wouldn't work—he was sure that damned sociopath Dr. Xu would supervise the force-feeding himself.

Poison was a possibility, but again, how could he poison himself with only the very limited means available?

That question had occupied the next day or so. To not be put on antidepressants, Liao appeared to come out of his depression and began interacting with the staff more. But all the while he was racking his brain for a solution.

The answer, of course, was a simple one. It came to him while he was relieving himself one afternoon. He rose and turned to flush the toilet when he caught sight of his feces floating in the bowl. He stopped and stared at it as the automatic system flushed it down. Might it be that simple?

He returned to his bed and sat, mind whirling with the possibility. An educated man, he knew that simply ingesting the feces wouldn't have the desired effect. For a moment he cursed his healthy lifestyle—an ulcer would have been perfect right now. But now, he was as healthy as a horse, more or less.

However, what if I introduce fecal bacteria to my bloodstream? All he would need is some kind of open wound and a judicious application of his own waste to the area.

Except they were watching him. They were *always* watching him. Only when he was asleep, he guessed, and the lights were out, were they not. The real issue was how he would conceal his infection plan from them, especially when all he had to wear was a flimsy hospital gown.

Again, the answer came while in the bathroom. He had been thinking about that problem while on the toilet when he realized that his entire body was covered by the gown when he sat. Also, he was as close to the infectious material as he was going to get right here, right now. But where to put it that wouldn't be easily discovered?

The answer came to him with such clarity that he nearly fell off the toilet. All he had to do was to break the skin near his groin and apply feces to the wound. It was going to hurt, but he was pretty sure he could scratch open the skin near his genitals, smear his waste on it and simply wait.

He put his plan into motion that night, scratching at the skin near his scrotum under cover of the thin blanket.

If anyone's watching, they'll probably just think I'm masturbating, he thought.

It took a few hours and his fingers grew stiff and sore, not to mention the area he was injuring did *not* feel good at all. But by morning he had a raw, red, open wound near his scrotum that he figured should do the trick.

Feeling better than he had in days, Liao got up and even whistled a little as he headed for the bathroom.

CHAPTER EIGHT

Now mobile and just another person in the tide of city commuters, Bolan was looking forward to the next part of the mission.

Since he hadn't been able to bring any weapons with him, Stony Man had reached out through encrypted web sites and list servers to various shadowy connections halfway around the world and arranged an armament package using third-party vendors.

In other words, Bolan was about to go weapons shopping on the black market.

Nobody had been pleased with that arrangement, as there were far too many things that could go wrong, the least of which included him walking into a trap or double-cross. However, bullets were going to start flying at some point during this trip and the Executioner needed some way to reply in kind.

Every building around him looked as though it had been built from neon. Glowing, flashing signs promising massage, go-go dancing, and other vague, suitably illicit pleasures lit the night. Strip clubs and the like were supposed to be illegal in Beijing, but as with most other crimes, where there was a will—which meant people willing to pay for it—there was a way. In this case, it meant they weren't advertised openly, but if you knew the right people, then just about anything could be had for a price.

Young men and women flooded the streets, looking, buying and selling. Spotting the place he was looking for, Bolan took a moment to confirm the address. The building was three stories high and its front was covered with floor-to-ceiling windows, in which comely young women sat and beckoned passersby to come inside, or danced to lure them. Judging by the steady flow of patrons entering, business was good—the better to get lost in the crowd.

That was also good news; the neighborhood seemed to cater to a diverse clientele. The crowd appeared to be a mix of various people and races. Bolan figured he'd have a better time blending in here. He parked the truck three blocks away, hoping it wouldn't get blocked in by the snail's-pace traffic creeping through the streets.

Pulling his baseball cap low again, he headed through the gawking, talking, drinking crowd, heading toward the club's entrance. Inside, he was met with a wall of noise and people, and the place was dimly lit by cheap colored-paper lanterns. Women danced on the bar to the loud approval of half-drunk men. It was hot inside, and reeked of grain alcohol, cigarette smoke, sweat and cheap perfume.

Bolan shouldered his way to the back, where a narrow stairway led to the second floor and the VIP rooms. He walked up, putting his back to the wall as a parade of young women dressed in American-label baseball jerseys, jeans and shirts paraded by. On the landing, he took out a pair of cheap sunglasses and slipped them on, blinking in the already dim red light, then walked down to the third door on the right and rapped on the frame three times.

"Yao?" The beaded curtain was pushed aside and a tiny woman with huge eyes, fake lashes and dressed in a

traditional Chinese silk dress stared up at him. Her eyes widened even farther in surprise, but she quickly masked her reaction and cocked her head at him.

"Chen song wo," Bolan replied, saying that Chen had sent him. He tapped his baseball cap, the only one he had seen in the room.

She raised a smartphone and looked at it for a moment, then nodded. "Come in," she said in English.

Bolan entered a small room lined with bench seats and pillows, with a small serving table in the middle. As with the rest of the upstairs, the room was lit with red mood lighting. The woman pulled a sliding door closed, immediately muting the cacophony outside to a dull roar. "Would you care for some entertainment while you wait?"

"No, thank you," Bolan replied as he chose a seat that allowed him to keep an eye on both the doorway and the woman keeping him company. "I'm here to pick up a package, and then I'll be gone."

"I am afraid it will be a few minutes," she said, extending a slim hand to the table, which had a single bottle and four glasses on it. "Something to drink, perhaps?"

"No, thank you." Bolan was well aware of the Chinese custom of sealing a business deal over alcohol, and he was just as determined not to let it interfere with his business. It was bad enough that he was in a public business, with not many escape routes if the deal went south. On the other hand, the fact that the handoff was going down here instead of in an isolated warehouse on the docks probably meant the black marketers had done this before and had a system in place.

Not inclined to make small talk, he glanced at the woman, who smiled shyly at him, then resumed watching the door. An ashtray sat in the middle of the table, surrounded by several books of matches. Bolan picked one up, studied the outline of a nude girl on it and slipped it into his pocket with a small smile.

In a few minutes the door slid open and an older woman poked her head in and rattled off a couple of sentences in rapid-fire Cantonese—at least Bolan thought it was Cantonese. He paid close attention to the young woman's reply, which was short and to the point. The older woman nodded, said something else and then left.

"Your package will be here shortly," she announced.

"You understand that I will wish to inspect it before I hand over the rest of the payment," he said, resting his hands on his legs.

"Of course," she replied. "Arrangements have already been made."

As she said that, the door slid open again and two suited men stepped inside, filling most of the rest of the space in the room. Each one carried a large nylon gym bag slung over one shoulder.

"Here is what is to happen," the small woman said. Bolan noticed she was now holding a stun gun in her right hand. "Under supervision, you will be allowed to inspect your purchase as you see fit. At no time will you be allowed to load or otherwise prepare any of it for firing." She pressed the stud of the stun gun, making the metal prongs crackle with electricity, for emphasis. "Once you are satisfied with the merchandise, you will hand over the rest of the agreed-upon payment. Do you agree to these terms?"

At Bolan's nod, the woman nodded to the man on the left, who stepped forward and set his bag on the table, then stepped back. Moving slowly, Bolan unzipped the bag and opened it to look inside before reaching in. Satisfied there were no surprises, he removed a heavy leather holster and opened it.

Inside was a stubby, matte-black pistol with cross-hatched grips that resembled a knockoff Walther PPK, only not quite as small and sleek. Holding the Type 59 pistol in one hand, Bolan glanced at the woman. "This is the PPM model, as agreed?"

She nodded. "Chambered in 9 mm Parabellum."

He nodded, pulled back the action to check the barrel and chamber, then swiftly fieldstripped it to ensure that any identifying marks or numbers had been removed—they were—that it was in decent shape, and that no parts—such as the firing pin—were missing. A cleaning kit was included, along with five magazines and two hundred rounds of 9 mm ammunition. Stony Man had promised to double the price if they could include a sound suppressor, but had no luck.

Bolan reassembled the pistol and worked the action again. It was in fair condition—the slide was a bit sticky, most likely due to lack of proper maintenance. If he had the time, he would remedy that. Under normal circumstances, he'd be more likely to throw the probably twenty-year-old gun at an enemy instead of trying to shoot them, but he had no choice in the matter. It was easily concealable, and fired one of the most common bullets in existence. He checked out the magazines, ensuring that the springs were clean and functional, and that they all fit into the pistol, then examined each box of bullets.

He was aware that if they were planning a sting or double cross, now would be the time. To them, he would just be one more foreigner who got in trouble while in their country and disappeared, never to be seen again.

Under the guise of inspecting the rounds, he palmed a bullet and then slipped it into the chamber when he "checked" the pistol one last time before zipping the bag shut and nodding. "It is acceptable. Next?"

The man on the right stepped forward and set his bag down. This one was the real test. Pistols were, of course, illegal for citizens to possess. What should be in this bag pretty much meant an automatic death sentence if these people were ever caught with it.

Bolan unzipped the bag and removed what resembled the love child between an AK-47 and an old World War II–era M-3 "grease gun." While it would never take any prizes for looks, the 7.62 mm Type 79 submachine gun was small and accurate.

Bolan fieldstripped this weapon as well, checking for removal of any identification as well as verifying that it would also fire when called upon. The subgun looked to be better cared for than the pistol. In fact, it looked so good, he wasn't sure it had ever been fired.

"Fell off a truck, eh?" he asked, receiving three stone-faced stares in return.

So much for breaking the ice, he said to himself as he reassembled the submachine gun and turned to the magazines and ammunition for it. He was expecting some sort of power play at any moment—like the "wrong" magazines had be included with the Type 79, and it would cost more to get the "right" ones. But everything was here. There was even the lock pick set they had also requested inside. For black market arms dealers, these guys were playing straight up—so far.

"It is also acceptable," he said, zipping the second bag closed. "I have the rest of your payment here, as well."

The woman blinked in surprise, then exchanged

glances with the two men. "You actually brought the money with you?"

Bolan shrugged as he rose, keeping his hands in plain sight. "I'm in a hurry." Keeping his right hand out, he reached under his shirt and undid a bulging, nylon waist pouch and handed it to the woman. She unzipped it and riffled through the contents, rapidly counting under her breath. The price had been extortionate—one hundred thousand yuan, half up front, the other half on delivery. Stony Man hadn't tried to negotiate. It was either this or have the Executioner walk around unarmed as he tried to accomplish his mission.

She finished her count and nodded. "Enjoy your bags."

Bolan was reaching for the two black bags when he heard raised voices on the landing outside. The two men immediately reached under their jackets as one cracked the door open and looked out.

Meanwhile, the woman had slid over to him and was holding the stun gun against his skin. "What is going on? Are you trying to double-cross us?"

Before Bolan could answer, four muffled thuds sounded from outside the door, and the two men both stumbled backward, clutching their bleeding stomachs.

CHAPTER NINE

Akira Tokaido yawned as he stretched his arms over his head, trying vainly to crack his vertebrae. Reaching for his most recent soda, he found that the plastic bottle had only a few drops at the bottom.

He stood and stretched his aching muscles some more, grateful that Kurtzman wasn't there breathing down his neck as he had been for the past five hours. While his boss had watched Bolan enter the building where the arms deal was going down, Tokaido had been tasked with locating the Liao family. Ever since then, he had been running through every permutation he could think of to figure out where they were.

And, so far, he had come up empty. The scant file they'd managed to assemble gave him very little to go on, although he had been surprised to learn that the wife had been a fairly famous model before trading that life in for the burbs, kids and a white picket fence. Normal tracking modes—license plates or cell phones—were useless, as her phone had been found with the crashed car, and Zhang Liao's BMW was still in its parking space at the government building where he worked. Hacking the Ministry of State Security's files had proved fruitless, as well—there was no trace of any information on the Liaos, indicating they either kept that sensitive information on an unconnected system or on hard copy.

Above his head on a large monitor, a loop of the attempted extraction played over and over. The young hacker had watched the feed until he knew it by heart. Even now his eyes strayed to it in time to see Mrs. Liao hustling her children off to the car behind Carstairs.

He'd run a very specialized program along the route the car had taken into the city and, working outward from where the smashed car had been found, trying to sift through the gigabytes of accumulated data from the hundreds of cameras in the area, searching for any sighting of the Liao family, but so far it had come up with nothing. He knew the chances of actually uncovering anything were on par with his winning the lottery, but he had kept the program trying, hoping for a second's glimpse that could help him figure out where they might have been taken.

Massaging his temples, Tokaido tried to think of anything he might have missed. He had access to the neighborhood cameras, as well as the security system to the Liao family's home. With nothing else to go on, he brought up the other feeds, running them forward at double speed, and just stared at the pictures of a wealthy Chinese family going about its day, coming and going, eating dinner, swimming in their pool. Playing electronic games—

Wait a minute… Tokaido leaned forward to pause the feed that showed the family clustered around their small pool. The husband and boy were goofing around in the water, whacking each other with water noodles while the mother watched them in between keeping an eye on their gas grill. But the computer hacker's gaze was drawn to the small game controller, complete with miniscreen, that the girl was absorbed in.

Sitting, he froze the picture and zoomed in on her. As he suspected, it was a wireless console with the capability to play games over the internet, no matter where she was.

Tokaido's fingers flew over his split keyboard as he hacked into Chinese telecom services to locate the Liaos' internet accounts. Three minutes later he was looking at their information and had everything he needed to trace the IP address of anything in their house. The computer was offline—no big surprise there, since they had seen operatives from the MSS carrying them out of the house—but the game console had been overlooked...and that was what the girl was playing in the video. What's more, it was still powered up.

Sending up a silent thanks to the powers-that-be in the universe regarding kids and their insatiable hunger for games and distraction, Tokaido began tracing the signal through the maze of various networks that intertwined in Beijing. Between the competing companies resorting to less-than-legal means to block or slow their competition, the stifling government, ready to leap in at a moment's notice to eradicate the slightest whisper of dissent and the myriad unlawful networks that sprang up on a daily, even hourly, basis, even Tokaido was hard-pressed to track the lone signal through the labyrinthine cyberspace that was China's internet. Add to it that he wasn't even supposed to be doing any of this in the first place, and for the first time in a long time, he felt beads of sweat forming on his forehead as he pulled out every trick he knew to stay on the trail of his target.

However, after several false trails, and evading dozens of enemy hacks on his signal—counterattacking would have been like sending up a red flag shouting, "Here I am!"—Tokaido was 90 percent sure he had located the girl. He leaned back in his chair and stared with weary satisfaction at the sleek high-rise where the signal was coming from. True to form, she wasn't using the network in the penthouse where she was staying—there were multiple unprotected wireless signals nearby that she was able to piggyback on.

Her captors probably just thought the controller was a self-contained game. And if she was there, he bet that her mom and brother were, as well. A few more keystrokes and the young hacker had pinpointed the floor and room she was in. But for how long…?

The acrid odor of Kurtzman's fresh cup of coffee alerted Tokaido that his boss had entered the room. "I trust you've come up with something concrete about the Liaos since I've been gone."

"Yeah, I have." The young man barely kept the triumphant smile off his face as he ran down how he had located the family, pointing at the address, building level and room the daughter was in. "If they were taken there since the abduction, I think the chances are fairly small that the ministry will move them any time soon," he ventured. "As far as they know, they snatched the family clean, and no one is looking for them—that they know of."

Kurtzman grunted and sipped his coffee. "What, are you looking to moonlight as a security analyst now?"

"No, it just seems likely that they'll be there until the MSS has gotten what they want from the family, or they have outlived their usefulness."

"Assuming you're correct, the problem is that we don't know what, if anything, they've told their captors, or how much longer the MSS is going to hold them before transferring them elsewhere."

Kurtzman spun his chair toward the door. "I'll go let Barbara and Hal know we've found the family. You start on getting us eyes and ears inside, as well as work up an entry plan for Striker and an extraction plan for him and the three targets."

"Already on it," Tokaido said, turning back to his computer as Kurtzman started to leave the room.

He paused. "Any recent updates from Striker?"

"No. He entered the arms meet about ten minutes ago, and there's no security system inside, so we're blind right now. He's also turned off his phone. But I'm expecting a ping from him any minute, and will let you know when it arrives."

"Okay. Good work, Akira." Kurtzman wheeled away, leaving the younger man in relative peace and quiet again. Donning his earbuds, he accessed his favorite artist, letting the steady, driving beat accompany him as he delved deeper into his work.

CHAPTER TEN

Taking advantage of the surprise caused by the two tong members getting shot, Bolan swept the stun gun up and away fast enough to avoid getting zapped. Drawing his hand back down, he stripped the nonlethal weapon from the woman's hand while standing and grabbing the bottle of *baijiu* off the table just as a gunman burst into the room, nearly tripping on one of his victims who had crumpled in front of the doorway.

Dropping a smoking plastic bottle with its end blown out, the newcomer glanced down for a moment to disentangle his legs. Bolan didn't need half that time. He swung the full bottle in a roundhouse arc, smashing it into the shooter's temple in an explosion of glass and rice liquor. The hardcase staggered across the room and dropped in a tangled heap against the far bench.

The woman wasn't stupid—she went for the smoking pistol that had fallen from his hand. Bolan gave her points for bravery even as he stepped over and hit the stun gun's trigger while pressing it between her shoulder blades. One three-second blast later, she was flat on the floor, moaning softly, but still moving her arms and legs.

"Stay down, and you'll stay alive," Bolan said as he kicked the gunman's pistol—a Beretta 92S—far enough away from her fingers to pick it up himself.

Now armed, Bolan tucked the stun gun into a side

pocket of the submachine-gun bag while covering the doorway with the Beretta pistol. Outside, he could hear shouts, screams and the sounds of panicked movement, but no one else seemed to be coming inside—at least not yet.

At the moment he couldn't be sure if he had just gotten made, or if he was just in the wrong place at the wrong time and had gotten caught in a fight between two rival gangs, but all he cared about was getting out and away with his cargo and himself in one piece.

The two injured tong members were still alive, and he took a moment to strip them of their pistols—an ancient, slab-sided .45 semi-auto that might have been from World War II, and a 9 mm Glock 17. He tucked the .45 into his waistband and tossed the Glock into the bag, then slung both bags over opposite shoulders, so one armament bag rested on each hip.

Stepping across the bodies on the floor, Bolan stood to the left of the doorway and checked the stairwell for more shooters. He didn't see anyone there, but shouts and screams from the lower level indicated more trouble. The only good thing so far was that he didn't hear any gunshots. Easing up to the edge of the doorway, he peeked out to the left, checking the rest of the hallway. A flash of movement alerted him to danger, and he pulled back as three shots sounded in the hall and splinters sprayed from the doorjamb as a bullet sliced through it.

He crouched. Taking a quick breath, he pivoted on the balls of his feet and swung himself out the door just enough to get target acquisition on the shooter. The gunman was waiting for him, but shot high, the bullets streaking over Bolan's head to drill into the staircase wall. His answering fire was dead-on, however; the three bullets hit the man's abdomen and chest, killing him instantly. He fell against the doorjamb and slid to the floor, his shirt a mass of dark red.

Immediately, Bolan stood and advanced, keeping his back to the rooms on the far side of the hallway so he could keep an eye on both sides of the corridor. As he thought, there was a door at the end of the hallway that he figured led to the third floor or attic space. From there, he should be able to find a way to the roof.

He was about to start down the corridor when he heard a blood-curdling scream followed by several men shouting from downstairs. The screaming continued until an even louder voice shouted and the person became quiet. Even though they were all shouting in Mandarin, Bolan had been in far too many similar situations to not know what was going on.

Gritting his teeth at the delay, he crept outside and toward the staircase, stopping just before the landing so he could peek out to see what was happening.

As he'd figured, the lower level was a panicked nightmare. The last of the patrons were shoving their way out the door while several men squared off in the middle of the deserted barroom floor. One of them had an arm around a whimpering woman's throat, holding a pistol to her head while he shouted at the four men who had backed him up against the bar but couldn't make a move with the guy threatening to blow her head off.

Drawing the Beretta, Bolan calculated the shot at about twenty meters—technically within the pistol's range, but he also knew it didn't take much to send a bullet wildly off course. Hollywood's action heroes making crazy pistol shots at impossible ranges were just that—

crazy and impossible. This one, however, was possible…
for a very skilled shooter.

Lucky for the hostage, Bolan was that skilled.

Lining up his sights on top of the man's forehead, he
took a deep breath and, just before the exhale, squeezed
the trigger.

The *crack* of the pistol shot made everyone below him
jump as the hostage-taker slumped over, blood spurting
from his cored forehead. Even from where he was, Bolan
saw brain and bone matter splattered across the bar. The
unhurt woman ran to the nearest man, and that was all
he needed to see before pulling back and heading down
the hallway toward the door at the end.

The Executioner was only a step away when he heard
the *whir* of another pocket door opening behind him.
Leading with the pistol, he turned in time to see the
muzzle of a gun lining up on him. He immediately swept
forward, using his hands on his own pistol to knock the
other gun out of the way as he bulled into the shooter,
using his greater size to force the man to retreat.

The back of the other gunman's legs hit the low table,
and he fell onto it, still clutching his pistol. Before Bolan
could line up a shot, the gunner tried to bring his pistol
into target acquisition.

Again Bolan lashed out with his gun hand, knocking
his adversary's aim off just as he squeezed the trigger.
This close, the report was deafening and the muzzle-
flash was like a flash-bang grenade exploding off to his
left side. Before the guy could recover, Bolan slammed
the butt of his pistol into the man's nose, flattening it
into his face. The would-be killer screamed and clapped
both hands to his pulped face, any interest in shooting
Bolan long gone. Just to make sure, the soldier rammed

him between the eyes with his pistol butt, then stripped the unconscious Chinese thug of his gun, a true 9 mm Walther PPK.

By now his bags were getting heavy with all of his new ordnance, and Bolan could also hear the singsong cadence of Chinese police cars as they approached. It was definitely time to go.

Stepping to the door, Bolan peeked out again but saw only empty hallway in both directions. As he stepped into the hallway, a man leaped out from the stairway, screaming and firing a huge chromed revolver in his general direction.

Although every instinct told him to leap for cover, Bolan fell forward instead, extending the pistol in front of him as he did to snap-shoot three times at the crazed gunman. Even while falling, his aim was such that the three bullets punched into the man's chest and lower abdomen, dropping him to the floor in bloody agony.

Getting back up, Bolan glanced around at the large holes the slugs had left in the walls around him. Turning to the door, he found the lock mechanism had also been mangled by a stray bullet. The doorknob now hung off the face plate. Bolan ripped off the knob and worked the mechanism through the hole, managing to open the door even as the first wave of shouting police entered the building through the main entrance below.

As he'd hoped, the door led to a narrow room that ran the width of the upper floor. Crammed inside was a bank of recording equipment tied to cameras mounted to cover each room. Apparently the gang that owned this club wasn't above engaging in a bit of blackmail alongside their sex and guns trade.

Quickly locating the camera that would have covered

his room, Bolan was relieved to find it was turned off. Just to be safe, he located the main computer that housed the digital files, ripped it loose of its wires and shoved it into the pistol bag.

As he'd also figured, there was a bolt-hole escape ladder in the corner that was shaking, as if it had just been used. The old wooden ladder led both up and down. Bolan looked down first and saw movement below. Looking up, he saw no one heading toward the roof. Sticking his pistol into his waistband next to the .45, he quickly began to ascend.

With the two bags, it was a tight fit, and more than once he had to stop and wiggle a corner of the bag free from where it had snagged on a piece of wood or nail. The ladder itself wasn't very stable, creaking and trembling under his weight.

After climbing several yards, Bolan spied a trapdoor. He pushed on it, but it seemed to be stuck. Looping his leg between the rungs, he shoved up with all his strength, and gradually forced the warped door open, all the while expecting the ladder to pull free of the wall and collapse with him still clinging to it.

He shrugged off the bags and shoved them up through the narrow, square hole, then squeezed himself through. The trapdoor was definitely not made for large people. For a brief moment his broad shoulders seemed stuck diagonally, but he was able to drop one and shove his other arm up and through.

He could now hear voices below and tried to break the ladder off so the police couldn't follow him. But although the dusty wood groaned under his blows, it refused to give. About to try once more, Bolan extended his leg to kick at the slats when the beam of a flashlight illuminated him and a powerful voice shouted at him to freeze.

Instead, Bolan pulled his leg out and shoved himself away from the trapdoor as a hail of bullets shot up and hit the roof over his head. Drawing the .45, Bolan stuck it over the lip of the trapdoor and returned fire, angling the muzzle away so he wouldn't hit any policemen below. As expected, the M-1911's thunderous roar made the approaching cops retreat.

Bolan aimed the pistol at the ladder and blasted it to pieces with the remaining rounds. He shoved the now free-floating section away from the wall hard enough to crack it off and let it drop through the shaft. Keeping the pistol, he closed the trapdoor and stomped on it to wedge it shut, then turned on the light in his smartphone to look around for a way out.

At first glance there didn't seem to be one—no doors, no hatches allowing roof access, nothing. Bolan slowed his search and looked around again, his gaze falling on a small ventilation grate on the far wall. It looked like another tight squeeze, but there was no other choice. Slinging the bags over his shoulders again, Bolan headed for the grate, stepping carefully on the trusses to make sure he didn't put a foot through the cheap ceiling tiles.

Reaching the grate, he found it screwed into the wooden wall, with a screen for bugs and thin metal slats to keep out the rain. With no time for subtlety, Bolan tore out the screen, grabbed the .45, reversed it in his hand and hammered on the slats until they bent outward enough for him to shove them free. With all of them gone, he figured he might be able to squeeze through the narrow opening. There just remained the question of what to do with the bags.

He poked his head out and looked around. As he had hoped, the roof was about six feet overhead. It was shallowly pitched, with red-clay tiles that he hoped were securely fastened to the building.

Moving the bags to right below the hole, Bolan shoved his upper body through, then grabbed both shoulder straps and looped them around his bent forearm. Holding on to the edges of the grate, he eased his legs out until he was supporting himself by his fingertips and right leg, which was bent over the lower sill. Thus braced, he pulled the bags to the hole and transferred one, then the other to the other side of his body, cross-slinging them so they would be secure.

With that done, he pulled his leg up and planted it on the sill, then reached up to grab the underside of the roof, which was covered in the detritus of decades of bird's nests. He knocked the encrusted material away, careful to avoid getting any of it in his eyes, nose or mouth. Then he looked at the lip of the roof and calculated the jump he'd have to make, off-balance and weighed down by about fifty pounds of weaponry.

He tensed, then leaped up and out, fingers scrabbling for a hold on the smooth tiles…

CHAPTER ELEVEN

Kurtzman had just returned to his station after updating Brognola and Price on the mission status when he noticed what looked like a panicked commotion at the doors of the nightclub Bolan had entered a few minutes earlier to purchase the rest of his equipment for the mission. Well-dressed men and scantily clad women were shouting and screaming as they rushed out the door and ran in all directions.

Still watching while downing a healthy swallow of coffee, he almost choked on it when he saw the first police car screech to a halt outside, and two officers get out and run into the building with pistols drawn.

"That can't be good." Setting his cup down, Kurtzman typed furiously, accessing highly classified eavesdropping programs used by the NSA to listen in to law-enforcement networks around the world.

While Kurtzman had complained earlier about the profusion of video cameras in the world, particularly America, he also recognized the need to keep tabs on others, including, sometimes, allies around the world in the fight against crime. The key, he had realized early on, was to use the collected data dispassionately, objectively, in the pursuit of justice, nothing more.

For him, there was never a personal agenda to the collection, no ax to grind against another government or nation—it was all done in the pursuit of a higher goal: making the scum of the earth accountable for their crimes. Finding other singularly minded people like that was a difficult task in today's world, but Stony Man had done it.

In Kurtzman's opinion, it was one of the main reasons they functioned so well in the shadowy world of covert ops and counterterrorism—everyone at the Farm knew their job and what they had to do. There were no turf wars, no political grandstanding or backbiting, just a near obsessive focus on getting the job done, period.

This particular case was an excellent example. Kurtzman's fact-finding would help them learn if Striker's cover had been blown, or if, however oddly, something else was going on inside that particular building. Once the data had outlived its usefulness, a transcript would be stored with the case file, and the master would most likely be deleted. If he did find something illegal or simply wrong, there would be no holding it over someone's head to extract a favor at a future time. He started the recording and began running the radioed dialogue through a burst translator to try to get a handle on what was going down.

The word was that an armed group of men had burst into the nightclub several minutes earlier, but the attack had been mysteriously foiled, with several of the suspects incapacitated or dead.

A wry grin creased Kurtzman's lips as he listened to the puzzled cops investigate the scene. Then he heard excited shouts and pounding footsteps, followed by a deafening flurry of gunshots and what might have been breaking or falling wood of some kind—it was hard to tell through all the yelling. Apparently they were chasing one suspect up into the top level of the building, but he was shooting back at them.

Throughout it all, Kurtzman kept listening for a familiar voice—Striker's, but never heard him. He wasn't worried. Bolan had near complete surprise on his side, and was an expert at creating his own escape routes, often when there didn't seem to be any in the first place.

Kurtzman listened a bit longer, just to make sure that Bolan was safely away. He heard the death count—three, but none were mentioned as being Caucasian, so he was pretty sure Bolan had escaped. He recorded a few more minutes of the officers' conversations, just enough to get the gist of what had gone down.

Sipping his coffee, he debated waiting to get the all-clear sign from Striker first, or possibly stirring up the hornet's nest by calling in Price and Brognola now.

As he pondered, his computer beeped with an incoming message.

Met cousins from wrong side of tracks.
Received presents, but others crashed the party.
Three won't crash anything again.
Was very popular. Had to leave without saying goodbye.

Grinning again, Kurtzman confirmed receipt and then forwarded the message to Price and Brognola.

"ARE YOU KIDDING ME?" Brognola said, the stub of an unlit cigar poking out of his mouth. "At the same time Striker's meeting with one tong to finalize his weapons purchase, another tong decides to raid the place?"

Kurtzman nodded. "Excellent summary, Hal. But to

be fair, the second gang did come in about ten minutes after Striker arrived."

"Jeez!" The big Fed ran a hand through his graying hair. "What the hell is going on here? Is this mission jinxed? Is there any chance that we've been hacked?"

"I think tongs have better things to do with their time than try to assassinate a high-level American operative, even if he did sneak into their home turf," Price said. "And I can't think of any reason one of the ministries would go to such extravagant lengths to false-flag a mission to this degree. If it had been a sting, they would have had him dead to rights on entering the country illegally and buying illegal arms—more than enough to throw him in a deep hole and throw away the key."

She folded her arms as she watched the translated radio communications between the officers at the club. "As far-fetched as it sounds, I think Striker was simply in the wrong place at the wrong time. The important thing is that he accomplished what he was there to do, and it looks like he got away clean."

Brognola watched through a street camera as the police cordoned off the block and began setting up their investigation. "That analysis does not make me feel any better. You know the old saying in covert ops—there are *no* coincidences. If Striker crosses paths with the wrong person, even inadvertently, it could jeopardize the entire mission."

"True," Kurtzman said. "However, unless you have anything you'd like us to do about this, we'll move on to Qincheng Prison and Liao's family."

"Keep us apprised of what happens at the nightclub while advancing both of those," Price replied. "Maybe we're getting all of the snags out early, so the rest of the op will go smoothly."

Brognola regarded her with a pained expression. "Want to bet?"

CHAPTER TWELVE

Ministry of State Security Agent Deshi Fang sat calmly in the back of his staff car as it inched through the crowded city streets, heading toward a nightclub that was the front for the White Lotus, a tong that ran drugs, girls and whatever else they could sell into and out of Beijing.

He was on his way to investigate what had been reported as an armed robbery and shooting that had occurred there earlier that night. Unconfirmed sightings of a foreigner being involved had been in the report that had crossed his desk, and something about the whole incident aroused his suspicions enough to warrant taking a look at the scene himself.

After sitting in the bumper-to-bumper snarl for a few minutes, Fang checked the remaining distance to their destination. When he realized they were less than two miles away, he decided to get out and walk. After telling his driver to meet him there, he left the car and joined the throngs of late-night revelers on the sidewalks.

A several-centimeters-taller-than-the-average Chinese man, Fang had no problem reaching his destination on foot. His calm sense of self-assurance and military bearing—gained from his years in the People's Army, where he had achieved the rank of major—dispelled the people in front of him without difficulty, many of them stepping aside without even realizing why. With a path clearing for him as if by magic, he reached the door to the nightclub, which was guarded by a trio of Beijing police, in less than ten minutes.

Showing his identification, he was allowed inside and was soon talking to the officer in charge. Most city cops were either obsequious to ministry personnel or barely civil, often thinking the MSS stuck its noses into cases it didn't need to, thus complicating the street officers' lives. For his part, Fang always tried to work with whomever he had to, without jealousy or rancor—life was too short for such pettiness.

This man, Sergeant Jiang Wei, with the Criminal Investigative Police, was neither. The weary-looking man, with heavily lidded eyes and pouches underneath them that reminded the major of a bulldog, was dressed in a wrinkled, light gray button-down shirt, collar unbuttoned and sleeves rolled up, and black slacks. Accepting the presence of the state security officer with a stoic blink, he offered him a cigarette, which Fang declined. Wei then tucked the battered pack in his pocket before launching into what his investigation had discovered so far.

"We had unconfirmed reports that guns were being run out of here for a few months now, contributing to the rise in violent crime and civilian casualties in the neighborhood."

Fang nodded; he'd seen the tragic incident reports, including one about a five-year-old girl killed on the street when a gunfight between two local gangs had broken out on her block. It had been splashed all over the city tabloids and had sparked a denunciation by the mayor's office, which had then immediately relegated cleaning up the mess to the already overworked city police department.

"However, we were never able to get a man on the inside. Since this was designated a top priority, we had been running surveillance for the past month, hoping to catch a lead—someone we could arrest and lean on. You know the story."

Fang murmured his agreement, content to let the older sergeant keep talking. He surveyed the room while listening, taking in the overturned chairs and tables, and the large blood pool and what looked like drying brains and skull fragments on the bar. He also spotted two young women wrapped in blankets—one trembling, one defiant as they were being interrogated by a female police officer.

"Tonight we were on eyeball detail when this tall Caucasian walks in—not completely out of the normal, the place gets a fair number of out-of-country tourists, but he was large enough that my men noticed him. Our man on the floor said he headed upstairs right away, as if he had an appointment with someone, so we thought we'd see what he came back out with and pick him up if we could. Except before he left—" Wei gestured to the chaos around them "—the Chaos Demons paid the White Lotus a visit."

Fang nodded again; he was familiar with both gangs. The White Lotus was more established and the Chaos Demons were the upstarts, making waves and taking territory any way they could. Fast, well armed and ruthless, they had been described in interagency briefings as "China's MS-13," referring to the powerful and fast-spreading Central American gang. He knew of several ongoing MSS operations against them, but none had been in this area. Making a note to follow up on that, he motioned at the sergeant to continue.

Wei paused as a badly wounded man strapped onto a stretcher was carried down the stairs by two paramedics. The middle of the blanket covering him was dark with blood.

"As far as we can tell, the Caucasian wasn't directly involved in this gang altercation. According to our preliminary findings, however, he killed several of the assailants."

"Killed several men armed with pistols?" Fang asked. "How did he do that?"

The sergeant nodded at the defiant-looking woman. "She claims he came in for a private show. Then, when the shooting started, he fought the attackers, smashing one in the head with a bottle, taking his pistol and shooting the others."

"Hold on—you're telling me some tourist off the street out for a lap dance suddenly decides to take on a bunch of armed gang members who burst into the club?" Fang asked with raised eyebrows.

"I'm as skeptical as you are, Major, but so far, that's what the evidence and eyewitness accounts are telling us."

"Right, the witnesses… Why leave them alive?" Fang mused. "For all he knew, she could have been in on the double-cross."

Wei shrugged. "She said he even told her to stay down and she would stay alive. She decided to follow his advice."

"Wait a minute. If she was on the ground, then how did she see him kill the other men?"

"All she claims is that he clobbered a guy with a bottle right in front of her, and when the smoke cleared, they were dead and he wasn't."

"Okay…" This entire incident was getting more and

more curious. "What about the man who got smashed with the bottle? Is he alive?"

The sergeant shook his head. "Caved in his temple. The guy was probably dead before he hit the floor."

"Pretty violent reaction for having his private show interrupted," Fang said while watching the trembling woman. He nodded at her. "What's her story?"

"She's another dancer. She was working the bar floor when one of the Demons grabbed her as a hostage," Wei replied. "Four of the Lotus surrounded him, so he wasn't going anywhere, but he had a gun to her head and told them to let him go or she was dead. Next thing she knew, a shot was fired and the guy was killed standing right next to her. She didn't get a scratch. From the angle of the entry wound—" Wei pointed to the top of the stair-case, about twenty meters away "—we figure it came from up there."

"Okay. What happened to our mystery customer?"

The sergeant ran a hand through his thinning black hair. "He escaped."

Fang's eyebrows rose again. "How did that happen?"

"The first officers on the scene came in right when the hostage situation was being…resolved. After securing the area, they headed upstairs and found three wounded men, two dead men and the woman dancer. A door at the end of the hallway was open and investigating it revealed a ladder that led up to an attic area under the roof and down below street level. The officers split up to investigate each potential escape route. The ones heading down say they lost any escapees in the maintenance tunnels under the street. The ones heading up, however, spotted someone ahead of them at the top of the shaft. They say their or-ders to stop moving were met with gunfire, which they returned. The ladder was damaged in the firefight and partially destroyed. By the time our men surrounded the building and gained access to the roof from the outside, there was no sign of the unknown subject."

The two men looked up as another wounded, groaning man was hoisted down the stairs on a stretcher. "I want updates on both of those men as soon as they're out of surgery. They are to be kept under guard until I say otherwise."

Wei nodded.

"I also want copies of all of the witness statements. The dancer, did she get a good look at the Caucasian?"

The sergeant shrugged. "She said he was wearing a baseball cap and sunglasses, so most of his face was covered. Our digital composite artist will be working with her down at the station."

Fang nodded. "Make that a top priority, and make sure the sketch is circulated throughout the city."

"What is the charge, sir?"

"The man is wanted for questioning right now, so just a be-on-the-lookout notice will suffice. Let's not try to spook him. Although it doesn't sound like he would gun down innocent civilians, I don't want to offer him the opportunity because some beat cop gets overzealous."

"So, add 'do not approach, may be armed and dangerous'?"

"Depends—how many guns do you estimate he took with him?"

Wei ticked off the count on his fingers. "At least four that we know of."

"Then, yes, add it to the notice." Fang looked at the stairs. "Let's go up there. I want to see what happened where and how."

"Right this way." The sergeant led him up the stairs. At the landing, they stopped while another police team busily wrapped up that part of the crime scene, zipping a body into a black plastic bag. A large dark puddle had soaked into the cheap carpet.

"Chou Lang, a member of the Chaos Demons for three years," Wei stated. "Armed robbery, drug trafficking, arms trafficking, extortion. He was blasting at someone with a .357 Magnum, took three in the chest and bled out right here."

Fang looked back, checking out the shot that had killed the hostage taker. It was a difficult one—in the dim light, with all the yelling and craziness that would have been going on. Fang wasn't sure he could have made it, and he practiced on the range three times a week. Whoever this person is, he knows his way around firearms, he thought.

The hallway looked like a war zone, with lights blown, bullet holes in the walls and the open door at the end missing its knob. Fang took it all in with a quick glance, then looked at Wei, who was standing by the third room down on the right.

"According to our eyewitness, he was getting his dance in here when the other gang busted in and starting tearing the place up. One came in here. He took out the man and left."

Fang surveyed the room, taking in the crumpled body of the man lying half atop a padded bench seat to his right. Two bloodstains on the floor near the door caught his attention. "Not enough here for deaths. Five people in this room at once?"

Wei smiled briefly. "There are elements of her story that don't quite check out."

"Why am I not surprised?" The two cops shared a wry grin.

"Those two wounded men being carried out of here were Jun Lu and An Zou, both White Lotus lieutenants. We found them in this room with her."

"Seems like an awful lot of security for just a lap dance," Fang commented.

Wei nodded. "We're thinking drugs or guns. Probably guns, since we've found no evidence of drugs anywhere, either in here or nearby."

"Plus, if the buyer felt he was being double-crossed or threatened, I doubt he would have much compunction about drawing a weapon and trying to shoot his way out."

The sergeant nodded again. "Indeed. Preliminary evidence puts him—" Wei pointed at the body "—as the shooter of the two men, who then got taken out by our unknown subject. If you'll follow me…" He stepped aside to allow Fang to exit into the hallway. "He comes out here and either takes out the gunman at the end of the hallway and then shoots the hostage taker or vice versa, we're not sure which yet."

Fang walked back to check the stairs. "No footprints in Lang's blood, and none on the landing. He killed the hostage taker first, then the gunman at the end of the hall when he came up to shoot his fellow gangster's killer. Also, I assume Lu and Zou were both armed?"

Wei nodded. "Both had empty holsters on them."

"So, our unknown assailant took their pistols, as well. Interesting. Where to next?"

"He walked down this hallway and was assaulted by another Chaos Demon hiding in this room." Wei stopped at the last door on the left, next to the broken one at the end of the hall. "One shot was fired and the man—Bao

Tan, Demon member for about nine months—is subdued with a broken nose and battery to the forehead. His pistol is taken, as well. The unknown subject then goes through this door and takes the computer that was storing the illegal media files the White Lotus was taking of their customers."

Fang nodded as the two men stepped into the crowded space. "Being very careful to remove any recorded trace of himself." So far, the evidence about this mystery Caucasian wasn't adding up to anything good. "Then he went to the ladder over there?" The major pointed at a brightly lit ladder with two uniformed police officers standing near it. A six-foot section of ladder, its jagged ends revealing where it had been broken, leaned against the nearby wall.

"Yes, sir. We've been working on rigging a replacement ladder to the trapdoor above," Wei told him.

"How's it going in here?" he asked, his tone indicating there was only one acceptable answer.

The upside-down head of a third man popped out from the hole in the ceiling. "Oh—hello, Sergeant. We've got a rope line secured to the top and were just about to open the trapdoor."

"This is Agent Deshi Fang, with the Ministry of State Security," Wei said, his tone neutral. "He is also working on the investigation." Which meant all of the men involved would now defer to Fang instead of Wei.

"The ministry appreciates your diligence in this matter, Officers," Fang said. "Now, I'd like to take a look at the upper level myself."

"We haven't opened the trapdoor yet, sir. Would you like us to do that before your inspection?" the man above him asked.

"If you don't mind, I'd like to examine the scene for myself," Fang replied. "I'll handle the door."

With a nod, the third officer pulled his head back above the ceiling, then reappeared a few seconds later, climbing down the ladder. "Be careful, sir, it's pretty rickety."

"Thank you for the warning, Officer." Fang climbed hand over hand, the ladder creaking and groaning under his weight, until he was at the broken part. The officers' solution to the missing portion was ingenious—they'd created a rope ladder and nailed it to the wall. He tested it first—just because they had built it didn't necessarily mean it was safe—but it held him easily. Climbing to the very top, he pushed at the trapdoor, only to find it stuck. He braced himself on the rope rungs and shoved with all his strength until the trapdoor creaked open.

Taking a small flashlight from his pocket, Fang climbed high enough to be able to peek over the lip of the floor but remained crouched below the opening. He turned the light on and raised the flashlight into the space, playing the beam all around. It wouldn't have been the first time a police officer had been caught by surprise by a criminal he thought had left an area, only to find him still hiding there. When no shot rang out, he poked his head above the floor edge and looked around.

The space around him was empty. The night breezes came in through a broken ventilation grate at the far end. Fang climbed up high enough to stand, and carefully walked to the square hole in the wall. He poked his head out again and looked down at the three-story drop into a narrow alleyway below, then up at the edge of the roof a couple meters overhead. One of the red tiles was crooked. That was all he needed to see.

He walked back to the ladder and climbed down to the men. "Sergeant Wei."

"Sir?"

"Getting that composite picture completed and distributed is your top priority this evening," Fang said as he pulled out his phone. "Also, once your men are done here, I want them to canvas the area in a one-block radius, every club, every apartment, looking for anyone who saw anything unusual. The unknown subject we are looking for is a professional, either police or military, or a former one or the other. He remains calm under fire, is able to engage and subdue multiple assailants and is careful to remove as much trace of his passage as possible. If he is spotted, I want to know about it immediately. Under no circumstances is any officer to approach him directly. Instead, they will call for backup and simply watch him discreetly. I will bring in the appropriate resources to apprehend him. Is that clear?"

"Yes, sir. I'll have the composite sketch forwarded to you as well, for dissemination as soon as it's finished."

"Thank you, Sergeant. Keep me apprised of your progress on this case, as well."

"Of course, sir."

"Excellent work, men, carry on." Fang headed to the main floor and out the door, where his car was waiting. Thumbing in a number as he got in, he told the driver to head to the safehouse, and made sure the door was closed before talking to the person on the other end of his call.

"I want the guard on Mrs. Liao and her children doubled tonight… I believe there's going to be an attempt to free her sometime this evening… I'm on my way there now… Notify all agents currently on duty there to report anything unusual, no matter how small, and include me in their five-minute check-ins… No, I have another matter to attend to first, so I won't be there until—" he caught his driver's gaze in the mirror, wincing as the man held up two fingers "—two hours from now… Yes, once I'm on-site, I'll oversee them personally this evening."

As the car pulled into traffic he ended the call and made another call, waking a sleepy-voiced man on the other end. "Da? It's Fang. The trap is still in place? Good, make sure your men are on alert tonight. I think the Americans are going to try something… I'm on my way right now… I know, they are crazy for wanting to break into a prison… See you soon."

After hanging up, Fang sat back in the seat and pulled out his pistol to check it. Although he had been on the job for almost eight years, this was the first time he was ever faced with the possibility of actually firing it in the line of duty.

I'm probably overreacting over nothing, he thought. I'll get there, and all of the men will have been on high alert all night for no reason.

On the surface, it was insane to try to break into a heavily guarded prison to free one man.

But as the car drove through the night, the nagging feeling in his gut told him otherwise. Fang leaned forward.

"Drive faster."

CHAPTER THIRTEEN

If I didn't know it was a prison, I would have thought it was some kind of retreat for the wealthy, Bolan thought as he stared through binoculars at the prison a quarter of a mile away in the foothills of the Yan Mountains.

After hauling himself onto the nightclub's rooftop, he'd crossed to the other side and leaped a five-foot alleyway to the adjoining building, which didn't have any kind of fire escape but did have a large drainpipe on its far side that he used to clamber down to the street. Bolan had been prepared to keep crossing roofs until he'd found a way to get down from the outside; the last thing he'd wanted was to go inside a building and possibly encounter any witnesses who might remember him later.

Once on the ground, he'd still been close enough to see the flashing lights from the police cars as they'd blocked off the street and to hear the shouts of the cops as they'd entered the building. By then he was at his truck and got inside, slouching in an attempt to disguise his height. He'd started the vehicle and pulled out into traffic, heading the opposite way before the streets became completely choked with stopped cars.

A few miles away he'd stopped at an overflowing garbage bin. Using a hammer he'd found in the pickup, he'd smashed open the computer from the nightclub and destroyed the hard drive, shoving the remains deep into the bags of garbage. Only then had he finally driven out of town, heading for the isolated prison a half hour north of the city.

Leaving the truck parked amid a stand of trees off the road a short distance from his insertion point, he made sure it was concealed from any casual passerby, repacked his equipment bag for this mission, got out and started to walk.

It was a good night for a walk in the country; the air wasn't quite as choked with pollution out here—it was bad, but not nearly as bad as the city proper. Bolan even heard some crickets, and once thought he saw a bat fly overhead, snatching insects out of the air as it went.

He kept his eye on his target as he moved. Unlike most modern prisons, Qincheng didn't have razor wire or guard towers. Instead, its primary fortification was a fifteen-foot wall, so wide that the guards patrolled the perimeter on top of it. The entire place was surrounded by fruit orchards—his data didn't say what kind—and there was even a fish pond on the land in front of the large iron gate.

Fortunately, Bolan wasn't entering the complex that way. The cyber team's research had come up with a more covert—although quite smelly—entrance, which he now stood in front of.

As with much of China's infrastructure from the middle of the past century, the prison's sewer system was rudimentary at best. The roughly five-foot-high pipe emitted a steady stream of waste onto a hillside that flowed out into a waste-slicked hill, with the run-off eventually flowing into the ditch and along the road below and meeting up with the nearest waterway. The pipe was blocked by thin metal bars. There had been concern they would be reinforced steel, but they turned out to be standard rebar.

Taking one last look around, Bolan took out a pair of latex gloves and pulled them on, then removed a butane torch from his bag and lit it, adjusting the flame until it was bright blue. It was short work to cut through two of the bars at their bottoms. He bent them just enough to slip through, then pulled them back into place so they would pass a casual inspection.

Bolan stuck his head back to the opening to take one last deep breath of the night air. After sending a short message to let Stony Man know he was in, he pulled on a black balaclava and a small, head-mounted flashlight.

He turned and started wading through the ankle-deep current of human excrement, counting his steps as he went.

After a while his nose acclimated to the stench and it became just one of the irritants in the pipe. There was also the fact that his height forced him to walk bent forward. The farther in he went, the higher the temperature, so he was soon dripping with sweat. All in all, it was one of the most unpleasant insertions he'd ever undertaken. Finally the pipe opened up into the sewer's main junction point underneath the prison. Streams of waste from the prison's various buildings collected here, pouring into a large pool that was slowly drained into the pipe from which he had just emerged. Although Bolan thought he had gotten used to the smell, the stench here was enough to make his eyes water.

Accessing his memorized map of the tunnels, Bolan counted off from his entry pipe four down, and sighed at the smaller pipe he had to traverse to reach his final destination. Roughly three feet in diameter, as all the others, it leaked a steady stream of waste. It was fifty yards to where Bolan could access the prison floor, and there was only one way to get there.

After finding a relatively dry spot to stash his gear bag, Bolan crouched and crawled inside, trying not to squirm at the warm stream of human waste that flowed over his hands and immediately soaked his pants from the knees down. He put it out of his mind and began crawling forward, remembering to glance up every so often to count the vertical shafts above him so he could come out as close to Liao's cell as possible. The pipe doglegged about twenty yards in, which was good, since it meant he'd only have to get that far for cover if someone was shooting at him.

This pipe was even more cramped, hotter and smellier than the first one, the combination teaming up to sap his stamina. Still, Bolan kept moving doggedly forward. When he reached the fourth vertical drain, he stood and used the crude rebar rungs set into the concrete to climb up to the grate in the floor.

He stood there listening for a few minutes, trying to see if any guards were on duty in the wing. Intel had showed that most worked outside, but they also conducted spot checks on prisoners during the night, making them sleep facing the peepholes in the door.

Even though the floor appeared quiet, he took out a small mirror and raised it high enough to see down the main hallway, then the other way. There was no one in sight in either direction.

The iron grate wasn't locked, but most of his strength was required to move it. He also had to be careful to not make a lot of noise, as he didn't want to alert any other prisoners to what was going on. After a couple of minutes of pushing it out of the way, he'd made a hole large enough for him to slip through. All that remained now was one padlocked door and he could grab Liao, take him back down the pipe and out.

Bolan hoped he wouldn't protest about their extraction route—it would be an ordeal to try to haul an unconscious body down that smaller pipe. Hoisting himself up, Bolan crept to the door to the cell Liao was supposed to be in and looked through the peephole. The light was on inside, showing a man lying on the bed, his hands above the covers as proscribed by the guards. He looked as though he was sleeping, with one arm over his face. Even though he already knew the dimensions of the room, Bolan was still surprised at how large it was, about twenty square yards. The bed was on the far side of the room, making a positive identification difficult.

Only one way to find out, Bolan mused as he went to work on the padlock securing the door. Working as quietly as he could took longer, but eventually the lock opened with a click.

He removed it and quietly opened the door, wincing at the high-pitched squeal. Easing inside, he crossed to the thin mattress and covered the sleeping man's mouth so he wouldn't shout when awakened.

The man's eyes flew open and widened at seeing the face of a masked man right above him.

"Zhang Liao?" Bolan asked. The man nodded. "I'm here to get you out. Do exactly as I say and we'll be clear of the prison in about twenty minutes. Do you understand?"

He nodded again and Bolan took his hand away from his mouth.

"Oh, thank you, thank you!" he whispered. "You have no idea what this means!"

"You can thank me once we're out of here," Bolan said, grabbing his arm and pulling him up. "Come on, we don't have much time—"

"No, just enough to hold you until the guards arrive," the man said, his hand diving under the blanket and coming up with a small pistol that he pointed at Bolan.

"I've caught him!" he shouted. "Guards! In here! Guards!"

CHAPTER FOURTEEN

Trying to keep his breathing steady, Liao lay back on his pillow and pulled the thin cover up to his neck.

Over the past day he had repeated the fecal matter treatment on his open wound three times. He had also managed to pass two health appointments, although once he swore the nurse wrinkled her nose and sniffed the air around him. He had immediately clamped his legs shut in the hope of cutting off any odor of waste she might have smelled. If they learned what he was doing before the infection could take hold, they'd probably install an armed guard to watch him around the clock or even worse, drug him so he couldn't do any harm against himself.

Even so, the moment the nurse had left, he'd gone to the bathroom and washed his injury clean, wiping it down with damp toilet paper that he immediately flushed. Inspecting the cut, he couldn't see any sign of immediate infection, but figured it was too early to tell. Cleaning it off also gave him the idea to try covering it in damp paper next time, as the warm, wet environment would hopefully speed the transmission of the bacteria and make him sicker quicker.

That thought brought a smile to his lips, which instantly died as the door opened and two guards entered, followed by Dr. Xu.

"Good afternoon, Mr. Liao. How are you feeling today?"

"All right, for a man who is going to die soon," he replied. Liao had decided early on to not fence words with the doctor or anyone here. He was going to be brutally honest with everyone. "But I imagine that doesn't concern you very much, does it?"

"Quite frankly, no, it doesn't," the doctor replied while reviewing Liao's chart. "No one ever arrives here accidentally. I know enough about you to know that the government has deemed you an enemy of the state, and therefore they have delivered you to me, so that I may recover what parts of you I can and give them to people in the hopes of prolonging their life."

"That's how you choose to rationalize your part in my death?" Liao asked.

"That's one way. I also take pride in knowing that I am helping to keep our glorious state strong by removing dissidents such as you who would seek to destroy it. So, while your ultimate goal may have failed, you should take comfort in knowing that your death will enable others to live." He said all of that as dispassionately as he might have ordered dinner at a restaurant.

Not if I have my way, I won't, Liao thought savagely. He kept his expression impassive, however, and stared at the doctor as he pored over the chart.

"Are you feeling feverish at all, or thinking slowly, perhaps?" Xu asked.

"No, my thought processes are very clear. Why?"

"The night nurse noticed a slight temperature variance over the past twenty-four hours, and you've been spending more time in bed than noted previously."

Liao waved at the empty room. "Where else would you have me be? Other than the toilet, that is?"

Xu's answering smile was thin. "We like our patients to be as healthy as possible, of course—"

"Of course—unhealthy organs wouldn't be nearly as useful to you, would they?" Liao asked.

"No, they wouldn't," the doctor replied. "Get out of bed."

"And if I refuse?"

The doctor's expression didn't change. "Then the guards will remove you from the bed by force if necessary. Any further insubordination will result in you being secured to the bed until your scheduled operation. Now, am I going to have to ask again or do you require assistance?"

"No, I can do it." Slowly, Liao got out of the bed, keeping his legs as close together as he dared without being obvious about it. Trying not to tremble in his nervousness, he stood impassively as the doctor checked his lymph nodes, then his limbs, then under his arms. He couldn't still the trembling in his limbs, particularly when he thought the doctor might be going to palpate his genitals.

"You're shaking, Mr. Liao," he noted as he placed his stethoscope on the man's chest. "Breathe in, please."

"That's because it's cold in here and that—" Liao nodded at the instrument on his chest "—isn't helping."

That actually brought a slight smile from the normally emotionless physician. "No, I suppose not. Turn around." He repeated the same breathing request, then removed the stethoscope, hung it around his neck and folded his arms. "You can return to your bed, if you wish."

"What's the prognosis?" Liao asked as he sat on the

bed and pulled his legs up, careful to not expose anything through the backless hospital gown.

"No sign of infection that I can find. We'll get you another blanket, and keep observing you for the time being, to make sure this doesn't develop into something. You just get plenty of rest, okay?"

"Sure. There's not much else I can do, is there?" Liao held the doctor's gaze for a few more moments, until he turned on his heel and left the room, the guards falling in behind him. Only when another minute had passed did he let out the breath he was scarcely aware he'd been holding.

It took every ounce of willpower he possessed not to bolt from the bed straight back into the bathroom and dig out some more feces to reinfect himself. However, since Dr. Xu had kindly informed him that he would be under observation, he didn't want to do anything to alert them of a change in his daily habits. Therefore, he would have to wait for at least a couple of hours before going again.

Liao lay back on his pillow, eager to see if his improvised poultice idea would bear any ill fruit.

CHAPTER FIFTEEN

The false Liao had barely finished uttering his shout for reinforcements before Bolan hurled the heavy padlock into his face. His nose crunched with a spurt of blood as the pistol went off—the bullet coming nowhere near the Executioner—and the man clapped both hands to his bloody face and screamed.

Drawing his own pistol, Bolan ran to the side of the cell door and waited as pounding footsteps approached. A man rushed in and the moment he did, Bolan chopped down on his neck with the butt of his pistol, sending him straight to the floor. Another man charged in right behind him, but couldn't stop in time to turn and shoot the intruder. Instead he tripped over Bolan's outstretched foot and fell on top of his partner. The big American drew his foot back and kicked the man at the base of his neck, stunning him.

Knowing the cell was a death trap, he took the PPK from his pocket. Sticking both pistols out the door, he fired four shots to the left and right, hearing startled shouts as guards scrambled to avoid the flurries of bullets.

In the confusion that followed, he ran for the sewer hole, still shooting in both directions. Some return fire sounded from one end, making him drop into a slide as he neared the sewer shaft. Once there, he scooted forward and stuck his feet into the hole, shooting in both directions. When the PPK locked back on empty, he tossed it aside, then slid into the hole, turning as he did so he could grab a rung with his free hand. He shoved himself down just as a spray of bullets split the air where his head had been a second earlier.

Not bothering with trying to pull the grate back, Bolan extended to his full height and dropped the few feet into the small tunnel. He crouched there, half in the horizontal pipe, waiting with his pistol pointed up until a shadow blocked the light. The moment he saw it, he unloaded the rest of the magazine, the thundering echo of the shots pounding his ears unmercifully in the small space. A spatter of blood rained down on him as the man fell over the hole.

Reloading his pistol, Bolan tucked it into the back of his pants, then scooted down and began crawling down the narrow pipe as fast as he could. He figured he had maybe eight to ten seconds before someone came along and sprayed the interior with bullets. He knew he had to make that dogleg before they arrived.

Distant shouts echoed down the passage and boots clanged against the rungs. Spotting the bend in the pipe a few yards ahead, Bolan put on a burst of speed as he heard someone splash down in the pipe behind him. It was either stop and try to shoot the guy or make it to cover. Bolan opted for the latter, lunging full-out into the muck as an automatic weapon opened up.

Bullets sparked and whined all around him. Lying full-length in the putrid stream, he pulled himself forward until he made it around the dogleg, then lay there for a few seconds. Sitting up in the pipe and gritting his teeth against the reports, he stuck his hand around the corner and fired six shots, trying to aim down the cen-

ter of the pipe. He heard splashing and shouts from farther back, and hoped he'd bought enough time to get out.

Turning back around, he crawled as fast as he could
to the junction, hoping he wasn't about to slide out of the
sewage into the arms of another squad of guards. As he
got closer, he tried to listen for any sounds of an ambush,
but he was making too much noise and the ringing in his
ears wasn't helping, either.

Leading with his pistol, the Executioner sluiced out
into the large space to find it empty. Pulling himself out,
he turned in time to see the flash of lights coming around
the bend. He crouched and waited until one of his pursuers turned the corner before unloading the rest of his
magazine. The light popped and died, and he heard no
more movement.

Reloading his pistol, he grabbed his bag and hit the
larger pipe. Once inside, he turned off his own light to
avoid being a target both from his pursuers or anyone
waiting ahead. The stifling, suffocating darkness pressed
in all around him, but he kept moving, knowing he had
a long way to go, and even then he might make it out
only to be captured at the end of the pipe. As he trudged
along, bent over so that he didn't hit his head, he tried
to stay alert for any sounds of pursuit, but soon realized
that his ears were still ringing from the shooting in the
small pipe. He settled for keeping his eyes open and his
pistol ready.

Replaying the step count in his head, he slowed when
he got to six hundred, knowing he was roughly one hundred steps from the exit. Although every instinct wanted
to charge ahead, he knew if he did that, it would likely
only earn him a long prison sentence in the best case or
a bullet in the head in the worst.

Panting and soaked in sewage, he approached the end of the sewer pipe carefully, his vision adjusting to make out the moonlit night through the blackness of the pipe itself. Twenty paces away, he stopped and tried to sense whether anyone was waiting outside, but didn't see anything, couldn't hear anything and realized he'd have to chance it.

He crept to the edge of the pipe and stopped, looking, trying to listen again. Quietly bending the bars apart, he slipped out, expecting to hear a shout to halt or to feel a hand on his arm.

Nothing…he was utterly, completely, alone.

But there were bright lights on at the prison, and Bolan knew they would be scrambling guards to come after him.

He turned and ran up the hill.

CHAPTER SIXTEEN

Akira Tokaido watched the alert unfold at the prison. Getting eyes on the facility while Bolan entered had been more difficult than usual. Due to its isolated location, the security cameras inside were self-contained, with no outside access. The young hacker had been able to access the regular computers—that's how they'd found Liao in the first place—but he hadn't been able to find a way in to the surveillance system.

Instead they'd grabbed time on a CIA satellite overflying the area, and had gotten the feed up just in time to see everything go south. Lights had gone on all over the compound, and guards were systematically locking down the perimeter and searching through every building. A heavily armed squad, complete with riot shields and automatic weapons, entered the building where the target had been located.

"No word from Striker yet?" Brognola asked.

"Not yet, Hal," Tokaido answered.

"And we have no eyes inside the building where the target was reportedly located, right?"

"You got it."

"Would someone care to take a *guess* as to what happened in there?" the big Fed asked.

"I'd say that they suckered us, Hal." Kurtzman pivoted

his wheelchair to face his boss. "They set a trap and we fell for it hook, line and sinker."

Brognola rubbed his hand over his face. "And exactly how did that happen?"

"Everything looked legit," Kurtzman continued, un-ruffled by the other man's laser-like stare on him. "He was the right type of prisoner to end up at Qincheng, the time frame was right and we did everything we could to confirm it in the limited amount of time we had. Based on all available evidence, Zhang Liao was in that prison cell—right up until Striker arrived. I'd like to tell you we're perfect, but that doesn't mean we can't be foxed, as well."

"No, you're right, Aaron. You guys do enough magic and mind reading on these things as it is. But Striker has walked into a trap and might very well be dead now. We need to put a team on standby to be ready to get him back ASAP."

"Not until he's missed his check-in deadline," Kurtz-man pointed out. "As per the mission protocol."

Price cleared her throat. "Bear's right, Hal. Also, while I don't like bringing this up, I need to remind you of the mission parameters that were handed to us by the President."

"I'm damn well aware of the parameters. I won't leave Striker hanging, Barb."

"None of us would, Hal. However, Aaron's still cor-rect. We need to wait until Striker's misses his next check-in," she said, hating every word that came out of her mouth. "Once we know his status, then we can plan accordingly."

Brognola grunted his acknowledgment of that brutal

fact. "With this part blown, what are the probable outcomes?"

"Bluntly, that depends on whether he's alive or dead," Kurtzman answered. "If he's alive, then it's only a matter of time before we're in a whole heap of trouble. Granted, there's nothing that officially ties him to us, however, as you've no doubt realized, the Chinese aren't that stupid. At some point, they're going to figure out that he's not from Russia or Eastern Europe. From there—and factoring in who his target was—it's not a huge leap to figure out who sent him. If that happens, the cat is out for good and we're left holding the bag."

"Technically, yes," Price said. "However, keep in mind that the Chinese don't want this to get out, either. It's very possible that they'll also sweep it under the rug, and Striker will have just disappeared in the line of duty. He knows the drill. The President will disavow all knowledge of any US assets operating in China.

"That said, I think I'll just wait here until we receive word from Striker." Price pulled up a chair and sat.

"I've never played the waiting game well," Brognola said. "I'm going back to the farmhouse to do some paperwork. Call me if you hear anything."

CHAPTER SEVENTEEN

"Traffic ahead, sir."

The driver's warning brought Deshi Fang out of his reverie and he looked out the windshield to see a truck from the prison drive by at a high rate of speed. It was followed by another one and he got a sinking feeling in his stomach. "Damn it—get us to the prison as fast as you can."

His driver stomped on the gas, and soon the sedan was flying down the dirt road. The moment he saw the prison, Fang knew he had missed whatever had happened there. It was lit up like high noon, with every light and spotlight in the place turned on. Guards scurried to and fro like ants spilling out of a kicked anthill.

The main gate was locked down tight, with a half dozen guards all carrying submachine guns at port arms. His driver stopped the car a few meters away and Fang got out slowly, aware that every guard was watching him as he approached.

He pulled his identification from his coat pocket and held it out in front of him as he walked to the nearest guard. "Agent Deshi Fang, Ministry of State Security. I must see the warden immediately."

The guard scrutinized his card closely, then said, "Come with me, sir."

He led Fang to the guard booth next to the gate, where

he called someone. Several moments later he opened the door that led into the prison. "You will find him in Yi Building, sir."

"Thank you." The guard's answer only deepened Fang's concern. He broke into a run toward that particular building, which was also surrounded by a ring of armed guards. Repeating the ID flash at the main door, he was let inside after another careful examination of his credentials.

Inside, there was activity everywhere, but the majority of it was centered around a sewer drain in the middle of the hall. Fang saw the warden, a man named Da Wen, directing guards who were hauling up something from beneath the ground. Over by the far wall, three guards were being attended to by a physician.

"Warden, what happened?" he asked as he joined the short, broad-shouldered man with buzz-cut, iron-gray hair and a pugnacious squint. He was smoking furiously as he oversaw what was going on.

"What happened?" He pointed to a limp, blood-and-sewage covered body that was just now coming out of the hole. "The trap we set worked—except the bastard fought his way out, that's what happened! I've got two dead and three injured guards, and he got away." He shook his head. "More than likely I'll end up in here myself, after a mistake of this magnitude."

Fang's ministry had joined forces with the Ministry of Public Security to set up a sting operation, in the event that the Americans tried to recover Liao. They had leaked the information about him being at Qincheng Prison in the hope of attracting some sort of extraction team. By the looks of it, they had attracted a lot more than they had bargained for.

"But it can't be all bad," Fang said. "Your people did flush out the team, right?"

"Team? Team!" Wen stared at him in mingled shock and anger. "This was all done by *one man*! He fought my guards to a standstill and got out the same way he got in—through the sewers. We had supposed that might be an entry point, but it ranked so low on our list we didn't reinforce it, figuring any sign of activity there might spook them, and anyway, we'd be able to capture them in here, right?"

Fang nodded, realizing *that* part would be the problem that would end the warden's career. "Look, you executed this operation by order of the Ministry of State Security. I'll do what I can for you in my report."

Wen took a drag off his cigarette, then lit a new one from it and tossed the butt away. "Sure, Fang, sure. You write it up any way you like…it won't make any difference." He shook his head. "A year before retirement, and it's all over."

The sad part was that Fang knew he was right. The central government didn't care about excuses or reasons why something hadn't worked; they only cared about getting results. If a person didn't accomplish the results the government wanted, that person was removed and another person was installed with the same orders.

With a start, he realized the same thing could happen to him. He looked up at Wen. "How long ago did this happen?"

The warden shrugged. "Maybe twenty, twenty-five minutes."

Fang nodded. "I have to get back to the city. Thanks for—" He wasn't sure what he could thank the other man for, as this mission had been almost a complete failure. "I'll be in touch."

Wen lifted a hand in a weak farewell as he stared morosely at the ruins of his once proud fiefdom crumbling around him.

Fang ran outside, through the front gate and to his car, jumping in the backseat. "Get me back to the apartment building right now!"

As the car sped down the road, he pulled out his cell phone and pressed one button. "He's coming. Tonight. Be ready. I want him taken alive."

CHAPTER EIGHTEEN

After reaching the truck, Bolan jumped in and drove until he found the nearest public restroom. Like many on the outskirts of the city, it was very simple, with squat toilets, barely operational sinks and watered-down pink soap. Bolan didn't care about any of that, and after what he had just gone through, he barely noticed the overpowering combination of urine and cheap incense.

Parking in the back to avoid any cameras, he kept his head down and carried his bag in. He swept through the stalls, making sure they were unoccupied, then stripped and threw away his clothes and boots, being careful to clean out his pockets beforehand to avoid leaving anything incriminating.

Running all the sinks, he cleaned himself with antibacterial soap, paying particular attention to any part of him that had come in contact with the raw sewage. After drying himself with scratchy paper, he dressed in clean clothes, finally feeling more or less his old self. Afterward, he drove a few more miles toward the city, then found a public parking garage and drove up to the roof, which contained only a few vehicles. Making sure no one was around, he turned on his phone and checked the mailbox for messages.

One was waiting for him: an encrypted data file. He transferred it to the tablet, then turned off the phone and turned off the tablet's wireless capability before opening the file. In it was everything he would need to recover the Liao family— Except for their father, he mused.

There was one odd bit attached to the file: a request to reply with the time he expected to begin the rescue op. There was no explanation as to why, but he figured there must be a good reason. Doing a bit of inner city navigating, he estimated it would take about forty minutes in normal traffic to get to the address. Bolan tacked on fifteen more minutes for unforeseen traffic and upped his estimate to a flat hour. He sent the reply immediately, figuring it would be better to do it from this location instead of right outside the target building. He also included the following about the blown op:

Could not meet with uncle—address incorrect.
Dogs near house were very angry. Will look for him in city. Assistance appreciated.

With that gone, he headed down to rejoin the sluggish, never-ending stream of cars and trucks winding their way through the city streets.

FIFTY-SEVEN MINUTES later the high-rise was in sight.

As he drove past the sleek glass-and-concrete building he noticed one of the metal garage gates slide up. On the way over, he had been pondering how best to gain access the building, but it looked as though his way in was being smoothed by the powers-that-be.

Those powers being Bear and Akira, no doubt, he said to himself as he realized why they had asked for the mission start time. Cranking the wheel, he turned into the lane and drove down into the parking level beneath the building.

Sure hope they can smooth the way out just as easily, he thought while parking the truck. There were no spots near the bank of elevators, which was fine, since he wasn't planning to take an elevator anyway. Finding a shadowed corner far away from the stairs, Bolan backed his truck into a parking space and turned the engine off.

Mission prep consisted of loading three magazines for the submachine gun and three magazines for the pistol, along with the Beretta's magazine. Loading each weapon and chambering a round in each, he placed the Type 79 gun back inside the nylon bag and slung it over his shoulder, with the top zipper open just enough for easy access. The Type 59 pistol was small enough to fit into his jacket pocket, with the Beretta tucked into the waistband of his jeans at the small of his back. An additional magazine for each weapon went into his back pockets, with the third ones in side-zippered pockets on the bag itself. Finally he put the stun gun into his other jacket pocket. When all was said and done, he looked like an everyday man heading home after a hard day's work—or at least he would have in America. He pulled on a pair of leather driving gloves.

Easing out of the pickup, Bolan made sure his ball cap was secure and kept his head down as he crossed the parking garage and headed toward the stairs. He noted that the garage door had closed.

The door to the stairs required a key card, but as he approached, the light on the card reader changed from red to green, and he heard a click from the door itself. Trying the handle, he smiled when it opened at his slight pull.

Bolan looked up at the seemingly endless flights of

stairs going around and around in a rising square above his head. He stopped on the first landing and listened, knowing that most stairwells were like huge echo chambers and the smallest sound was often magnified along its entire length. The whole space was as quiet as a tomb. Pulling off his baseball cap, he pulled a thin, black balaclava over his head, covering everything but his eyes and mouth. Shaking his head to make sure it was comfortable, he glanced up one more time and began to climb.

The steps were a bit shorter than he was used to, and it took a couple flights until he got into a comfortable rhythm. Once he did, his legs ate up the distance with surprising quickness. On the way up, he reviewed the plan.

With Stony Man now clearing the way, he hoped to gain entrance to the penthouse without alerting any of the guards. If necessary, he would shoot his way out, but if he could at least get in without firing a shot, so much the better.

With two floors to go, he slowed and slipped a hand into his pocket to flick off the safety on the Type 59 pistol.

With one floor to go, he slowed to a walk. On the landing below his target floor, he stopped and listened for a minute, trying to hear any noise from the nearby hallway. Hearing nothing, he slowly ascended the last flight of stairs, every sense alert, checking the next flight above him just in case his hearing had been affected by the blasting traffic and street noise he'd been subjected to. He still didn't hear any noise from either the stairs or the hallway. There was no security on the access door. He reached for the handle, his other hand tight on the butt of his pistol, and began to pull the door open— only to hear the soft chime of the elevator door opening a few yards away. Voices speaking Mandarin carried to his ears and Bolan quickly let the door fall closed. Leaping to the upper staircase, he headed up two flights before he stopped.

The door to the stairwell opened and a two-man team in suits checked both up and down, although they only gave a cursory glance at the upper level, as Bolan suspected they would. In the absence of a sighting-verified threat, even the best counterintelligence teams tended to concentrate on the most obvious entrance points, often showing a characteristic lack of imagination about ways enemy operatives could gain access to areas—as he had just done.

However, this definitely complicated his mission, as the team didn't seem to be executing a standard sweep-and-clear. They looked to be on a higher level of alertness, as if specifically looking for someone. As though he had somehow been made. Bolan had no idea how that might have happened, since no one outside the handful of people at Stony Man knew he was in China. It was theoretically possible, though practically impossible, that someone might have detected Kurtzman's and Tokaido's hacking of the apartment building's security system, but whatever had occurred didn't change his mission parameters. How it was to be accomplished, however…that might be a different story.

Stepping slowly, carefully, back down the stairs, Bolan edged low enough to glimpse the doorway. A flash of movement made him pull back, but he'd seen enough to confirm his suspicion: one of the men was stationed on the landing by the hallway entrance.

Shooting the man was out of the question. The echo would bring every agent in the building running. The trick would be to subdue him without allowing him to raise the alarm. Bolan crouched and listened for the next fifteen minutes, long enough to establish that the security team was on a five-minute check-in cycle.

Bolan ran through several plans to take out the guard, but they all either relied on equipment he didn't have or were impossible to execute in the space. After ditching the idea of trying to drop on the guy from the space between the stairwells—it would have been a tight but not impossible fit—he realized there was no other way to do it. He would have to rely on speed, strength and skill.

That said, the only thing left was to wait until the man checked in again. Bolan used that time to slowly remove his nylon bag and set it down beside him. Three minutes later the man returned.

Hearing the murmur as the agent replied to one of the other team members, Bolan waited until the stairwell fell silent again, then made his move by noiselessly creeping down two more steps, enough to be able to vault the chest-high barrier that ran alongside each flight of stairs. The real problem would be making sure he landed fully on a step. If he missed and sprained his ankle, it would be all over. Glancing behind him to gauge where the proper step would be, Bolan moved.

Planting his hands on the sloping railing, he flung his legs over and landed lightly on the third step down, exactly where he'd intended. Crouching to absorb the impact, he immediately leaped forward again, sailing down the rest of the flight of steps to land directly in front of the man.

The Chinese agent reacted immediately, one hand darting inside his suit jacket, the other going up to his earpiece.

Stepping forward, Bolan whipped around the butt of

the Beretta and dealt a savage blow to the man's cheek, snapping the bone and sending the agent staggering across the small landing to the wall, where he managed to stop himself from hitting headfirst. It didn't help, however, because before he could activate his transceiver or cry out for help, Bolan was on him again and a hard blow to the back of the head put him down for good.

Pulling the radio receiver out of his former adversary's ear, Bolan stripped him of his pistol, used his own handcuffs to secure the unconscious man to the railing, and gagged him with a handkerchief taken from the agent's pocket.

He then ran upstairs for his gear, headed back to the door, listened for any signs that the alarm had been raised, then opened it just enough to glance down the hallway.

The floor plan placed the stairs in an alcove next to the elevators, with the doors to the large apartments on this floor on either side of the hallway's T-intersection. Working carefully, Bolan was able to ease himself through the door into the alcove.

Peeking out into the hallway, he saw two men at the far end, walking around and watching the elevators. Pulling back before they could spot him, he tried to figure out a way to incapacitate both men. Aware of the countdown ticking away in his head until the next check-in period, Bolan prepared to take down the pair, ready to shoot if he had to.

The chime of an arriving elevator caught his attention and he heard footsteps on the tiled floor as the men approached it. Hoping these weren't more reinforcements, Bolan listened as the two conferred quietly. The doors slid open. They chuckled and then started heading back to the other end of the hallway.

A second chime, on the far side of the hallway from the stairway, made them pause. Bolan peeked out again to see them watch the second arriving elevator, their hands also going under their suit jackets.

The elevator chimed and Bolan drew the Type 59 pistol as the doors slid open. When this one was also revealed to be empty, the two men frowned and one of them reached up to his ear.

That was when Bolan moved. Stepping out from the alcove, he walked up behind both men in two large strides and rammed each one on the back of the head with the pistol butt. Both collapsed to the floor and he quickly pulled out the earpieces, removed their pistols and handcuffed them together. Dragging the agents back into the elevator, he hit every button between the twenty-fifth floor and the fifth, then got out and let the elevator start its long ride down.

With a silent thanks to Kurtzman and Tokaido, he started down the hallway, searching for the door of the apartment where the Liaos were being held.

CHAPTER NINETEEN

"That was inspired thinking with the elevators, Akira."

"Thanks. Maintenance programs are the best, aren't they?" The young hacker rubbed his eyes, then returned his attention to the screen showing Striker taking out the two Ministry of State Security men on the other side of the world. "Locking that elevator between floors...now. Okay, those two guys will be out of commission even after they wake up."

Everyone had different reactions when the email from Striker had arrived. Tokaido had pumped his fist in the air, while Kurtzman had simply nodded soberly, as if he had already known the outcome. Brognola, who had returned from the farmhouse, merely grinned.

And behind the three men, Price had simply thanked the powers-that-be that Mack Bolan was still alive.

She caught Kurtzman looking at her and she nodded. He nodded back and then returned to what he had been doing.

Now she, along with the three men, watched Bolan neutralize the guards around the Liao apartment.

Pinpointing his location from the last brief email they had received, Kurtzman had picked him up on a traffic camera. He'd tagged him so that the cameras along his route would automatically show him on their feed as soon as he appeared in their view, then scrub the data afterward on every camera that had caught him to remove any trace of his presence. Since they were already on-site in preparation to scrub the building's security data as well, they'd assisted with getting him inside and also overridden the elevators to provide the crucial moment's distraction that had allowed him to take out the guards.

"Keep in mind we can also lock the elevators so any incoming reinforcements have to take the stairs. Or, even better, we can trap them inside one, like I just did, to allow Striker to get the targets out," Tokaido noted.

"Great thinking. Since you're already there, you might as well assist him into the apartment," Price replied. "As long as he can maintain the element of surprise, he should be able to take out those guards and get our targets out and away quickly."

"I can get him through the door no problem, but the rest of it will be up to him."

"When you have a moment, Bear, check in with our extraction team to make sure they're ready to go," Brognola said. A thumbs-up was the bearded man's only reply and it didn't interrupt his typing in the slightest. Ever since Bolan's email had come in, he had been busy trying to locate Zhang Liao. So far, he has having no luck.

"How do you want to handle this complication with Washington?" Price asked. "If the President gets wind that Liao's missing, he'll probably want to scrub the op."

"He probably would, which is why I'm not updating him until absolutely necessary," Brognola replied. "If Striker can pull the family out, that should be enough leverage for us to keep the mission green. Of course, none of that will matter if we can't find him."

"Hopefully it won't come to that," Price replied. "Too bad about the guards."

"Well, I wouldn't say 'risks of the job,' but if you try to set a trap for a lion, you'd better damn well expect a lion to show up." Brognola grinned. "They're lucky he didn't burn them all down."

"I just heard from the extraction crew. Stony Air touched down fourteen minutes ago and is awaiting arrival of cargo," Kurtzman said.

"Thanks, Aaron," the big Fed replied. Under the guise of a test flight, Brognola had sent Jack Grimaldi and Charlie Mott the other way around the world, flying to the West Coast and over the Pacific to Kunsan Air Base, on the west coast of South Korea. They had been cooling their heels there until their mission window had opened, at which point they had taken off and flown across the Yellow Sea to Beijing's Xijiao Airport, a military airport that, oddly, also accepted charter flights. They were sitting on the tarmac right now, awaiting Bolan's arrival with the Liaos. The moment they received any members of the family, they were to go wheels up and get them out of Chinese airspace ASAP.

"I just hope this 'hide under their very noses' plan is going to work," Price mused. "It was tricky enough getting Jack and Charlie into the country in the first place."

"Worked so far, hasn't it?" Brognola grunted. "Those boys know how to keep their heads down."

"Damn! You might want to see what just went out over the Beijing police wire," Tokaido said, making all eyes turn to him. "Remember that nightclub where we set the meet for Striker to pick up his weapons? Well, from the looks of things we chose the same night that a rival gang made a hit on the place. Apparently, Striker got caught in the middle of it somehow and is now wanted in connection with the incident."

"How so?" Price asked, staring at the digital sketch of a man with Bolan's jawline and face shape, partially obscured by a ball cap and sunglasses.

Tokaido squinted at the screen. "It doesn't give a lot of details, just that he's wanted for questioning. If it makes you feel any better, it's for internal dissemination only. Apparently they're not releasing this to the public yet."

"Damn it, I knew that buy was too dangerous! We should have had weapons sent over by diplomatic pouch via the Gulfstream," Price said.

Popping an antacid from his never-ending supply, Brognola offered one to Price, who declined. "They didn't grab him on the scene, and the fact that the MSS is keeping this on the down-low means they don't want it getting out, either. Striker may be wanted, but he's supposed to be staying on the move until he leaves the city. All he's got to do is stay ahead of the guys trying to nab him—"

"And not run into any more friction along the way," Price said, folding her arms. "With the way our luck's been running so far, they'll have an entire Special Police Unit guarding the Liaos, and since he's on radio silence, we couldn't even warn him!"

"Even so, I'd still give Striker even odds on coming out with what he came for," Brognola told her. "He's been doing this a long time, and under more adverse conditions. He'll bring them out."

"I hope you're right, Hal," she replied, turning back to face the screen to see Bolan at the door to the apartment. "I hope you're right."

CHAPTER TWENTY

Baozhai Liao tossed and turned on her narrow twin bed, finding sleep as elusive as safety. The rest of her day after the failed interview had gone steadily downhill, with her being served a bland, tasteless meal of watery rice and chicken, which she had eaten mainly because it was something to do other than constantly dwell on her children and husband.

True to his word, Agent Fang's orders had prevented her from seeing her children that evening. Making matters worse, they had been let out of the bedroom they were confined to for at least two hours, talking to their captors loud enough that Baozhai could hear the conversations. Well, at least one of them.

Unsurprisingly, the government agents had drawn Cheng out of his shell and he was now peppering them with questions. Each time he laughed was like a dagger in her heart. She heard nothing from Zhou, however, but the beeps of that damn video game she was always playing. Baozhai made a solemn promise that, if they got out of this alive, she was going to smash that thing against the closest wall, although she regretted the impulse the moment she'd thought of it, knowing it was probably the only thing keeping her daughter calm.

Forced to listen to her children in the next room, but for all intents and purposes a million miles away, she finally decided to try to ignore the sounds and go to sleep.

But even though physically and emotionally exhausted, she ended up lying there for hours, staring at the walls or the ceiling, unable to find a moment's respite.

Finally, she sat up in bed, licking her dry lips. Her bladder was becoming insistent, and she could use a glass of water, as well. The kids and she were in the second and third bedrooms. The master, with its attached bathroom, had been taken over by the MSS agents.

Sliding out of bed, she walked to the door and knocked softly.

"What do you want?" The answer came immediately from the other side of the door.

"I need to relieve myself and to get a drink of water."

There was a moment's pause. "Very well. Step back from the door."

Baozhai did as ordered, retreating to the middle of the room and standing there with her hands at her sides. Once, she had made the mistake of moving a bit too slowly from the entrance and had nearly gotten shot. She had made sure never to make that mistake again.

The door opened wide and one of the agents, Liu, she thought, stood in the doorway. If ever there was a mold somewhere that MSS agents came from, he was it: short, black hair, an alert, guarded expression and a lean, quick body under a plain black suit. He regarded her for a moment, then stepped back and waved her forward. "Two minutes."

Baozhai trotted into the hallway and into the bathroom on the left, closing the door. The locking knob had been replaced with a simple handle. She sat on the toilet with great relief, then quickly washed her hands and her face, the tepid water feeling as refreshing as the finest eau de toilette she had been given during her modeling career.

She looked around for a glass to drink from, but there was nothing on the sink. Other than a small roll of toilet paper, there was nothing extra in the bathroom, not even a shower curtain rod.

She could have stayed in there for an hour but knew that Agent Liu had meant what he'd said. When the two minutes were up, he would come into the bathroom and drag her out.

Still, she savored the privacy for as long as she could before exiting. He pointed her toward the bedroom, making her frown slightly. "What about my water?"

A larger frown creased his brow. "Go back to your room. I will bring you some."

She spoke as he began turning. "Please, I have been trapped in there all day. Just let me have one minute to go to the kitchen and get it, and then I will return to my room and not bother you for the rest of the evening."

His face remained impassive during her plea and, for a moment, Baozhai didn't think he was going to allow it. Then his expression relaxed and he stood aside to let her walk to the kitchen. "One minute."

Despite being a large penthouse apartment, it had been designed fairly oddly. Instead of opening up to a central living space, the apartment was bisected into halves, with the divider being the wide hallway that cut through the middle. On her left was the entry into the living room, where she heard the murmur of other voices—two, maybe three men—and could detect a hazy pall of cigarette smoke. To her right was the kitchen, with two entryways, the one near her and the other farther down and across from the dining room.

Baozhai walked into the kitchen, the lights automatically coming on as she entered. It was sleek, with stainless-steel appliances and light maple cabinets. She took a bottle of water out of the fridge and grabbed a glass from a cabinet. As she pulled it down, something—she never knew what had caught her eye—made her look over at the corner, where she saw a large man, dressed all in black from head to toe, staring at her with ice-blue eyes. He was holding a gun in one hand, holding a finger over his lips with the other.

Startled, Baozhai managed not to scream, but her hand twitched and the glass fell and smashed against the edge of the cabinet. Within three seconds Liu was beside her, his hand on his holstered pistol.

"What happened?" he asked.

Baozhai blinked and glanced back at the corner, but the man was gone. "I—I just scared myself, that's all. I was getting the glass when I thought I saw something over there—" she pointed to the other side of the kitchen, near the stove and dishwasher "—and jumped, dropping the glass. I'm so clumsy."

She bent to start picking up the pieces, but was stopped by Liu. "Don't bother with that. I'll get it cleaned up."

"All right."

"Get your drink and I'll take you back to your room."

"Thank you." Baozhai retrieved another glass, her mind spinning. She *had* seen that man in the corner, she was sure of it. And what was more, he was a round-eye. An American? She didn't know how they had found her, but she had to take advantage of this opportunity. But how?

She poured some water into her glass and drank, trying to prolong the experience while thinking furiously. All she knew for sure was that the men obviously didn't know the intruder was here. But how could she use it to her advantage? Any sort of attack on her captor—like smashing the glass into his face—would just bring the others into the room. No, she had to figure out a way to distract him that would allow the other man to kill him silently.

Figuring he had to be either in the dining room or more likely on the other side of the hallway, she decided to gamble on walking to the dining room while Liu was distracted. She finished her drink, then turned and headed for the second exit. "I'm just going to stretch my legs in the hallway, okay?"

"Wait, what?" His head popped up as she walked into the hallway. The moment she was out of sight, she scurried to the entrance to the dining room, then paused long enough until she saw his shadow fall into the hallway. "Mrs. Liao, you cannot—"

She walked into the dark room, the only window at the far end shrouded by vertical blinds. She didn't see the other man anywhere and barely made out the long wooden dining table in time to avoid smacking her leg on it. As soon as she saw it, the idea came to her and she sank to the ground, rocking back and forth. "Ow!"

"You are not supposed to be in here!" Liu said as he appeared in the doorway.

"I'm sorry. I banged my shin on the table," Baozhai said while clutching her leg. "Just give me a moment and I'll be able to get back up again."

He stepped over to her and started to bend down. "Let me see… You really need to go back—"

His words were cut off with a small yelp, and she looked up to see both his arms flailing as what looked like two black bands had appeared out of nowhere to encircle his head and throat. Although caught off guard, Liu made a valiant attempt to draw his pistol, but it slipped from his limp fingers even as he pulled it from its holster. In a few more seconds his eyes fluttered closed and he sagged to the floor.

The man behind him kept the sleeper hold on him for a few more seconds, then released the unconscious man to the floor. He picked up the pistol—not that Baozhai could even think of reaching for it—and quickly searched the agent. Pulling out a pair of handcuffs, he secured Liu's hands behind him around the leg of the dining room table. Pulling off the agent's tie, the man gagged him and then turned to her. He stood and offered her his hand.

Still trembling at the sudden attack, she took his hand and he helped her to her feet, keeping his finger to his lips. He leaned forward and set his mouth next to her ear.

"I know you can understand English, so please listen very carefully," he whispered. "I'm from the United States, and I'm here to get you and your children out of here. To do that, you are going to have to trust me implicitly and do exactly as I say. Do you understand?"

Baozhai nodded. "I will do whatever I must to save my children."

"All right. To disable the men on the other side of that room, I'm going to pretend to take you hostage. Just play along, and I promise that no harm will come to you or your children. Do you understand?"

"Can't you just go in there and shoot them?"

"First rule, no questions. We're doing this my way. If you don't like that, you're free to go back to your room—"

Baozhai clutched his arm with a strength she didn't know she had. "*No!* No, please. I'm sorry. I'm sorry. I'll do whatever you say."

"All right. You'll translate my commands to them. Let's step out into the hallway and get ready."

"May I—may I ask one question?"

The big man looked at her for a moment. "Go ahead."

"How do you know they won't just shoot us both?"

"Because they think you know things and they want to find out what." He raised a finger as she opened her mouth. "No more questions."

They walked into the hallway and he positioned her in front of him, with an arm around her throat and a pistol pointed at her head. "There's no round in the chamber, so don't worry. Now, let's go. Just remember, trust me, listen to me and translate my commands, and we'll get out of here shortly. Do you understand?"

She nodded and they began walking down the short hallway toward the living room. Pausing just before the entrance, he asked, "Are you ready?" She nodded again and he pushed her gently into the living room.

"Nobody move. Everyone stay where you are!" he barked, and Baozhai stammered out the orders in Cantonese as the three men all looked over and froze at the black-masked man holding a pistol to the head of their witness. They were all sitting in armchairs around a low coffee table, their jackets off and slung over the backs or arms of their chairs. Scattered, dog-eared magazines and newspapers and an overflowing ashtray indicated they had been killing time here for at least a few days.

The three also more or less resembled the other agent, with slight differences. One was taller and very skinny; one was chubbier, with the beginning of a potbelly poking out his button-down shirt; the third man was several years older than the other two and had salt-and-pepper hair, possibly the agent in charge.

"Don't touch it or she dies!" he said as Beanpole slowly began reaching for his earpiece. "Take off the radios and place them on the table. Do it now!" He pressed the muzzle of the pistol harder into her temple and Baozhai didn't have to fake the fear in her voice as she translated. At a nod from Salt-and-Pepper, the all three men complied, sliding their radios across the table.

"Now the guns, very slowly! Anyone tries anything and you'll be wearing her brains!"

Baozhai nearly fainted at that, but repeated the words. Again the older man signaled the others to do as the big man ordered. Three sleek, black pistols appeared and were placed on the table.

"Now your handcuffs! And keys! On the table! Right now!" Again the equipment came out and was set on the table.

"All right, all of you step back and raise your hands!" Once the three men had done that, he prodded his "hostage" forward until they were both at the edge of the coffee table. "Now, you, woman, grab the table and pull it back."

Blinking, she reached down and grabbed the edge of the coffee table and pulled it several feet back, out of reach of the three agents. "Pick up the pistols and handcuff keys and put them in this bag."

She did as instructed.

"Okay, move that table over to this wall, then pick up all of the handcuffs." She hauled it over, leaving a large empty space in the middle of the room, and picked up the matte-black metal cuffs.

"Now, keeping your hands up, you three slowly walk into the middle of the room," the American said while shrugging off the nylon bag.

The three men did so, never taking their eyes off the man and his hostage. "Stop!" he commanded, then pointed at the tall, skinny one. "Step forward and hold out your right hand. Have the other two sit down."

Baozhai translated again and the three men did as instructed. "Put the handcuff around his wrist. Make sure it's snug." She did so. "All right, tell Beanpole to sit right where he is, and have Chubby come over here."

The second agent came over. "Have him place the other cuff around his right foot. Make sure you tell him the right foot."

She did so, making him frown, but the man behind her thumbed back the hammer on his pistol, the *click* ominously loud in the silence. He did as he was told, sitting and facing the other man so as to place his right foot next to his fellow agent's right hand. "Now, have Chubby hold out his left hand." She did so, and shortly afterward, there was a cuff encircling his wrist.

"All right, Salt-and-Pepper, you know what's coming next. Get over here." Frustration darkening his features, the older agent slowly approached. "No funny business or she gets a third eye. Sit and cuff your left foot."

He did so, obviously hating to obey but having no other choice. "Now toss him the last pair and have him cuff his right hand to Beanpole's right foot."

Baozhai tightened the last cuff around the skinny man's ankle, making sure it was secure. With their hands cuffed to feet, the three men would find it practically impossible to move together in any sort of coordinated fashion.

Bolan removed his pistol from Baozhai's head and covered the three agents. "Wake your children up and get them ready to go," he told her. "You have one minute."

Baozhai stumbled away from him, relief at not getting shot flooding through her body. Telling herself to be strong, she ran to the second bedroom and flipped on the light. As expected, both children had slept through the entire incident in the living room. They were curled up together in the single twin bed, the sight making Baozhai's heart break all over again.

"Zhou, wake up! Wake up right now!" she said as she pulled the covers off and picked up the still-sleeping Cheng—it would be easier to carry him than to try to wake him.

"What—what's happening?" To her credit, Zhou awoke fairly quickly, blinking sleepily as she stared at her mother. "Are they moving us somewhere?"

"No, we're leaving. The Americans have come for us! Come on!"

Thankfully, her daughter had been sleeping in her clothes, so all she had to do was slip on her shoes and she was ready to go. She snatched her video game off the floor as they ran out of the room.

Zhou's eyes widened at the man in black looming in the living room entrance. He glanced at her with cold, blue eyes, then at the sleeping boy in Baozhai's arms.

"Tell your daughter she must do exactly as I say, when I say it."

Before Baozhai could say anything, Zhou nodded. "I understand," she answered in English.

He nodded. "Good. Take your children to the door, but don't open it."

With Zhou walking in front of her, Baozhai hurried to the apartment entrance. She turned to see the man backing toward them, the nylon bag slung over his shoulder and his pistol trained on the opening to the living room. "Stand to one side," he whispered.

She did so, and he walked to the door and put his ear

to it. After a few seconds he opened the door and peeked out into the hallway.

"It's empty. I'm going to check the stairway. You stay here until I come back for you." She nodded and he stepped outside.

Baozhai edged up to the door, casting a worried glance behind her at the living room.

A flurry of shots rang out down the hall and, moments later, the man ran back into the apartment, his pistol smoking.

CHAPTER TWENTY-ONE

If Mack Bolan had ever thought about how many close calls he'd had in the line of duty, this one wouldn't have ranked very high on the list. He'd been expecting reinforcements to arrive at some point. It was only a matter of time before the five-minute report-in was missed and someone was sent to check on them.

What he hadn't been expecting was a five-man team coming down the hallway. Bolan had opened fire first, but they had been ready, scattering for cover as his fusillade was buried in the back wall. Fortunately this entire floor was empty, making injuries to bystanders all but impossible.

Retreating to the apartment door, he slipped inside and informed them of the complication. As he did so, he heard a *thump* from the living room, and glanced over to see the head and shoulders of one of the agents sticking out past the wall as he aimed a small pistol down the hall. He'd had a backup.

Snapping his arm out, Bolan pushed Baozhai into the dining room and shielded her daughter with his body as he fired three shots. At least one hit the other agent, making him jerk and drop the pistol even as he fired. The bullet blurred past Bolan's head to core through the door, and the wounded man was pulled back into the living room.

"What are we going to do now?" Baozhai asked, still holding her son.

"You're going to cover the living room entrance," Bolan replied as he took her son and placed him on the dining room floor. He stared curiously at the sleeping child for a moment, then shook his head. He pulled one of the QSZ-92 pistols from the bag and yanked the slide back.

"Hold out your hand."

Baozhai extended her left hand and he placed the butt into it, wrapping her other hand around her fingers. "Push forward with your left hand, pull back with your right. It will steady your aim."

Leading to her to the edge of the doorway, he positioned her to cover the entire hallway. Bolan wasn't concerned about the door at her back—Tokaido had gotten him inside and he was confident t the hacker would lock out the Chinese agents for as long as possible. "Anything moves down there, you fire two shots, okay?"

She nodded, her face pale. Bolan noticed she was breathing shallowly. "Take a deep breath."

She did so.

"Now let it out."

Baozhai complied and began breathing normally.

"All right, you'll do fine," Bolan said. "All you have to do is watch the living room doorway. Anything moves—"

"Two shots."

He nodded as he took the submachine gun out of the bag, extended the stock and flicked off the safety.

"What about me?" Zhou asked.

"Stay behind your mother. When she moves, so do you."

"What are you going to do?" Baozhai asked.

"Find another way out of here. I'll be back."

Before she could reply, he poked his head out into the hallway. When no fire came his way, he ran across into the kitchen. Stopping inside the entrance, he put a short burst through the front door, then turned and put another burst through the living room wall, high enough to avoid hitting the agents on the other side—unless any of them had been standing. There were no cries of pain, so he guessed not.

He walked to the middle of the room and put two longer bursts into the wall next to the refrigerator in a X pattern, blowing off large chunks of shattered wallboard and exposing the metal studs beneath. Bolan put his boot through where the two lines of bullet holes met, kicking out a narrow, three-foot-high opening. Checking the space between the steel framework, he found just enough room for him to squeeze through.

He went back to the opening to the hall in time to see Baozhai squeeze off two shots, flinching each time the hammer fell. She didn't drop the pistol, however, and kept aiming down the hallway.

"Good work." Bolan checked the living room opening but saw no one there. He crossed over and picked up the boy. "We're leaving through the kitchen. I'm going first, then you bring your daughter."

"What? How—"

"No questions. Come on!" He turned and ran into the kitchen, then stopped by the doorway and waved her in with the submachine gun. Taking her daughter's hand, Baozhai ran across the short space.

Bolan held her boy out. "Take him and get through the hole. Go, go, go!" As they left, he put another short burst into the entrance door, then a second one near the living room entrance.

Spotting the gas stove, he opened the valve. Removing his gun's magazine, he stripped out three bullets, tossed them in the microwave above the stove and set it for ten minutes. Running to the hole, he squeezed through it, coming out in a reversed version of the same kitchen on the other side, where Baozhai and her children waited for him. She had set her son down next to Zhou and taken up a position where she could cover the front door. Bolan's eyebrows rose in admiration.

"What now?" she asked when she glanced at him.

"First, keep moving into the hallway," he replied, jerking a thumb over his shoulder. "There's going to be a big bang in there any second. Then we try to get the drop on them. Come on."

He led them to the door of the empty apartment, conscious of the sudden silence. Bolan looked through the peephole and found his view blocked by something. Putting his finger to his lips, Bolan pointed at the door, then held up one finger.

Just then, there was a small *bang* and then a giant *whump* from the other apartment, and a tongue of flame rolled out into their kitchen, making Baozhai and Zhou press closer to Bolan.

He looked out the peephole to find the man who had been using the doorway for cover had left, apparently to investigate the explosion.

"Okay, here we go. Stay here and watch the hole until I tell you to come out."

Opening the door, he slipped out and checked left, seeing a man there raising his pistol at him. With no choice, Bolan fired his submachine gun from the hip. The short burst chewed into the shooter's stomach, dropping him to the floor with a groan.

Bolan immediately turned and rushed for the door of the agents' apartment. Getting there just as a man holding a pistol was rushing out, he stuck his gun in the man's face. "Stop."

The man stared at the gun and raised his hands. "Drop it," Bolan ordered, nodding at the pistol.

The agent let the gun slip from his fingers. Bolan turned him around and stuck the muzzle of his gun into the back of the man's neck. He glanced backward but was careful to keep the man between him and the open door. "You understand English?"

The man nodded.

"Okay, walk backward with me." Bolan tugged on his arm and pulled the man back as two more men burst out of the room, pistols raised.

For a moment everyone in the hallway froze. The only sound was the moaning of the gut-shot man on the floor.

"Tell them to drop their guns and kick them away, or you're dead," Bolan said.

The man rattled off a string of Cantonese. When the other two agents hesitated, he barked, *"Xianzai!"*

Both men set down their pistols. At the same time two shots sounded from inside the apartment where Baozhai and her children were standing. The three men all twitched, but no one went for their guns again.

"You okay in there?" Bolan asked, now seeing smoke starting to drift out of both doorways.

"Yes! Are we going now?"

"We're leaving now. Come into the hallway," Bolan said, shielding Baozhai and her children with his body and that of the MSS agent.

"You won't escape, you know," the agent said in impeccable English. "Reinforcements are on the way. You don't have a chance."

"We've been doing pretty good so far. Also, you forget—we have you," Bolan replied. Taking Baozhai's pistol hand, he stuck her gun into the man's neck. "Don't move."

He dropped his submachine gun into the nylon bag and drew the Beretta, curling an arm around the man's neck and putting the pistol to his temple. "Cover the—" he said to Baozhai, but she was already watching the door she had just come out of, with Zhou between her and Bolan.

"Okay, we're all leaving now. If everyone stays calm and doesn't try to make a move, you'll all stay alive," Bolan said. "Come on. Baozhai, watch behind us. I'll cover the door."

As he started backing toward the T-intersection, the fire alarm went off, its piercing Klaxons blasting through the hallway. Bolan half walked, half dragged his hostage around the corner, then kept backing up to the elevators.

Come on, Akira, come on…

"Why are we stopping here?" Baozhai asked. "We can take the stairs!"

"Because that's exactly what this guy wants us to do," Bolan replied. Just then the elevator car—the one without the two guards—dinged, and he pulled everyone to one side, just in case it was carrying more reinforcements. It should be empty. Once the op had started, Bolan was fairly sure the young hacker had locked down the entire bank, but he couldn't be sure the MSS didn't have its own version of the young genius working on their side.

The doors opened to reveal an empty car and Bolan hustled everyone inside and hit the button for the first floor.

"I can still smell the sewer on you," their hostage said. "You are an incredibly skilled man."

"On your knees," Bolan ordered the agent after taking his handcuffs. "Who's downstairs?"

"At least ten more men are in the lobby," the agent replied as he knelt. "As I told you, there's no way out. If you surrender, I can at least try to help you."

"Really?" Bolan replied as they passed the twentieth floor. "Face the corner and place your hands behind your back." Once the man had complied, Bolan looped the handcuffs through the railing and cuffed him, finishing as they passed the fifteenth floor.

Bolan turned to face the dome light set into the corner of the ceiling. "Override the elevator lights and take us to Parking Level One."

"Who are you talking to?" the man asked. "This isn't Japan. We don't have voice-activated elevators."

Bolan didn't answer as they continued descending past the tenth floor. "You three stay on this side," he said, moving them to the front corner diagonally across from the captive MSS agent. He swapped weapons again, trading the Beretta for the submachine gun.

"Even if you do manage to escape the building, you will never get out of the city," he said. "Every police officer, every army soldier, every civilian will be on the lookout for you."

Bolan checked the ammo load in Baozhai's pistol, then gave her a new, fully loaded one. "Good luck finding me among everyone out there."

The agent snorted. "A one-point-nine-meter Caucasian man among twenty-one million who are a dozen centimeters shorter? It won't be hard."

"Yeah, that's what your boys up north thought, too."

The elevator reached the first floor and the floor light stopped there, as if the door was going to open. But the car kept going, descending into the parking level as Bolan took up a position across from Baozhai and the kids. Amazingly, the boy was still fast asleep in her arms.

"Hackers…" the agent seethed. "American hackers who infiltrated the building network."

The elevator stopped and the doors opened. Bolan covered the immediate outside, then stuck his head out fast enough to check left and right. The parking level appeared empty.

"Keep the door open and wait here." Steeling himself, Bolan stepped out, scanning the huge concrete room in a 180-degree arc as he tried to spot any hidden gunmen before they opened fire. When none came, he took two more steps out and then waved the woman and her children forward.

"Follow me." Keeping an eye on the stairwell door, Bolan made sure the elevator door closed, confident that Tokaido would strand the agent between floors. He got Baozhai and her kids to cover between a row of cars and used that to hide them as he herded them toward the white truck.

They reached it unmolested, with the scuff of their shoes on the concrete and their panting breathing the only sounds. At one point, Bolan thought he heard a sound near the elevators, but couldn't see anything when he looked back, so he kept them all moving.

When they reached the truck, he put her and the kids in the passenger seats, then slid in behind the wheel. He put the submachine gun away and tucked the Beretta on the seat between his legs.

"If I say get down, you get down," he said as he started the truck.

"Something smells in here…smells bad," Zhou said.

"Yes, what is that?" Baozhai asked.

"A long story," Bolan answered.

"How are we getting out of here?" she asked.

"Same way I came in," he replied, putting the truck into gear and heading toward the exit ramp.

"But what if—" Her question was interrupted by the *crack* of a small-caliber pistol and the rear window starring and shattering.

"Down!" Bolan stomped on the gas and the truck shot toward the ramp. He glanced back to see the same MSS agent he'd left in the elevator running after them, firing a small pistol.

"What, does everybody carry a holdout here?" he muttered as they hit the ramp. "Get that gate open, Akira—"

It was half open when they were about twenty yards away and closing fast. "Hang on!" Bolan said as more bullets hit the truck's cargo bed.

The speeding vehicle rocked as the front windshield slammed into the metal gate, shoving it out as they scraped underneath. The truck shuddered as it passed, then they burst out into the night—and right past two police sedans pulling into the entrance to the parking level.

Bolan didn't even have time to try to shoot one of the cars' engines, they were moving so fast. Instead he just cranked the wheel and guided the truck into a sliding turn onto the road. Glancing back, he saw one car turning to pursue them and the other being stopped by the Ministry of State Security agent.

"Damn," he said. "Looks like we aren't in the clear just yet."

CHAPTER TWENTY-TWO

Deshi Fang now knew exactly how Warden Wen felt—
he'd never been so humiliated in his entire life.

To have his secured, reinforced position cut through
like tissue paper and his men outwitted and outmaneu-
vered at every turn was bad enough. But the fact that it
had all been done *by one man*—that was the part that
really stuck in his throat.

Making matters worse, he had also been taken hostage by this lone, heavily armed intruder. He was using
Chinese weapons and had nonchalantly escorted the ministry's prize witness to Zhang Liao's treason and her children down to the parking garage and out the elevators,
leaving him handcuffed and fuming.

But not finished.

Even while they had been heading down to the garage,
Fang had gotten his hands on the spare handcuff key he
always attached underneath his belt—an old policeman's
trick. The moment the doors had closed, he had lunged
for the door open button, but pushing it had done nothing.
Then he slammed the emergency stop button, and that,
being a mechanical system that couldn't be overridden,
had brought the car to a shuddering stop.

Prying the interior doors open, he saw that there might
be just enough room for him to slip out to the parking
level. Drawing his backup 9 mm police revolver from its

ankle holster, he wedged a hand into the exterior doors and forced them open, as well. Sticking his head out, he made sure the American wasn't waiting to ambush him before sliding out to the ground.

Landing in a crouch on the stained concrete, he listened intently, trying to hear anything in the large space. Some kind of noise reached his ears, but he couldn't be sure what it was, or where it was coming from. The *clunk* of a car door closing, however, was much clearer, and he headed toward where he thought it had come from.

A few seconds later he heard an engine start up and Fang quickened his pace. A white utility truck pulled out of a space several cars ahead, and he raised his pistol and fired as he broke into a run after the escaping vehicle.

The rear window burst into fragments from his shot, and the truck leaped forward as if he had just goosed it. He put on a burst of speed, firing all the while, but the truck pulled away, heading up the exit ramp and colliding with the half-raised gate in a burst of sparks and a screech of metal on metal.

Fang didn't stop, pounding onto the ramp and sprinting forward with everything he had. He saw the truck shoot past two Beijing city police cruisers, both of which skidded to a stop. Lungs burning, legs aching, Fang ran toward the first one, shouting and waving his arms.

"Stop! Stop...the car!" He reached the driver's side and pulled out his identification. "Ministry of State Security! I need you to follow that truck!"

"Of course, get in!" the female police officer replied.

Fang ran around the front and jumped into the passenger seat. He hadn't even pulled the door closed when the driver threw the car into Reverse and backed up, then cranked the wheel and slammed on the brakes, executing a perfect 180-degree turn. Shoving the car into drive, she pressed the accelerator, pushing the cruiser to catch up with the other pursuing police car.

"Thank you for the assistance. I'm Agent Fang," he said after jamming his seat belt on and taking a moment to catch his breath.

"You're welcome. Patrolwoman Cai, pleased to assist," she said, never taking her eyes off the road. "Who's in the white truck?"

"People who must be recaptured due to their importance to our nation's security," he said. "They are armed and extremely dangerous. Please radio for all available units in the area to assist."

"Yes, sir." She grabbed her radio microphone and began talking into it while Fang watched the truck attempt to fend off the police car ahead of them, which had turned on its light bar and siren. It was trying to get close enough to use a pit maneuver on the back of the truck, but the fleeing driver was good enough to cut off the cop every time he tried to pull up alongside. Swerving back and forth, he played cat and mouse with the chasing cruiser, always just managing to cut him off before he could get into the proper position.

Near the apartment building, they were following a fairly deserted road, but as they headed into the city, the traffic became heavier, slowing the pursuit. Fang thought they were going to lose the truck when it squirted through an intersection right before a large tractor-trailer was about to cross, but the lead car didn't hesitate, plowing right through, as well. The semi slammed on its brakes and skidded to a stop, leaving just enough space for them to shoot through the gap.

"Additional units are on the way," Cai said. "Whether

they try to get on the freeway or use the city streets, we should be able to set up a roadblock in the next few kilometers or so."

"Very good. If we are able to capture these insurgents, there will be a commendation for you."

"Thank you, Agent Fang, but I am simply doing my job," she replied as she jerked the wheel to the right, narrowly missing sideswiping a street-cleaning machine. Even with the more crowded city streets, they still hit speeds of fifty and sixty miles an hour. Fang clenched his teeth at the thought of an innocent bystander—or even worse, some drunk tourist in the wrong place at the wrong time—getting splattered all over the road.

To her credit, Cai was driving masterfully, but she couldn't control everything that happened outside her car. As if to illustrate, the truck ahead seemed to falter and slow. For a moment Fang was hopeful that one of his bullets had hit something vital and they would be able to take the occupants prisoner without any more danger. However, it proved to be a feint. As the lead patrol car sped up to take advantage of the momentary lapse, the truck braked even further and the driver rammed into the patrol's car's front fender. Caught off guard, the police car fishtailed back and forth on the road before T-boning a parked car and spinning to a stop facing them, its one working headlight nearly blinding both Fang and his driver.

Cai swore as she twisted the wheel and they shot the gap between the stalled car and the velo-taxi parked on the other side of the street. This time they weren't so lucky. The speeding car scraped both sides, shoving the three-wheeled taxi onto its side on the curb and rocking the police car back and forth on its axles. However, she maintained control and they were soon gaining on the truck again.

"They're heading for the freeway. Left! Left!" Fang said.

"I see it!" she replied, turning onto the on-ramp and accelerating into the lighter but still busy traffic on the eight-lane highway. The white truck was already trying to lose them among the larger trucks and other vehicles cross the city, but Cai was just as determined and doggedly pursued their target.

As they got closer to the white pickup, it pulled alongside another tractor-trailer, and as Fang watched, an arm extended out the passenger window and aimed something at the truck's large tires.

"They're trying to crash the tractor! Hit them, hit them now!"

Cai stomped on the gas and her car leaped ahead. Orange flame spurted from the pistol in the shooter's hand, but nothing seemed to happen—the tire didn't explode and the truck kept going.

As the passenger shot again, they had gotten close enough to smack the truck's rear bumper. The white vehicle surged ahead and the pistol was drawn back inside the cab.

"There isn't a lot we can do without potentially causing a much larger accident here," Cai said. "We may have to fall back and try to take them once they take an exit."

"However you think it is best to apprehend them," Fang replied. "Is there any way to head them off ourselves?"

"Maybe," she replied. "But we might risk losing them completely— Wait! What's happening up there?"

Fang squinted through the exhaust and pollution-choked night to see movement in the cab of the truck. It slowed again then sped up as the head and shoulders of a masked man appeared out the passenger-side window and he leveled a submachine gun at them.

"Down!" Fang cried, scrunching low in his seat as the criminal let off a burst of rounds. Even as he fired, Cai deftly turned the wheel, sending them into the left lane and dodging most of the bullets coming their way. Their right headlight blew out in a flare of sparks and glass, but the car kept going without further damage.

"Nice driving," he said.

"Thanks," she replied. "I don't suppose you could shoot back, could you?"

"My pistol doesn't have the range," he said.

"I'd have you use mine, but that would complicate matters tremendously," she said. "Uh-oh."

"What—oh, damn!" Fang said as he watched the white truck pull alongside another tractor-trailer, this one hauling two trailers. Unable to do anything but watch, they stared as the masked man put a long burst into the semi's front tire.

The bullets exploded the wheel, making it disintegrate in a spray of rubber and sparks as the steel rim bit into the roadway. The semi slewed left, almost taking out the white truck as it crossed three lanes in seconds.

"Don't stay behind it!" Fang shouted, gripping the door handle as Cai fought to avoid rear-ending the crippled big rig.

"I'm trying not to!" she said as the semi jackknifed across the freeway, making other cars, vans and trucks skid to a stop in its wake. Cai yanked the wheel hard left and punched the gas pedal, aiming for the widening gap at the end of the trailer as the semitruck careened into the right concrete barrier.

"I think we're going to—" Fang began. But even as he spoke, the tractor hit the barrier with such force it rebounded and started coming back over again. The stress on the coupling was so great that the second trailer broke free and began heading straight back into traffic— directly toward their car.

"Punch it!" Fang shouted as he saw their escape hole quickly closing.

"It's on the floor right now!" Cai screamed back. It was too late to brake or to turn as they streaked toward the narrowing opening. Fang wanted to close his eyes but couldn't as Cai hunched over the wheel, as if somehow she could impart the extra bit of necessary velocity needed to make it through.

They shot through the gap and Fang instinctively glanced left to see a wall of tractor-trailer door inches from the driver's side. Then, with a *thud* that almost sent them into the left concrete safety divider, they were through. He looked back to see five lanes blocked by the semi, with the other three already clogged with cars trying to avoid the sudden traffic jam.

"That was incredible," he said.

"It will be all for nothing if we don't catch these people," she replied as they once again began gaining on the white truck. It suddenly crossed four lanes of traffic, making three cars hit their brakes, their drivers all honking angrily as it took an off-ramp at an insane rate of speed.

"Keep on them!" Fang said as she turned the wheel, crossing behind the slowed cars to take the ramp at a slightly less suicidal rate of speed. For a brief moment he hoped they would find the truck in a smoking wreck at the bottom of the exit. It would be worth it to lose them all to a fiery collision, but that was not the case.

"Whoever's driving that thing has the devil's own luck!" Fang growled.

"It won't last forever," Cai said as she grabbed her mike again. "They left the freeway and now they are ours. It's only a matter of time."

Speaking into the mike, she arranged for local units to set up a roadblock a few streets away. However, every time she did that, they seemed to know when it was happening, and turned off before they could spring the trap.

After the third time, Fang had had enough. "Damn it! Bring in more squads ahead of us! We'll trap them between us, and stop them that way!"

Cai did as he ordered, and soon two cars were a half kilometer ahead of them and closing in fast.

"Just stay on him. We keep him on this street and we can box him in on the next block," Fang said.

Cai just nodded grimly, every sense focused on traversing the road, which was in poor condition in this neighborhood.

Thirty seconds later they were almost on the other cruisers. "Steady…steady…*now!*"

The cruisers ahead turned on their roof lights and both turned into each other, blocking the road in a V formation, with the front of one car pointing directly at the side fender of the second one, ensuring that the truck wouldn't be able to smash through without sustaining crippling damage. Both sides of the road were filled with parked cars, leaving no way out.

But the truck didn't stop. It didn't even slow as it approached the roadblock. "Are they trying to kill themselves?" Cai muttered.

Fang was wondering the exact same thing.

Then, maybe fifty meters before they were about to crash into the two cruisers, the truck's brake lights flared then winked out. Along with that came a long screech of rubber, followed by the sound of scraping metal as the vehicle disappeared from view.

"Stop, stop, *stop!*" Fang ordered, making Cai almost stand on the brakes to bring the car to a screeching, shuddering halt in a cloud of smoking rubber. Fang looked both ways to see what might have been the rear of the truck as it turned right out of a narrow alley that he could only see because they were perpendicular to it.

"Left, left, left!"

Already radioing the two lead cars to pick up the chase on the next block, Cai backed up and headed into the narrow alley. Fang saw a long scrape of white paint on the side of the building, confirming they were back on the trail. They squeezed into the alley, snapping off both side mirrors. Cai had to go slowly to make sure she didn't wedge the car and trap them there.

It took most of a minute but eventually they came out the other side and took a sharp right, accelerating to catch up to the white truck. But as they sped through the now-quiet city blocks, Cai got a call on her radio that made Fang's brow furrow.

"We're on our way," she replied. A few moments later they turned into an automated parking lot packed with cars. Two other police cars, their lights still flashing, blocked both entrances.

Cai stopped her car behind the first one, making sure their suspects couldn't ram their way out through them.

Fang and she got out and, staying low, ran to the driver's side. "Where is it?" he asked.

The officer pointed at the crumpled rear end of the pickup sticking out behind a van with tinted windows. "Pure luck that we spotted it. I thought we'd lost them, but then Jun saw the rear of the truck there, and we immediately blocked them in."

"Call for backup. They're armed and very dangerous," Fang said. He glanced at Cai as he drew his revolver again. "You ready?"

She also drew her service weapon. "I cannot promise to take them alive."

"You don't have to take the man alive, just the woman and children if possible." Fang didn't elaborate on why, feeling his reasoning was obvious. "Apprehend them any way you can. We'll parallel each other on the approach. I'll take the front, you take the rear, all right?"

She nodded.

"What about me?" the other patrolman asked.

"You stay here and back us up if needed," Fang replied. The officer nodded and checked the load in his own revolver.

"Let's go." Staying low, Fang headed around the car's hood to the front of the row of vehicles. He waited until Cai had reached the back of the row, then they started walking toward the van in front of the truck.

It took less than a minute to reach the large van, and Fang held up three fingers, counting down silently. On one, he rushed forward to cover the driver's side with his pistol.

"Don't move! Don't—"

It was definitely the same truck they had been chasing throughout the city, but there was no one inside.

A flash of movement alerted him that Cai had reached the passenger side. She glanced up at him and shook her head. Fang reached for the driver's door handle and jerked it open, only to be greeted by an empty seat. He checked the rear cargo area, but they were gone. A scattering of brass cartridge jackets on the floor was the only evidence that a gunman had ever been inside in the first place.

Fang stood on the floor of the truck and lifted himself up to look around, trying to find any trace of where they might have gone. The parking lot was framed by two multistory buildings to the west and south, and the open street on the north and east, all of which were framed by more buildings with narrow alleys in between. Even with the Caucasian, all they needed was a one-minute head start to get to cover, and it would take a small army of police to search every direction they might have gone.

He slammed his fist on the truck's roof hard enough to dent it, then got down and walked over to Cai. "Come on."

They trotted back to the other two cars. "Get on the radio and get every patrol car in a ten-kilometer radius here right now," Fang said. "The three of you start a street sweep in your cars, you take east, the other two split up west and south. I'll wait here for the reinforcements and direct them where to go. You're looking for a one-point-nine-meter-tall Caucasian man with blue eyes, and three Chinese—a woman in her late thirties or early forties, and two preteen children."

"Got it." Cai began talking on her vest mike while running.

Fang was left to look around in frustration, wondering how they could have gone to ground so quickly. It's not over, however, he thought as he pulled out his phone and dialed headquarters. Not over by far.

CHAPTER TWENTY-THREE

The Mercedes-Benz sedan was incredible. Even though it was a six-figure luxury car in China, Bolan still felt invisible behind its tinted windows, which he suspected were illegal in the city, but right now he didn't care.

He checked on the kids, who were now both slumped over, fast asleep in the soft, wide backseat. Then he looked over at Baozhai, who was fighting to stay awake.

"You might as well get some sleep. We won't be there for a while," he said.

After abandoning the white truck and disappearing into the neighborhood, they had walked a dozen blocks then paused to catch their breath. Bolan had taken the still-sleeping boy from Baozhai halfway through their trip, and had looked around to find that they were near a cluster of sleek high-rise buildings surrounding a small park. A large backlit sign was prominent.

"Let me guess, it's an insurance company?" he'd asked.

Baozhai shook her head. "Commercial real estate. One of the largest in the city."

"Even better. Come on." He started walking toward the nearest brightly lit lobby.

"What are you doing?" Baozhai said as she hurried to catch up with him. "They have cameras everywhere!"

"That's not a problem." He walked up to the door and

stood in front of it for a few seconds. After about a minute the light changed from red to green, the door clicked and Bolan pulled it open.

"Where are we going?" Zhou asked.

"To get a new set of wheels," Bolan replied. They walked to the elevator and down to the parking level, which was much cleaner than the previous one. Outside the elevator, Bolan stepped into the middle of the first row and just stood there.

"What are we doing here?" Baozhai asked. "We need to keep moving, right?"

He nodded. "Right. And—" he waited until the lights of a car halfway down the row flashed twice "—that's our new ride."

Walking over to the burgundy Mercedes-Benz S63 AMG, he opened the driver-side door.

"We're really going to steal this car?" Baozhai asked.

"Well, it's at least forty kilometers to the airport we need to reach," Bolan said as he opened the rear passenger door and deposited the boy on the backseat. "So unless you like walking, this is how we're getting there. Don't worry, I'll drop it off at the airport parking lot, the police will eventually find it, and it'll be returned to the owner none the worse for wear. Now come on, everyone's been through enough tonight as it is. "

She hesitated only long enough to sit, but once she sank into the dove-gray leather seat, it was all over. She had put her seat belt on, and only when they were out of the parking structure—with the gate and barrier both rising as if by magic in front of them—did she truly start to relax.

"Where—" she spoke through a huge yawn "—are we going now?"

"You and the kids are being dropped off at an airport, where a private plane is going to take you out of the country. You'll be safe."

"Thank you." She exhaled a quavering sigh. "I know I have no right to ask this, but what about my husband?"

"He's why I'm not coming with you," Bolan replied. "I'm going to try to find him, as well."

"Oh—" Her eyes shining with tears, Baozhai clapped both hands over her mouth. "Oh, thank you, sir, you have no idea what that means to me."

"Don't be thanking me just yet. We're still looking for him," Bolan replied. "We found you and your kids easily enough, but there are a lot of places where your country sends its political dissidents that are way off the radar."

"But you will find him, right?"

"We've got our best people on it right now. If there's any possible way, we'll locate him."

Baozhai leaned back in the seat and watched through the darkened windows at the passing streetlights. "I will pray for your success."

Bolan glanced sidelong at her. "Are you a religious woman?"

She smiled ruefully. "Not until tonight."

"What's that old saying about no atheists in foxholes?"

That brought a true smile from her, which Bolan matched. "It was unfair of your country to persecute your husband for doing what he thought was right."

"But when they are saying that what he is doing is acting against China's best interests, who is right, then? It is just like your Edward Snowden, yes? But I do not see your President offering him a pardon."

"It's true, he broke the law," Bolan replied. "But at the same time, he did what he thought was right to uncover what he saw as illegal activity undertaken by our government. There comes a time when too many secrets held by a few against everyone else becomes as limiting as open aggression. While I may not agree with his methods, I have to respect his conviction to risk everything to do what he felt was right." Bolan glanced at her. "Just like your husband is doing."

She nodded. "I just hope you can find him in time."

"We're doing everything we can to locate him," he replied. "You should try to get some rest if you can."

She shook her head wearily. "I don't think I've slept more than two hours at a time ever since this whole thing started. First there was the constant fear that they were watching us, waiting for any of us to slip up so they could come to get us… And then once my husband disappeared, I see him every time I close my eyes. I won't feel truly safe until I am out of this country. And I won't be able to truly sleep until I have my husband back…or at least know what happened to him."

"The plan is to bring him out alive," Bolan replied. "But you know I can't promise anything."

"I understand. But if there is anyone who can find him, I believe it's you."

"Thanks for the vote of confidence," Bolan said, deliberately keeping it light. However he knew the odds were even higher against him now, since they knew why he was here. Although this part of the mission had been successful, it had just tripled the difficulty of actually locating and recovering Liao.

"We're coming up on the airport now," he said as they passed a sign stating Xijiao Airport 3 KM.

"Xijiao?" Baozhai asked. "Isn't that a military air base?"

Bolan glanced at her. "How do you know that?"

"I was a model before I was a housewife. We did a shoot there several years ago. So, we are going to the air base?"

"Yes, they also handle charter flights there, oddly enough. We're driving the right car for the plane I'm taking you to, and we should have no trouble clearing the gate…assuming my people have already smoothed the way."

"All right…it's not like I have a lot of choice in the matter, is it?"

"Just sit tight. In a few more minutes, you'll be on a plane heading out of the country."

"Won't the authorities lock down all of the airports?"

"That's what I'm thinking, which is why we're getting you out right now. Also, my people are probably making sure that particular message doesn't reach this base until you're out of here."

They turned off the main road and approached the fenced-in airfield. A manned checkpoint broke the seemingly endless line of razor-topped, chain-link fence.

"Remember, I do the talking. Just stay calm and quiet," Bolan said as he tucked the Beretta under his left leg.

They pulled up to the guard post and Bolan rolled down his window. The armed guard—carrying a submachine gun much like the one Bolan had on his shoulder—walked over.

"May I help you, sir?" he said in accented English.

Bolan held out his smartphone. "Carter Edwards, US Embassy. I'm here to deliver a package."

The guard took out a tablet and scanned the electronic ID showing on the phone screen. While he read what was coming up on his screen, Bolan dropped his left hand to his pistol, just in case.

"Yes, I have you down for this morning, but not arriving until 5:00 a.m.," he said.

Bolan stayed calm and nodded with an air of exasperation. "I know, but they moved my schedule up, which is why I'm giving you something to do here in the middle of the night."

The guard cracked a smile and handed Bolan's phone back. "If you'll wait here for just a moment, I'll be right back." He headed inside the booth, where he picked up a handset.

"What's going on?" Baozhai asked. "Are we in trouble?"

Bolan subtly shook his head. "We're doing fine. We're not in trouble until he draws a weapon or reinforcements arrive. Most likely he's just double-checking to make sure that everything is in order. All we can do right now is wait. Just sit back and relax. Looking worried or getting upset now is not going to help us."

Baozhai took a deep breath, then let it out. "Okay... I'm all right."

He turned to look at her. "For everything you've been through tonight, you've done a fine job. I don't know many women—hell, I don't know many men who would have done half as well in the same circumstances."

"Thank you." Her faint smile at his compliment disappeared and she nodded at the guard post. "He's coming back."

The guard returned to the gate and activated the crossbar. "Thank you for your patience, Mr. Edwards. You can go right in. Your party is at Hangar Eight."

"Thank you, and have a good morning," Bolan replied, receiving a nod from the guard. He hit the gas and they drove on.

"All right, assuming these are in order, we're coming up on Hangar Eight right about...here," he said.

Even if they hadn't been able to read the posted signs, the sleek Gulfstream G-650 sitting outside the hangar would have been his first and only clue that they'd reached their destination. With a cruising speed of 0.86 Mach and a range of seven thousand nautical miles, the jet would easily get the Liao family to Hawaii, and then on to the mainland, where they would apply for political asylum once safe in Washington, DC.

Bolan parked the car a safe distance away. "All right, you wake your daughter and I'll get your son on board."

They got out of the car, with Bolan looking every direction just to make sure this wasn't a trap. Except for the idling jet, the area was deserted.

He went to the back of the car and picked up the still-sleeping young boy. Carrying him in his arms, he headed toward the jet, which was dropping its stairs. A man roughly Bolan's age appeared and walked down.

"Morning, Sarge." Jack Grimaldi sniffed the air and grinned. "What is that? You switch colognes or something?"

"Or something," Bolan replied.

"Anyway, you sure cut it close," the ace pilot continued. "Eight more minutes and I was supposed to take off, passengers or no passengers."

Now Bolan smiled. "And what are the odds that you would have developed some baffling mechanical trouble that would have been miraculously fixed just as I arrived?" Like him, Grimaldi had no trouble bending rules when he had to. He had pulled Bolan out of hot spots around the world more times than either man could count.

"About one hundred percent. I see you've brought our

passengers." Bolan quickly handled the introductions, and the Stony Man pilot looked at the three, but recovered quickly and nodded. "Welcome aboard, ma'am. I'm afraid there isn't much in the way of five-star dining, but we've got sandwiches, coffee and juice and milk for the kids."

"Is Charlie in the cockpit?" Bolan asked, referring to Stony Man's other pilot, the quiet, calm Charlie Mott.

"He's already running through our preflight," Grimaldi replied, then lowered his voice. "Aren't we supposed to be carrying five?"

"Complications arose. Let's get them aboard and get you wheels-up. I'll fill you in," Bolan said as he turned to Baozhai.

"Both these men both work with me. You can trust them implicitly."

She nodded, but didn't say anything.

"Right this way, folks." Grimaldi led them into the sumptuously furnished cabin, complete with soft leather seats, thick carpet and soundproofing that reduced the noise of the two powerful Rolls-Royce BR725 engines to a dull rumble. The interior normally sat eight but had been converted into a personal jet, complete with a bedroom. Bolan tucked Baozhai's son under the covers, then slid the pocket door shut.

"Nice ride," Bolan said.

"Yeah, you can thank our neighbors south of the border for this one—it was seized by the DA as part of freezing a cartel leader's assets."

"I wouldn't have figured it for drug lord's airplane," Bolan said as he admired the cream-colored leather seats and plush matching carpet. "It's far too tasteful."

"I know, right. So, what's the SNAFU?"

"Liao wasn't where he was supposed to be." Bolan quickly filled Grimaldi in on the situation. When he finished, the pilot whistled low.

"Damn. So you got the family and are bugging out with us, right?"

Bolan shook his head. "Still missing one."

"Far be it from me to tell you how to run the show, Sarge, but you've already pulled off enough heroics for a month, much less one night."

"It doesn't matter. I came here to find him and I'm still going to try to do that. Besides, they still have very little idea as to what I look like, and even less of an idea where I am at the moment. I figure I'll give it twenty-four more hours, see if Stony Man can come up with something, then, if we still don't have a location, I'll head west. You, however, need to get the hell out of here ASAP."

Grimaldi grinned. "Haven't popped up on any law enforcement or military no-fly orders so far," he said as the two men headed to the front of the cabin.

"That doesn't mean it's not headed this way right now, even with the Farm working overtime on an intercept," Bolan said. "I'll get out of your hair and let you get out of here."

"One for the road before you go?" Grimaldi opened the refrigerator and took out a tray piled high with wrapped sandwiches.

"Yeah. It might be the only food I get until I leave the country." Bolan selected two roast beef and one ham sandwich and set himself up with a travel cup of steaming coffee. "Thanks."

"Anytime." Grimaldi pitched his voice low, making sure it didn't carry to their passengers. "You sure you don't want us to stick around, wait for you to bring Liao back? It would be a hell of a lot easier than that secondary extraction plan. Our 'mechanical problem' could pop up anytime, you know."

Bolan shook his head. "It's just too risky. Like I said, they may not know exactly where I am, but the bad guys know I'm around, and it's only a matter of time before they throw their net over the whole city. You need to get out while the getting's good. We don't need Chinese fighter jets chasing you out of here."

"All right. You just be careful out there, Sarge, and bring him and yourself back in one piece, okay?"

"That's the plan." Bolan turned to Baozhai. She sat beside her daughter, who was strapped into the seat, her attention buried in her video game, not noticing as her mother stroked her hair. "The next time we meet, Mrs. Liao, I should have your husband with me."

She nodded and tears welled in her eyes again. "Thank you…for everything."

Bolan nodded then turned to head back to the ground. "See you back in the States, Jack."

"You got it."

Walking to the Mercedes-Benz, Bolan got in and sat behind the wheel. He took the lid off his coffee and set it in the cup holder to cool, then unwrapped a roast beef sandwich and took a big bite, watching the Gulfstream taxi onto the tarmac and head for the runway.

Bolan looked around, wondering if there was going to be some sort of ludicrous chase scene, with military jeeps or trucks pursuing the leaving jet like in the movies. But other than his car and the Gulfstream jet starting to gather speed at the end of the runway, the area was deserted.

He watched, sipping his coffee and eating the rest of the sandwiches, until the jet vanished into the early morning air. Balling up the plastic wrap, he tossed it into his armament bag as he started the car and left the airport.

"Three down, one to go."

CHAPTER TWENTY-FOUR

"Yes, sir… Yes, I will notify the flight tower immediately."

Akira Tokaido spoke calmly and pleasantly into his headset. Only the single bead of sweat on his forehead betrayed any hint of his nervousness.

Barbara Price stood next to Hal Brognola a few feet away, both remaining stone silent. Besides the young man's voice, only the soft sounds of Aaron Kurtzman's keyboard could be heard in the command center as he ensured that the cell phone hack remained solid.

After helping Bolan acquire a new ride and executing the usual erasure of any and all signs of his passage, the Stony Man team had turned to the daunting task of making sure that Xijiao air base remained open long enough for Grimaldi and Mott to take off.

Tokaido kept speaking in his usual voice, but to the person on the other end—one Deshi Fang, an agent with the Ministry of State Security—he sounded like any other Chinese military man, complete with proper inflection and accent.

The near-AI translation program had been dreamed up by Kurtzman a few years earlier, working with all three members of his cybernetics team: Huntington Wethers on the program's framework, and Tokaido and Carmen Delahunt on creating it and integrating it with their already-existing systems and capabilities.

Intercepting a cell phone call was already difficult enough. Intercepting one and being able to reroute the call to a person who sounded like the one the caller had intended to reach was akin to juggling chainsaws while walking a tightrope coated in ground glass over Niagara Falls barefoot.

Kurtzman stared intently at his screen, not only making sure the rerouted signal stayed at full strength, but also kept at least two more channels open, in case the one they were using began to degrade.

"To repeat, all flights, both incoming and outbound, are to be delayed until otherwise notified by the ministry... By you personally, understood... Yes, sir, I will. Thank you and good night."

Tokaido disconnected the call and leaned back in his chair, resting his head against the black leather. "Okay, that guy's pacified for now. Damn, I wouldn't want to be the real duty officer when Fang finds out a plane left this morning."

"Well, ideally we won't be scuttling someone's career over this," Kurtzman said as he began running the suite sweeper that would erase any electronic trace of the flight or Bolan's presence at the air base. "Once I've wiped all of the data, we'll simply go in and log the call as received and pass it on to the appropriate personnel. The gate guard and tower crew may remember an early morning departure, but there will be no record of it in their logs. What's more, they'll have a direct order from the MSS to ground all flights that morning until otherwise directed. Faced with that evidence, do you think any of them will break ranks to speak up about a mystery flight that may or may not have existed?"

"I would say that's highly unlikely," Price replied.

"Exactly," Kurtzman said. "If you don't mind, once this op is completed, I want to send the recording of this conversation over to Hunt and Carmen for analysis. It seemed to do fine, but we can always make it better."

"Once we're done, and after you scrub the copy of any identifying names and places," Brognola said, frowning as he noticed Tokaido stifle a huge yawn. "How long you been in that chair, Akira? Eighteen, twenty hours?"

"Something like that… I'm all right, though—"

"Experience says otherwise," Brognola interrupted. "I want you to sack out for four hours in the dark room. That's an order."

"But we still haven't pinpointed Liao's location," the young hacker protested.

"And you've had your data-sifting programs searching for clues for the past day and a half," Price added. "Unlike your stroke of genius with the daughter's game, we don't even have that clue to go on here. It's time to let them do their work—and for you to take a break. Once we locate him, we'll need you at your best to assist with getting Mack inside."

"Listen to them, kid," Kurtzman said as he stretched his hairy arms over his head. "I'll hold down the fort until you get back, and then you can do the same for me, *capisce*?"

"All right, all right, I'll go. See you in four." It took two tries for Tokaido to pry himself from the chair and then slowly trudge out of the Computer Room.

Kurtzman watched him go. "I'd suggest watching your step when you leave. You might trip over him sleeping in the hall."

Price and Brognola both cracked smiles at the idea,

but they just as quickly sobered. "Akira does bring up a good point, Bear. Where are we on locating Liao?"

The computer genius combed his bushy beard with his fingers. "According to our files, he's still supposed to be at Qincheng Prison. There's been absolutely no trace of him in any prisoner transfer log or government holding facility. It's like the man disappeared into thin air."

"Is it possible that they terminated him already?" Price asked.

"Possible, but not likely," Brognola said. "Not until they've figured out exactly what he took and what he's told us. They'll want to make sure they know every single thing he's done before they've finished with him. Most likely he's being held in some extraordinary rendition site that's so far off the grid they cart in their electricity."

"Even so, wherever it is has to be connected to the rest of the country in some way," Price stated. "The power grid is a good place to start."

"Agreed, but it's hard to do a search when I don't know what I'm looking for," Kurtzman noted.

Price tapped her lips as she considered the problem. "Everything we've seen about this man indicates that the Chinese do not want any knowledge of his existence leaking to the general public. They'll need someplace to keep him isolated as they interrogate him…" She trailed off as a fragment of the conversation she'd had with Brognola a couple of days earlier resurfaced. "What if…"

She looked up to find both men staring at her.

"Go on," Brognola urged.

"What if you're right, Hal?" she said. "What if those transplant hospitals you'd mentioned are just fronts for organ trafficking? And what if they dumped Liao in one to keep him on ice and extract whatever information they need until—"

"Those damn butchers are ready to cut him open and sell his insides to the highest bidder! Of course."

"Well, that's great, except it still doesn't get us any closer to locating the man," Kurtzman observed.

"Yes, but we know the locations of those places, so that's a start," Price pointed out.

"You know, the easiest thing to do would be to just have Striker tail this Deshi Fang guy," a weary voice said from the doorway, catching everyone's attention.

"He was the one overseeing the team holding Liao's family, so he's obviously running the case," Tokaido said, regarding them through drooping eyelids. "I'd be stunned if he didn't go and visit the only asset he has left now, if only to check up on him, but most likely to interrogate him. Follow him and he'll lead you right to Liao. And with that, *now* I'm going to sleep." He turned and started shuffling out the door, only to bump into the jamb. Recovering, he continued on his way.

"Was it just me, or did it look like Akira just sleep-walked in here to tell us how to do our job?" Kurtzman asked.

Price and Brognola exchanged a puzzled glance. "Normally, I would have said no—until he walked into the door," the big Fed replied. "But, honestly, I don't care, as long as his idea's good, and it is."

"Risky, but with the best chance of success," Price agreed. "Bear, notify Striker of the change in plans. We're going to either have to get him a new license plate or another new vehicle, since I'd imagine the car he's in has been reported as stolen."

"Barb, please, give me *some* credit," Kurtzman muttered. "I didn't choose that Mercedes for its looks, I chose it because the owner is on a week-long business trip to Australia and won't be back for four more days."

Price and Brognola shared a grin. "Excellent. Then let's get Striker tailing Fang, and hope he leads us to Liao," the mission controller said.

CHAPTER TWENTY-FIVE

Zhang Liao lay under his blanket in his room, not feeling well at all.

He was flushed and thought he was running a mild fever, which wasn't good enough. He was concerned that the nurses would notice his condition and treat him with antibiotics that would knock out the infection before it really even got started.

On the plus side, the damp toilet paper poultice he'd made seemed to be doing a great job of keeping his waste warm and moist. He had kept it on for the entire night, and thought he was definitely coming down with something.

Now he lay on his side, with his legs together and brought up to his chest. Just as quickly, he got cold as a chill swept over his body.

The door to the room opened and the guards escorted in one of the silent, efficient nurses to check on him. That was a surprise. Usually they didn't come in this early. Liao covertly wiped his face with the sheet before sitting up and greeting her. Despite his antagonistic tone with the doctor, he was always polite to the nurses. It just seemed to be something he couldn't help.

The woman wheeled a small tray over to him. "I'm going to take a blood sample, all right? It will just take a few minutes."

She swabbed his arm, then wrapped a blood pressure cuff around his upper arm and inflated it. "Make a fist and hold, please," she said before inserting the needle. She filled three small test tubes, then cleaned and bandaged the puncture site.

"Are you feeling all right?" she asked. "You feel a bit clammy."

"I'm fine," Liao lied. "It was warm earlier and I may have been sweating a bit."

The nurse eyed him but didn't say anything. He breathed in and out evenly as he stared back at her.

"All right, then, you can go back to sleep," she said. With that she gathered her things and wheeled the cart back out the door, leaving a worried Liao to watch her go.

What if they test that blood and find the infection? he wondered. As soon as he thought it was safe, Liao hid the poultice in his hand as he got up and headed to the bathroom, where he flushed it down the toilet. He also examined his wound, which had turned an inflamed, angry red, making him smile. He just needed a bit more time for it to truly take hold…

Returning to bed, he lay down and curled up, trying to shake off the surprise visit and get some sleep. It felt as though he had just closed his eyes when he was roughly shaken awake and opened them to stare at the stern face of Dr. Xu, flanked by two guards.

"Restrain him."

Liao tried to struggle, but his arms and legs were pinned as they were placed into straps attached to his bed and cinched tight. In seconds he was securely fastened and unable to move.

"What is the meaning of this? Why are you doing

this?" he asked, even though he knew exactly why they were restraining him.

"Did you think you could hide an illness from us for long, Mr. Liao?" Xu asked. "When I saw the nurse's report, I immediately tested the blood she had drawn from you and what do you think I found?"

Liao tried to shrug, but his pinioned arms made that impossible. "I don't know. What?"

"The early stages of what appears to be sepsis," the doctor replied while pulling on a pair of latex gloves. "I'm unsure as to how you managed to contract it in here, since we keep our facilities scrupulously hygienic, but rest assured, I am going to find out. Now, I advise you to lie still while I am conducting my exam, otherwise—" he nodded at the guard standing on the other side of the bed, who was holding a stun gun "—you will be punished. Do you understand?"

Liao clenched his fists but nodded. "Yes."

"Very good. Now hold still."

Xu bent and began closely examining his prisoner's body.

Gritting his teeth, Liao put up with the exam, hoping that the doctor might still miss the injury, since it was at the joint of where the leg met the pelvis. If he didn't look too carefully…

It took a few minutes but eventually Liao's hopes were dashed by the doctor's surprised gasp. "Well, well, you have been a busy patient, haven't you?"

Holding Liao's legs apart, he leaned down and sniffed the wound. "Introducing your own fecal matter into your bloodstream—very clever indeed." He straightened and shook his head. "All that will do is prolong the inevitable, you know."

Liao spit in the doctor's face. "I was hoping to poison my body and organs enough so that my corpse would be useless to you."

Xu took out a handkerchief and wiped the saliva off his cheek, then shook his head. "A not uncommon scenario, I'm afraid. When faced with oncoming mortality, a patient often seeks to avoid that…finality by whatever means necessary, even to the point of infecting himself— or herself—with disease in the hope of being treated and gaining a few more precious days of life."

He regarded Liao not with a look of anger but of pity. "It is the only worthwhile goal, is it not? To survive, to continue your existence for as long as you possibly can. Sadly, however, for some, that is not possible. For you, this is certainly true. We will cure you, and what was going to happen is still going to happen, but first…"

He nodded at the guards, who had been standing by the door now that Liao had been restrained. They opened it and in walked the same nurse he had seen earlier that morning, along with a man carrying a small leather satchel who looked vaguely familiar. With a start, Liao recognized him as the MSS agent who had questioned him about four months earlier.

Had they known about me that long ago?

"We will be starting you on an antibiotic drip to fight the infection before it goes too far. However, Agent Fang has some questions he would like to ask you first."

"Hello, Mr. Liao," Fang said as he set the satchel on the end of the bed and opened it. "I am afraid that I have some unfortunate news—your wife and children were all killed earlier today in a botched attempt by the Americans to get them out of the country. I am sorry for your loss."

Liao stared at him in shock, trying to comprehend the words the other man had just said. Baozhai? Zhou? Cheng? All…gone… Tears welled in his eyes and ran down his cheeks.

"Even with this unfortunate news, there is still the matter of finding out what you have already given or told the Americans," Fang said as he removed a hypodermic syringe and small glass vial. "I am afraid that we must know everything." He inserted the needle in the vial and drew out 30 ccs of a clear fluid, tapping the syringe to make sure there were no air bubbles in it.

He nodded at the doctor, who assisted the nurse in preparing Liao's left vein for an injection.

Normally Liao would have struggled or fought against them, but he was still too stunned by the news about his family.

"We will begin in a few minutes…once the Sodium Pentothal has had time to take effect," Fang said as he expertly injected the drug into Zhang's arm. "I think we will start with the first time you contacted the Americans…"

CHAPTER TWENTY-SIX

Bolan sat in the Mercedes-Benz on the top level of a parking garage, looking through a pair of knockoff Zeiss binoculars at the fenced-in and heavily guarded facility, where, according to Tokaido and Kurtzman, the Chinese government was holding his target.

With his lack of appropriate armament and gear, Bolan thought it would be just short of impossible to infiltrate the facility. The easiest part had been finding the place. Once turned on to Agent Deshi Fang, the Executioner had picked up his staff car coming out of the MSS headquarters and pulled into traffic behind Fang's sedan.

But once they had reached the so-called "organ transplant" center, his trained eyes had immediately seen that although the place wasn't heavily fortified, it was heavily guarded. Two-man patrols circled the inner perimeter of the fence, and the only way in and out was manned by three guards, one of whom always stayed in the guardhouse. They were alert and very thorough, using mirrors to check underneath cars and searching the trunks. They also searched both the top and cargo area of a laundry truck that had driven up. Bolan had also spotted what he thought were motion sensors attached to the tops of the fence posts and ceramic capacitors wound with razor wire, telling him the fence was electrified. No doubt the place was well lit at night, too.

Lowering the binoculars, he stared at the otherwise nondescript four-story building. The fence could be neutralized, the sensors hacked and the entrance security could be taken care of, but even if he did find Liao, how would he get him out of there?

It didn't matter, however, how difficult the mission was. Bolan had taken it on and he was going to execute it, come hell or high water.

Over, under, around or through, he thought. The four ways of achieving an objective. So far, it would seem through was the best way...

He grabbed his new burner phone—the other one and the first tablet he'd used had been wiped and smashed beyond repair, the fragments divided up among three different garbage bins in the city. Tapping a quick email to the anonymous drop that would eventually get back to Stony Man, he sat back and waited.

Less than ten minutes later, there was a reply.

Feasible. Working on it. Check every 30 for update.

Bolan picked up the binoculars and began looking at the grounds again, taking notes on security patterns and weaknesses. He might have come up with a way to get in quietly, but more than likely he was going to make a hell of a lot of noise getting back out.

FIVE HOURS LATER Bolan drove the Mercedes-Benz sedan up to the front gate. He was dressed in an ill-fitting, dark blue suit with a white short-sleeved shirt underneath, and had plastered his hair down with gel until it gleamed. He'd also picked up a pair of horn-rimmed reading glasses with no magnification, so he could still see while looking the part. On the seat beside him was a thick, expensive-looking briefcase that was crammed to the gills with what he'd need to get inside—he hoped.

He rolled down the window and held out his cell phone to the approaching guard. "John Randine, General Electric Healthcare Service Division. I understand you folks are having a problem with your CT 750."

The guard blinked at him, then took the phone and looked at the electronic identification as he spoke into his vest mike. It took a few minutes, but eventually he gave the phone back. A man started walking around the car with a lighted mirror on a pole, using it to scan the undercarriage as the first guard said, "Open the trunk, please, sir."

"Of course, of course, just a sec." He popped the trunk release and waited patiently while they looked through the immaculate space. All the while, his fingers, drumming a nameless tune on the armrest, were only inches from the Beretta pistol, although if he had to put these guards down, the mission was already over.

"Please show us what is in the briefcase, sir."

"Huh? Oh, sure. Boy you guys sure take your security seriously." Chuckling, Bolan picked up the heavy briefcase and opened it to reveal a dizzying variety of electrical equipment. "Be happy to tell you what these all are." Bolan picked up a fiber-optic scanner. "This is the X85 small-bore fiber-optic—"

The guard raised his hand. "No, no, that is fine." The guard looked at the empty passenger seat and rear seat. The trunk lid slammed down with a thud, and the crossbar in front of him lifted. "Please go in, second parking lot on your left, then through the main doors. The receptionist will escort you from there."

"Oh—okay. Thanks a lot, guys." Bolan drove forward, noting the pop-up spike barrier on the road. Pulling into the parking lot, he picked up his briefcase, then got out of the car and went to the trunk. Opening it, he was relieved to see that the compartment holding the rear tire didn't seem to have been tampered with. That was good, because if they had lifted the carpeted panel, the mission would have gone wet really quickly.

Bolan pulled it up now to reveal the spare tire and underneath it the black nylon bag containing his weapons. He picked the bag up, slung it over his shoulder, made sure the Beretta was secure at the small of his back, and headed toward the double doors of the main entrance. Thunder rumbled overhead and he looked up at a dark sky that appeared ready to unleash a huge storm. That might work in my favor, he thought as he pushed the door open and walked inside.

The lobby was simple and bare, with cream-colored walls, white tile underfoot and a simple, high desk, where a neatly dressed, middle-aged woman sat. Bolan walked up to her and presented his phone again, with the identification still displayed on it. She took it and scanned it under an IR reader next to her desktop computer. "Welcome to the Guaw Li Center for Organ Transplanting and Research, Mr. Randine. It will be just a moment while we create your visitor's pass."

"All right." Bolan took the minute to look around the room. He spotted the electronically controlled double doors behind the receptionist's desk, and hoped that Tokaido or Kurtzman had taken note of them, as well. There was no other furniture in the room. Apparently visitors who had to wait got to stand.

"Here we are, Mr. Randine." Bolan looked back to see

her proffering a small laminated card. "If you will please clip this to your lapel, it will allow you access to the areas where you need to be. If you will follow me, please?"

She walked to the double doors behind her and pushed them open. Bolan saw what was unmistakably a guard on the other side. He carried a nightstick, but no gun. The receptionist muttered something in Cantonese to the guard, who nodded and waved Bolan forward.

"I will escort you to your destination and introduce you to the team you will be working with," he said in clear but accented English. "Please do not deviate from where you must work. The penalty for going into unauthorized areas is very severe."

"You don't have to worry about that, sir," Bolan replied as he walked into the beginning of a long corridor, lined with several doors and broken up every so often by an intersection. "My only goal here is to get your body imaging scanner up and running again."

The guard nodded as they continued down the corridor. So far, the layout corresponded with the plans the Farm had sent him, which Bolan had memorized. The full body scanner he'd be working on was located near a stairway that led to the below-ground level where Zhang Liao was being held.

About a hundred yards later, the guard knocked at a closed door. Bolan noted the stairway across the hall. The door opened after a few seconds and a middle-aged doctor in a white lab coat with salt-and-pepper hair looked out at the two men through thick-lensed glasses. *"Shi de?"*

"The service engineer is here," the guard said in Cantonese, pointing at Bolan.

"Ah, excellent!" The doctor switched to thickly accented English. "Thank you for coming so promptly. Come in, come in!"

Bolan entered a small antechamber and stuck out his hand. "John Randine, General Electric Healthcare Service Division. We treat all technical problems with the same attention, no matter if it's a country clinic or the biggest hospital in Beijing."

The doctor pumped his hand heartily. "Good, good, well, it's only the MRI we have here that you have to worry about today." He chuckled and Bolan smiled with him as they walked across the small room and into a larger one. "Well, here it is."

The machine was one of the most advanced imaging units in the world. Bolan knew that without Aaron Kurtzman's tutorial, he would have been completely lost. As it was, he walked to the nearby computer station and looked at the error message flashing on the screen.

"Yup, I've seen this before. You've got a firmware conflict with your Gemstone Spectral Imaging program. I'm going to need to update it and recalibrate the system." As expected, the doctor smiled and nodded politely at what Bolan was saying, but he doubted the other man understood a single word. "I can take care of it, but it's going to take a bit of time, that's all."

"Very well, please get started. I will be in the next room if you need anything."

"All right, thank you." Bolan couldn't believe his luck—he would be mostly unobserved to perform the next stages of the operation. Unslinging his bag, he set it on the floor as he pulled out the chair and sat, setting his briefcase on the desk next to the computer.

Opening it, he removed the new tablet and set it on the desk. He then found a browser in the operating system and logged on to the dead-drop address and sent a blank email message.

A reply came less than thirty seconds later. A few seconds after that, Tokaido had control of the computer and, less than a minute after that, the building's entire system. While they could have hacked in using back-door programs, it was just so much easier with a man on the inside.

Bolan spent the next two minutes readying his weapons, then the next three waiting for the Stony Man cyber team to set up everything.

Finally Ok, we're set on this end, Tokaido typed. You ready?

Do it, Bolan replied.

There was a moment's pause, then all the lights winked out at once, replaced by red emergency lighting. Startled cries and exclamations of alarm were quickly drowned out by a high, piercing electronic alarm. The shouts and cries grew louder and approaching footsteps could be heard. Bolan slung his bag across his shoulder and stood as the doctor rushed into the room.

"You must come with me right now. The fire alarm has sounded, everyone must evacuate building!"

"Lead the way, Doc!" Bolan followed the man into the hallway, where other white-coated personnel moved briskly but calmly through the halls. The doctor headed off down the main corridor, but Bolan took two steps to his left and pushed open the door to the stairwell.

Drawing the Beretta, he kept the pistol near his leg as he went down two flights of stairs. The few people using the stairwell to go up paid him little attention, even as out of place as he looked.

At the second sublevel, a knot of people rushed past,

escorted by a security guard who did notice his presence and rattled off an obvious question in Cantonese.

"Sorry, I don't speak Chinese," he said and held out his ID card. The guard brushed it aside and grabbed his elbow to escort him back upstairs. When Bolan turned and saw that the last of the evacuating personnel ahead of them was out of sight, he brought up the butt of his pistol and hammered it into the guard's forehead. He slumped over and Bolan relieved him of both his identification and his pistol, another QSZ-92.

After dragging him under the stairs, Bolan walked to the secured door and tried it, expecting it to open. As the Stony Man team had suspected, the fire alarm overrode the door locks, allowing for faster evacuation. Cocking the Beretta, he stepped into the hallway, which was also bathed in red light. This level was nearly deserted, save for a couple of desk personnel, who were leaving, and two guards still at their stations near a door at the far end of the hall. Assuming Deshi Fang hadn't set another trap for him, the man being held prisoner behind that door was Bolan's target.

Noticing a fire extinguisher in a nearby cabinet inset into the wall, he opened it and grabbed the red-metal canister. Prepping it to fire, he began walking straight toward the guards. He got to within five yards when the man on the left looked over, his eyes widening at the tall foreigner who was pointing a fire extinguisher at his face.

"Shenme shi—" was all he got out before getting blasted with a thick cloud of white foam. The chilly stream caught him off guard and sent him staggering back into his partner, who shoved the blinded guard away as he brought around his submachine gun.

Stepping forward, Bolan swung the extinguisher,

smashing the end into the guard's arm and making him cry out as both the ulna and radius snapped. He clutched his broken forearm, allowing Bolan to finish him off by whipping the end of the extinguisher into his face, breaking his nose and knocking him unconscious.

The first guard had clawed the dissipating goop out of his eyes enough to see again—just in time to watch the bright red fire extinguisher swing toward his face. With a dull thud it smashed him to the floor, also out cold.

Bolan stood to the side as he turned the knob and pushed the door open, but didn't enter. Instead he poked the nozzle of the fire extinguisher inside and let it rip, squeezing the trigger until container was empty. Only then did he go inside, heading toward the bed at the center rear of the room, stepping carefully in the slick foam. *"Halt!"* He'd taken only one step before a body burst out of the fog on the left side of the bed, pointing a pistol at him. As the chemical cloud dissipated, Bolan saw the same man he'd taken hostage at the apartment building, the man who had led him here—Deshi Fang. If Bolan was going to get Liao out of here, he'd have to go through this guy.

"Don't—" the Chinese agent began when Bolan lifted the extinguisher tank and hurled it at the man's head. The Executioner dropped to the floor on his side of the bed and fired three rounds at where he thought the man's feet or legs might be. There was no cry of pain indicating that he'd hit Fang, but that was okay. The important thing was that Fang was distracted by either the extinguisher—which hit the floor with a loud clank—or by the bullets flying toward him.

Springing to his feet, Bolan found his opponent out cold on the floor on the other side of the bed, a nasty welt springing up on his forehead.

He ran around the bed and grabbed Fang's pistol and extra magazines, then looked at Liao, who was out cold and strapped to the bed. Bolan checked his vitals, which were strong, then unstrapped him and set him on the floor.

He looked at the unconscious MSS agent, then at Liao. "This'll only take a minute."

CHAPTER TWENTY-SEVEN

"He's got him!"

Akira Tokaido's excited shout, accompanied by his exuberant fists shooting into the air, came as no surprise to anyone in the Computer Room, as they were all watching the same security feed he was. What did surprise them was what Bolan did once he'd gotten Liao out of the bed. It was done in less than a minute, and by the time it was over, everyone in the room was grinning.

"Bear, we need to verify the backup extraction plan," Brognola stated.

"I've been doing that since he first entered the room," Kurtzman replied. "It's going to be tight, since once Fang gets free, he'll probably focus all of his resources on capturing Striker, but it should be doable if they can get clear of the city."

"I still wish we could have gotten them on a boat to South Korea. It would have been so much easier," Price said.

Brognola nodded. "Maybe so, but it would also be expected. By now the airports have all been alerted, along with all the harbors on Bohai Bay. There's too much chance of being spotted there. Since they'll be looking for them to try to reach Shanghai or Hong Kong and fly out, heading north is the safer bet—it's the last thing they'll expect."

The original backup plan had been to take either a train or bus north to the border town of Erenhot to get onto the Trans-Mongolian Express and ride to Moscow, where papers would be waiting for Liao at the US Embassy.

"Right," Kurtzman said. "Or, we could alter the plan and possibly have Striker and Liao out of there and over neutral airspace in less than twenty-four hours. You know, since the bus and train stations have most likely also been alerted."

Price and Brognola looked at each other. "What's your idea?" she asked.

"Well, according to my most recent data, Jack and Charlie are still in South Korea—"

"What!" Barbara interrupted. "They were supposed to be in the air ninety minutes ago."

The computer wizard shrugged. "I know that, but Jack said their number two engine was running rough, and they didn't want to start a six-thousand-mile flight if it was going to conk out on them. It sounded reasonable to me."

"A Rolls-Royce engine with less than twenty thousand miles on it 'running rough'?" she pressed. "Really?"

Kurtzman spread his arms. "Hey, don't be shooting the messenger. I'm no pilot, so if you have questions, grill Jack when they return. The point is, since they're still in the area, we could reroute them to the airport at Dalanzadgad, in the south of Mongolia, which is just about the same distance from Beijing as Erenhot. Since Striker's got a decent car, he could drive there. They connect at the airport and *whoosh*—they're flying over to Mumbai or Dubai or Moscow, or anywhere else they want to go.

Hell—" Kurtzman tapped more keys "—with that Gulf-stream's range, they could make London no problem."

"Okay, let's consider this alternative. And believe me, it's not that I don't want to get Striker and our target safe, but is the risk in altering the extraction plan at this late stage worth the payoff?" Price asked. "I mean, it's not just Jack and Charlie we're risking here, but the rest of Liao's family. With the car, he could still drive to Eren-hot and make the train as originally planned."

"Look, you guys all know I'm not a fan of winging these sorts of things," Kurtzman said. "However, if this guy is going to blow this wide open, then about twenty thousand cops and other personnel, including toll booth operators and ticket sellers, are going to be on the look-out for a six-three, blue-eyed, black-haired Caucasian with a Chinese man in tow. We all know Striker's great at going to ground, but there he's gonna stick out like a big white thumb. This plan gets them both away from the public faster, and minimizes contact with locals, any one of whom could blow the whistle on the whole thing.

"My analysis of the revised extraction is that if we can make it happen in the next twelve to twenty hours, there is a less than ten percent chance of capture, with the percentages going up by around five percent, plus or minus two, for every six hours afterward—and that's in-cluding the original train time, by the way."

"That's all I need to hear," Brognola stated. "Make it happen, and inform Striker of the change in plans. The sooner we get all of them out of China, the better."

Price noticed him watching her and he motioned her off to one side. "Are you okay? You look like you just drank a cup of stale coffee."

"No, it's—" Price sighed and uncrossed her arms.

"Look, I know this all works out in our favor, but...you know Jack delayed their flight on purpose, right?"

"I don't *know* it specifically, but let's just say I have a strong suspicion about it," Brognola replied. "Look, you know part of everyone's job is to execute their mission parameters as they see fit. And just like Striker volunteered to stay behind to try to recover Liao, if Jack got a hunch that they were still going to be needed, and 'arranged' it so they were available, then so be it."

"I know that, and normally I'd agree with you, except that he's risking the rest of the Liao family, too," she replied. "Mongolia and China have grown really tight over the past thirty years—infrastructure investments, mining partnerships, security, you name it, they're working on it. If anything goes wrong, Mongolia will hand them over on a platter rather than antagonize their best buddy to the south, and this whole thing will have blown up in our faces in the worst possible way."

"All very true," Brognola agreed. "So we'd better do our best to make sure that everything goes smoothly until they're on that plane."

"The biggest issue at the moment is getting across the border. If they can manage that, then they'd be ninety percent of the way out."

Brognola nodded. "Then let's make sure that ten percent is as simple as possible, right?"

"Right, starting with figuring out the best way to get them across that border unnoticed." Price walked back to Kurtzman's workstation.

"You guys gotta check this out," Tokaido said, pointing to the wall screen. "Striker's got the perfect disguise for waltzing right out of there in plain sight."

Price looked up, smiling as she saw him wheeling the

motionless Liao in a wheelchair down the main hallway. "Good, keep tabs on him, and notify me when he's clear of the facility," she said. "Meanwhile, here's what we're going to do…"

CHAPTER TWENTY-EIGHT

Garbed in a white lab coat, and with a paper mask covering the lower half of his face, Bolan wheeled the unconscious Zhang Liao out of the facility's main doors. The fire alarm was still going off, and many of the evacuated technicians and patients were gathered in the parking lot.

Noticing Bolan as he exited, a guard said something to him in Cantonese and pointed to the rest of the patients, who were grouped together under three more guards' watchful eyes.

Keeping his head down, Bolan nodded and wheeled him over to the group of patients, then stood nearby, trying to figure out how to get him away from the hospital without starting a bloodbath. He could see his car, about a hundred yards away, but it might as well have been in Mongolia for all the good it did him now.

But that wasn't the only problem, he realized. He was wearing a lab coat and had his face partly covered, but he couldn't do anything about his height. He was still several inches taller than every single person around him. If he didn't get Liao out of here fast, they were both dead.

The wailing siren of an approaching fire engine gave him the distraction—and the plan—he needed. As it drove into the parking lot, Bolan looked around for the doctor who had been with him in the MRI room. He found the man standing with a few other doctors away from the rest of the group. The others turned to watch the fire engine arrive, allowing Bolan to move alongside the man. "Just stay calm and don't make any sudden moves."

"What do you mean?" The man looked down at the muzzle of the gun, hidden by Bolan's crossed arm, that poked into his side. "What is—"

"Not another word or a lot of people here die," Bolan said. "Come with me."

He led the doctor a few steps away from the others so they could talk without being overheard. "It's very simple. You're going to help me get a patient out of here without raising an alarm, or you and many people here will die. Help me right now, and you can save all of them. What's your answer?"

The doctor looked down at the black pistol again, then up into the Executioner's ice-blue eyes. "I—I will help you. What do you want me to do?"

"We're going to go get that man." Bolan nodded at the unconscious Liao. "When we do, you're going to come up with a reason why he needs to go to another hospital, and then you and I will take him in my car. I'll be watching you during your conversation with the guards. If I see *any* hint that you're trying to warn them about me, you'll die first, followed by whoever's closest—guards, doctors, nurses, I won't discriminate. Now, I don't want it to come to that, and I'm sure you don't, either, right?" The doctor nodded. "Okay then, let's go."

He escorted the man to the slumped-over Liao. The doctor put on his stethoscope and checked the man's heart, then thumbed back his right eye and shone a penlight into it. He rattled off a sentence to the nearest guard, who asked one question but was cut off by the doctor, who jabbed a finger at the road. The guard started saying something else as he pointed at the facility, but was cut off again by the doctor, who grabbed the wheelchair's handles and began pushing him across the parking lot.

"Good work, Doc, you seem to have put him in his place," Bolan began as they went, trying not to walk faster than the man beside him.

"Don't look behind you," the shorter man snapped. "If they see you acting suspicious, they'll stop us for sure."

They were about halfway across the parking lot when they heard a shout from the group in front of the building. Bolan looked back to see two guards and a doctor walking toward them. When he saw Bolan look back, the doctor raised his hand and shouted again.

"I think they're on to us," he said. "Move faster. You get into the passenger seat. I'll get him into the back.

As they approached the car, it turned on by itself. Bolan made sure the doctor got into the front seat, then pushed the wheelchair to the driver's side. There he turned and aimed his pistol at the small group of men, firing several rounds over their heads and making them hit the ground.

Opening the rear door, he shoved Liao across the backseat, tossed in his weapons bag, then fired three more shots to make sure their heads stayed down before jumping into the car and speeding toward the guard post.

"Keep your head down!" Bolan said as shots rang out behind him. He didn't hear any bullets strike the car, which was fortunate, since bullet holes would be a dead giveaway, and finding decent wheels would be harder the farther away from the city they got.

The guard post was coming up fast, with one of the two on duty there stepping out and raising a hand to stop them—something Bolan had no intention of obeying. He stepped harder on the gas, making the luxury car leap forward as he lowered the driver's window. Sticking his pistol out, he fired bullets at the guard and the shack, making both men dive for cover—and more importantly, not activate the spike barrier.

"Hang on!" he said as they hit the crossbar hard enough to soar a foot off the ground then crash back to the road. The Mercedes-Benz handled it well, with Bolan making a minor correction before recovering and accelerating into traffic.

"Are you okay?" he asked the doctor, who had gingerly straightened and was now looking back at the quickly receding building in the distance.

"Yes, I am unharmed, thank you."

"Great, since you're here, do me a favor and check on him." Bolan jerked a thumb at Liao, who was sprawled half on, half off the backseat.

"Yes." The doctor unbuckled his seat belt and twisted to take a look at Liao. "My name is Heng Gao. What should I call you?"

"Nothing right now," Bolan replied. "If you do talk, I'll be pretty sure you're addressing me."

"Well, I don't know what your plan is right now, but you may be interested to know that this man really is sick."

"What?" Bolan asked. "You mean something more than the aftereffects of whatever they doped him with?"

Dr. Gao nodded. "I'm afraid so. I won't show you, but he has a rather inflamed wound near his groin. He's showing the first signs of sepsis."

"Sepsis? How the hell did he get that?"

The doctor shrugged. "I'm not sure myself. Our facility is kept very clean, so there should have been no chance for him to come into contact with anything that would make that sort of injury." He rubbed his chin. "The only thing I can think of is he somehow inflicted it on himself—perhaps, once he learned where he was and what was to happen to him, he decided to contaminate his organs so they would be of no use to us."

"Great," Bolan muttered. "What's the prognosis?"

"From my very cursory examination, he looks to be in the first twenty-four hours of the illness. But without some kind of treatment, he will quickly grow more and more sick. Eventually his organs will weaken and shut down, and death follows soon after."

"Is there any way to stave off the infection?"

"Intravenous broad-range antibiotics are usually the first line of treatment. Of course, you can only find that at hospitals."

"And as you've no doubt figured out, that's not possible," Bolan replied. "Is there anything you can get at a pharmacy that would at least slow the infection down? I just need a day or two to get him to a safe place where he can be treated."

"Well, depending on where we are going, there are several antibiotics that would normally be available at a pharmacy."

"Okay, what's the easiest one to administer?"

"Ceftin would probably be the simplest one, as it can be ingested either orally or as a powder dissolved in liquid."

"Let's see if we can find one near a gas station. We've got a long way to go." He sighed. "Unfortunately, I'm going to need to keep you with us for a bit longer. Sorry."

The doctor regarded him intently. "I must say, you are

the most unusual criminal I have ever met, and I've met my share over the years, let me tell you."

"Have you now?" Bolan glanced at him. "Given where you work, how many of those people are you absolutely sure were criminals, and how many were turned over on trumped up charges?"

"I cannot say, although you would be surprised at how many confessions I have heard," Dr. Gao replied. "But that was not my task. My job was to process them, ensure that they were healthy enough for the operation and ensure that we got as much out of them as possible. The 'why' of how they got there did not matter to me. If I questioned any of it too much, then most likely I would end up on the operating table next."

"So, instead, you just kept your head down and did what they told you?" Bolan shook his head. "I suppose that's easier than risking your neck to speak out about your government silencing dissenters and cracking down on those who want more freedoms, and even basic human rights."

"Quite honestly, yes, it was." The doctor shrugged. "I suppose I was more idealistic once, when I was younger. But…my country's government has a way of chipping away at that, a bit at time. And before you know it, you end up in a place like that—" he jerked a thumb behind them "—doing what I was doing. But my original point was that you are not a regular criminal, are you? You came here with a singular purpose—to rescue this man." He glanced at the unconscious Liao. "Does he mean that much to you?"

Bolan nodded. "He was willing to risk his life to come to us. When your government took him, I was willing to risk mine to help free him."

"He must be very important to you. Most interesting," the doctor replied and then pointed to a sign on the left. "If you take this next off-ramp, there should be both a gas station and a pharmacy where we can get what we need nearby."

Bolan regarded him for a long moment. "I truly have no wish to hurt you, Doctor, but if you try to trick me, you'll leave me no choice."

To his surprise, the older man shook with laughter, actually chuckling at the threat. "Mr. American, I am your hostage, but I have seen too much in my life to be scared by your threat, which I have no doubt is very real. Rest assured that I will not act against you or this man in any way. My countrymen, however, will no doubt think quite differently."

"I've been aware of that since the moment I entered the country."

The off-ramp was coming up and, with a last look at the doctor's face, Bolan took it. He didn't have any real choice, as the car was low on gas and he needed to fill up for the long journey ahead.

"We'll stop at the gas station, then the pharmacy. I'll be with you for both places, so let's keep the visits brief, and we'll be on our way."

"As you wish," the doctor replied.

CHAPTER TWENTY-NINE

Fang sat in the bed, gritting his teeth as a guard undid the straps holding him on the bed. "Free my arms. I can do the rest myself." The man was too professional to smile or laugh as he worked, but the MSS agent knew what he was thinking.

He had awakened to find himself strapped down and gagged in Liao's bed, with his gun gone and no sign of either Liao or his rescuer. Even worse, the blow Fang had taken had given him a blinding headache, which intensified every time he tried to think of what the man looked like. But the face of his attacker eluded him, lost in his concussed mind.

He had endured what seemed like hours ticking by, but in reality had been less than ten minutes before people had returned to the floor and discovered him. The moment the guard freed both hands, Fang tore off the straps on his legs, threw his feet over the side of the bed and stood—then promptly vomited on the floor.

"I am afraid that you probably have a concussion, Agent Fang."

Wiping his mouth, he looked up to see Dr. Xu standing in the doorway. "If Liao escapes, that will be the least of my problems, Doctor." He straightened and held his aching head, every thought agony.

"You should really allow us to examine you. If left untreated, your injury could be very dangerous—"

"And I told you it does not matter!" Fang snapped. Just raising his voice made his head swim and he sat on the bed. "Before the interrogation you had said something about giving him antibiotics. Why?"

Xu pursed his lips, as if he had just bitten into a lemon. "The patient had infected himself with his own bodily waste, creating the condition for sepsis to manifest in his body. When you were finished, we were going to give him a broad-range antibiotic IV—"

Fang cut him off with a slash of his hand. "So you had not administered the medicine before the—incursion?"

"No, sir."

"In your professional opinion, will he need that medicine soon?"

Xu considered the question for a second. "If by 'soon,' you mean within the next two to three days, then, yes. As the infection grows, he will weaken. If they do not catch it in time, there is a good chance he will die. However, the intruder took Dr. Gao hostage when he left, so there is a strong possibility that they already know Mr. Liao is ill."

"Thank you, Doctor, this has been a great help." Taking a deep breath, he pushed himself off the bed and stood next to it for a moment until his nausea passed. "I want you to contact every hospital, clinic and pharmacy within a fifty-kilometer radius of here and warn them of a Caucasian or Chinese doctor who comes in and tries to acquire any sort of antibiotic." He gave the other man a card. "Anyone who has contact with such a person is to call me immediately. Do you understand?"

Xu took the card and stared at it. "We're not really equipped for this sort of thing—"

"Then tell me, Doctor, are you equipped to answer questions from the Ministry of State Security regarding the lapses in security here that allowed an American to enter this facility and remove a high-ranking traitor?" Fang asked. "Because if you are, then you're right, there's no need to worry about the fact that they are getting farther away with every second that you stand there looking at my card!"

His face paling, the doctor ran out of the room, shouting for receptionists as he went.

Fang clutched his head until the sharp throbbing passed, then walked to the doorway and called to the nearest guard, a man also rubbing his head. "Yes, sir?"

"Before you get checked out, you will isolate the security footage of the car the suspects are driving, and forward all of the information to the ministry." Fang held up his ID card. "Tell them I have authorized a citywide alert for the car and the three suspects—a six-foot-three, blue-eyed Caucasian, a male Chinese accomplice between forty and fifty years of age, and Dr. Heng Gao, who is their hostage. Go now!"

He pulled his phone from his pocket, thanking the heavens that the man hadn't stolen or smashed it as well, and dialed a number. He hated doing it, hated admitting that he had failed yet again, but he couldn't handle this by himself. The only path to redemption lay in capturing both of these men, and if he was to have *any* chance of doing that, he needed help—lots of help. Fortunately, Fang was able to call on his own resources—ones outside the ministry.

"Put me through to General Zhao immediately," he said when he was connected. While he was waiting, he walked to the door and looked out to see three women at the main desk, all talking urgently into phones. Xu himself manned a fourth, also talking quickly to whoever was on the other end.

His attention was brought back by a click and a smooth voice saying, "General Zhao's office."

Repressing the urge to scream at the secretary, Fang said, "This is Agent Deshi Fang of the Ministry of State Security for General Zhao."

"Yes, sir. I will put you through immediately."

True to his word, the general picked up less than ten seconds later. "Agent Fang, to what do I owe the pleasure?"

"Shanghai, February 10, 2006," Fang replied. "You know the particulars."

They both did. Before being stationed in Beijing, Fang had been an agent in Shanghai at the same time as Zhao, who was a lieutenant then. One night he had answered a call about a disturbance involving an army officer, and entered a hotel room to find Zhao sitting in a chair, staring at the body of a local prostitute, dead of a drug overdose. The scandal would have meant the end of his career, but Fang had been convinced it was simply bad luck on the lieutenant's part, and had managed to cover up the incident to everyone satisfaction. Of course, handling such a favor came with certain assurances, and Fang had held tightly to that fact as Zhao had risen through the ranks. In fact, the incident had actually bonded the men, and each had done the other smaller favors over the successive years.

"It's time?" the other man asked, his voice firm.

"Yes."

"Very well. How can I help you?"

"I need at least two platoons of soldiers and supplies and transportation for a two-day trip. Call it a training exercise, call it maneuvers, call it whatever you want, but I need them mustered with full gear and sent to me within the hour. You need to manufacture the paperwork to make it all aboveboard."

"I can handle that. Where are you?"

Fang gave him the facility's address. There was a pause on the other end.

"What are these men to be assisting you with?"

"Recovering an item that has been lost," Fang replied through gritted teeth.

"An important one, I assume?"

"Of course it is. I wouldn't be bringing you in on it otherwise."

"I understand. I just needed to ascertain the gravity of the situation for myself," Zhao replied. "I will assemble the units myself within the hour and lead them personally. I have never forgotten that day, Deshi."

Fang took a deep breath upon hearing those words. "Thank you, General. I will be at the main gate awaiting your arrival."

"See you soon." The general hung up and Fang turned off his phone off, feeling somewhat better. Since he had a bit of time to kill, he decided to go to see if there was anything they could give him for the concussion.

I've not given up yet, American, he thought. Oh, no, not until you are dead.

CHAPTER THIRTY

Zhang Liao clawed his way back up to consciousness to find himself in an uncomfortable position, with one arm trapped and asleep underneath him. Blinking to clear his bleary eyes, he focused on what should have been the ceiling of the hospital, only to see the curved, cloth-covered roof of what looked like—*a car?*

Turning his head, he looked at the leather seat back next to him, then the other direction to see a middle-aged man's face looking at him kindly through thick glasses.

"Ah, you're awake! Good. Tell me, how do you feel?"

"Wha—" He pushed himself upright to find that he was indeed in the backseat of a car, and still dressed in his hospital gown. He only got halfway before the world began spinning around him, and he quickly lay back down, clutching his head. "Everything's spinning…"

The man chuckled. "Yes, I'm afraid that most of those sorts of hypnotic drugs have unpleasant side effects. It will pass in time. You're probably better off staying out of sight for the time being anyway."

When his vertigo subsided a bit, Liao risked looking at the man again. "Who are you and how did I get here? The last thing I know, I was being interrogated by that man who told me…told me…" He put a hand to his mouth as he remembered the emotionless way the MSS agent had informed him that his family had been killed.

"I don't know what to tell you, as I've never seen you before," the man replied. "My name is Dr. Heng Gao, and I work on the main floor in the MRI department. Whoever you are, you're apparently quite popular, as there are all sorts of people interested in you, my friend."

Liao was about to reply when the driver's door opened and another, larger man got behind the wheel.

"He's awake!" Gao said.

The new man glanced back at Liao with the coolest pair of glacial-blue eyes he'd ever seen. Liao stared back at his round eyes. "Are you from…?"

"Don't say anything right now." The driver nodded at the doctor. "He's here under duress."

"A fine way to treat the man who's helping you!" the doctor replied. "Look, I know you're American, so I have a pretty good idea of what this is—"

He swallowed his words when the driver started the car with one hand and poked the doctor in the side with the muzzle of a pistol that appeared to come out of nowhere. "We're not out of the woods yet, Doc, and that means you aren't, either. Just relax and get ready to get that prescription we need."

"All right, all right." The doctor folded his arms and stared out the window.

Liao wasn't sure, but he thought the doctor might actually have been pouting a bit. He frowned as the driver's words sank in. "You know I'm ill?"

"Well, we do have a doctor with us." He checked the rearview mirror. "I'm not thrilled with that attendant. I think he was giving us the hairy eyeball."

"I told you, you should have let me deal with him," the doctor said. "And what is that? 'Hairy eyeball'?"

"I meant he looked like he was suspicious of us," the

driver said as they pulled into traffic. "I overpaid him and left before he could give me the change, so hopefully he'll just pocket it and look the other way."

"Yes, hopefully," the doctor said. "Although I'm sure not many tall Westerners come to this part of town."

"Thanks, that makes me feel so much better." The driver watched Liao in the rearview mirror. "We're getting some medicine for your illness. Hopefully it will stave off the infection long enough for us to get you out of the country, and then we can get you fully treated once you're safe."

"Um…thank you. I owe you my life," Liao said, not ready to talk about his lost family yet. "I don't suppose we might be able to get me some clothes when we stop?"

"I can't make any guarantees, but we'll see what we can do," the driver replied, then glanced at the doctor sitting next to him. "For now, give him your coat. We already look odd enough as it is. No need to be running around in that, too." Bolan shrugged out of his own lab coat.

"If I must," the doctor said, shrugging out of his white coat and passing it back. "The place you want is up here on the right."

They pulled into the parking lot of a standard pharmacy. The driver looked at Liao before getting out. "We should be back in a few minutes. Just stay down and stay here, and we'll be back on the road in no time."

Liao nodded, his world turned upside down again in the past hour.

The two men got out and walked inside, either talking about something or perhaps arguing good-naturedly. The door closed, leaving him alone in the car.

Despite the American's instructions, he couldn't help

looking around fearfully, worried that every passerby might be calling his location in to the police. Becoming aware of what he was doing, he scrunched down in the backseat, growing more terrified that someone was going to spot him and summon the police, or even worse, that awful MSS agent.

A flash of light from the front of the car caught his eye and Liao looked at the dashboard to find that the electrical system had come on, apparently all by itself. There was a ten-inch screen in the center console, and as he stared at it, a small green light in a button in the roof winked on, as well.

"Hello, Mr. Liao," a man's voice said.

Liao blinked and looked around.

"I know this must seem odd, but the car is not talking to you," the voice said. *"I am talking to you from the United States."*

"Okay…you are with the man who freed me from the organ harvesting facility?" Liao asked.

"That is correct. He works with us, and he will be doing everything he can to get you out of there safely," the voice said. *"But since he couldn't explain the plan with that doctor there, we thought we'd contact you directly and let you know what's going to happen…"*

CHAPTER THIRTY-ONE

"It looks just like a regular pharmacy," Bolan said as they walked inside. The one thing he wasn't pleased with was that the windows all had large advertising decals covering them, with gaps here and there, so it was hard to see inside or out. Otherwise, except for the Chinese letters everywhere, it might have been any pharmacy in America.

Gao snorted. "What did you expect? Incense and herbs and dried chicken heads hanging from the ceiling? I mean, we have those—without the chicken heads—so if you want to swing by one after here, I'll be happy to take you."

"No, thanks. Just get that prescription and let's get moving." Bolan was acutely aware that his presence was attracting attention. The other patrons were discreetly— or not so discreetly—staring at him and whispering as they headed down the middle aisle, which was loaded with Asian versions of cold medicine, vitamins and even condoms, toward the pharmacist's counter.

As they approached he tapped the doctor's shoulder. "Just remember," he said quietly. "I still have a pistol on you and I'm watching you carefully, so don't try anything."

"Try anything?" The smaller man grinned. "I haven't had this much fun in years!"

Bolan shook his head, mystified by the man's chutzpah. "Just get in line."

He joined him behind what looked like two housewives, one grandmother, and a young professional woman in a pencil skirt and cream blouse, talking on a cell phone. All of them turned to look at the new odd couple that had joined the line, then gradually turned back to waiting, occasionally sneaking glances at the tall foreigner in their midst.

His phone buzzed in his pocket. Bolan pulled it out to see a new message with the subject line: Vacation Itinerary. He opened it and scanned the contents, smiling at what he saw.

Change in plan.
Head north to border, go to AIV (+III).
Brother-in-law will pick you up.

Good old Jack, he thought. Translating the simple code turned the three letters into DLZ, which turned out to be Dalanzadgad Airport in southern Mongolia. A quick check of the distance put it at about 380 miles from their current location, which was easily drivable in their current vehicle.

Closing the message, he turned off the phone and slipped it back into his pocket. The line moved forward more quickly than he'd expected, and the doctor was being served now. He was engaged in a rapid-fire exchange with the pharmacist, who seemed either bemused or reluctant to fill the doctor's request.

Knowing every second counted, Bolan came up alongside the short man. "Is there a problem?"

The doctor turned to him and threw his hands up. "I

don't know. He says he's not sure they have it in stock, and he has to check. It's a common antibiotic. No pharmacy should be without it."

The pharmacist's face had grown steadily paler as the doctor had been speaking. Bolan looked around and noticed that they were more or less alone at the back of the store. His instincts told him the pharmacist was delaying for a reason. "Then to hell with it," he said, pulling his pistol from his pocket and pointing it at the man behind the counter. "Tell him not to move."

Gao did so and the man remained frozen while Bolan cleared the counter. "Come on, Doc."

"Are you kidding? I'm too old to vault over a counter—"

"You either get your ass over here or I'm coming back there and throwing you over!" Bolan growled.

"Er...coming." The doctor turned, hoisted himself up so that he was sitting on the counter and then swung his legs over, almost kicking the pharmacist in the chest as he did. He scooted to the other side and hopped down. "There, happy?"

"Ecstatic," Bolan replied. "Just get in there and find the stuff, will you? And if they have anything stronger, grab that, too."

Gao seemed to be taking his time choosing the items he needed.

"Come on, Doc, let's go!" Bolan said, dividing his attention between the small man scurrying around the shelves and the space in front of the counter. "Coming, coming!" The doctor returned to the front of the counter, carrying a plastic bag filled with four containers. "It's a rather crude cocktail, I'm afraid, but with enough water, it should do the trick."

"Great, let's grab some bottles and get the hell out

of here." About to leave, Bolan realized he had to stall the pharmacist from contacting the police. Noticing the skinny young man was wearing running shoes, Bolan told the doctor. "Tell him to lie on the floor."

Gao did so and the pharmacist complied. Bolan swiftly untied his runners and hogtied him with the long laces, connecting his hands and his feet.

The pharmacist began to say something, only to have Bolan hold up his hand. "Right!" He quickly pulled off the man's tie and gagged him with it.

The doctor clambered over the counter, followed by Bolan, who concealed his pistol in his pocket again.

"All right, grab some water and let's go. I didn't see any clothes, so he's out of luck."

"Yes, our drugstores aren't really minimarkets like you have in America," the doctor replied.

They found the water aisle and filled a basket with several plastic bottles. Bolan thrust a large handful of yuan at the doctor as they headed for the front. "Here—pay for it."

They joined the line, which was moving much more slowly, with people using coupons and apparently wanting to pay with exact change. "Can you just toss the money at them and we'll go?"

"It would draw more attention to us—" Gao began to say when they heard a scream from the back of the store.

"Too late!" Bolan replied. "Come on!"

While everyone else was looking toward the rear of the store, Bolan hustled the doctor toward the front doors. The man said something as he tossed the wad of money at the cashier.

"What'd you tell her?" he asked as they hit the door.

"'Keep the change,' of course!" he replied with a grin.

Coming out into the sunlight, Bolan blinked as he realized that a police car had just stopped behind the sedan and an officer was getting out. "Damn! Get in!" he said as he drew his pistol and pointed it at the cop. He had no intention of shooting the man, as he would never kill a cop. However, the cop didn't know that.

"Stop! Raise your hands!" he commanded the officer, who stared at him blankly, one hand hovering over his holstered pistol.

"He doesn't know what you're saying!" the doctor said.

"If he doesn't want to die, tell him to get his hands up!" Bolan ordered.

The doctor repeated the command in Cantonese and the cop's hands shot up. "Step away from the car and lie on the ground," Bolan said as he opened the driver's door. The doctor repeated it and the officer complied. "Okay, get his gun."

"Me?" the doctor replied.

"Yes, you!" Bolan said, glancing back to see several drugstore patrons staring out the window at him, some on smartphones, some recording what was going on. He turned and put a bullet into the glass window over their heads, making them duck for cover.

"Get it and let's go!" Bolan shouted, putting a bullet into the police car's right front tire. The doctor yanked the officer's gun from its holster and brought it back to Bolan, who grabbed it and pushed the smaller man toward the car. "Get in!"

Gao scrambled over to the passenger seat as Bolan piled in behind him. The car was already on, and he shoved it into Reverse and floored the accelerator.

The large Mercedes-Benz shot backward, the powerful V8 engine driving it into the lighter police sedan and shoving it out of the way. Bolan didn't stop, but cranked the wheel hard so he was now facing traffic. Putting it into gear again, he peeled out of the parking lot as he heard several bangs behind him, their rear window shattering into tiny pieces. Damn it, did every cop carry a backup piece? he wondered.

"Both of you stay down!" Bolan shouted as they roared into traffic, nearly sideswiping a passing window-washing truck. As it slewed away, one of its ladders fell off its hooks and made two other cars screech to a halt. Within a minute, a mini traffic jam was escalating behind them.

"Where's the nearest on-ramp to the highway? We need to get on the G110 heading west!" Bolan said.

"There should be an entrance within the next two or three kilometers," Gao said. "Might I advise slowing down a bit? Our speed is likely to attract attention."

"Right now, Doc, I don't think we could possibly attract any more attention than we did at the pharmacy," Bolan replied, but he slowed anyway. "Were either of you hit?"

Gao looked down at himself, as if the very idea had never occurred to him. "I seem to be all right. How about you, Mr. Liao?"

"I am fine, as well," he answered, slumped in the rear seat amid dozens of pebbles of safety glass.

Between glances behind them for any signs of pursuit, Bolan kept an eye on him in the rearview mirror. Despite the excitement of the past few minutes, Liao actually seemed calmer, if a bit pale. "I must admit that I am not feeling very well."

"You got the bag, Doc. Can you whip something up for him?" Bolan asked.

"I will once we get on the highway and headed in the right direction," Gao answered. "The farther out one goes, the most desolate the countryside becomes."

"Good," Bolan replied. "I've had enough civilians watching me here to last the rest of my life."

CHAPTER THIRTY-TWO

"You know, I'm starting to think that Striker can't go *anywhere* in China anymore unsupervised," Tokaido said. "Everywhere he goes, there's some kind of trouble."

His attempt at humor fell a bit flat; there were a couple weak smiles, but no one said anything else. The young hacker rolled his eyes. "Why the long faces? At least they got away, and with the medicine, right?"

The team in the Computer Room had just finished watching the drugstore debacle, as he was already calling it.

With Kurtzman and Brognola both going off to get some much-needed rest, it was just Tokaido and Price now.

Price would have slept if she could. She'd tried, but every time she closed her eyes, her mind filled up with all of the possible things that could still go wrong on the mission. Although she was far too much of a professional to voice them aloud, it was nearly impossible to not think of them. And after forty-five minutes of tossing and turning, she'd admitted defeat, gotten up and headed for the Computer Room.

Now she shifted from side to side as she saw the stolen luxury sedan smash aside a Beijing police car and speed off into traffic, almost causing two accidents as it got away. As it was, traffic was still snarled up at the site, which did help matters a bit.

"You're right, Akira. It just would have been good to have been able to get in and out without causing so much...commotion," Price said. "This is definitely going to attract Fang's attention, and the closer he gets, the closer they get to being caught."

"Yeah, it was pretty bad timing for a joke, especially after everything that's happened, right?"

She smiled and patted his shoulder. "It's all right. They can't all be winners." Refocusing on the tasks at hand, she studied the different views of traffic from the cameras, watching as the Mercedes-Benz, now missing its rear window, joined the rest of the sluggish traffic on the superhighway. "If only there was some way to mislead the MSS as to where they're going..."

"Only some way?" Tokaido sniffed in mock insult. "You wound me, Barb. Watch this."

His fingers flew over the keyboard as he brought up a video-editing suite. She watched over his shoulder as he isolated the car and seamlessly inserted it over a similar car in the traffic flowing the other way. Using digital editing tools, he swiftly modified its appearance to match the angles of the other cameras on that stretch of highway and inserted the car, allowing for the time it would take to reach each camera, at the proper point in the file. "It won't pass a really close scrutiny," he said while placing the last one, which showed the car taking an off-ramp heading south, "but it'll pass a cursory or even midlevel inspection. For our purposes, it should be fine."

"That's fantastic work," Price said. "Well done."

"Well, it is what you pay me for," he replied. "Now I just have to remove him from all city cameras on the western road, which should take a couple of minutes." He used a similar model car, but with a different color and license plate, to replace Bolan's car in the heavy traffic. "And...voilà! One disappearing car, moved around to be seen heading in the opposite direction—" His quick grin vanished just as quickly as his main screen flashed red. "Crap."

"What's going on?" she asked.

"Someone got footage of Striker at the drugstore, and it's being uploaded to a government server right now."

"But I thought you scrubbed the gas station and pharmacy cameras?" she asked.

"Of course. It's standard operating procedure," Tokaido replied as his fingers blurred over his keys. "This is on the cell data network. Damn smartphones make our job harder."

"And easier, don't forget," she gently chided.

"Yeah, yeah. It all comes out to about fifty-fifty in my book," he muttered. "Still, this isn't that hard to mess with. I don't even have to wipe it, just manipulate it so that they can't get anything usable out of it..." He tapped more keys then hit Enter with a flourish. "And two for two! One blurry smartphone movie later, it could be any six-foot-three, black-haired man pointing a gun at that police officer."

Price breathed a soft sigh of relief. Next to acquiring the Liao family, making sure Striker's appearance didn't appear on any media was the second highest priority. So far, they were winning that battle, but it was a constant slog, and for every piece of footage they cleaned, there was always the unverifiable idea that they might have missed something. But that couldn't be helped. She had to have faith that Stony Man's resident team of geniuses could get the job done.

"I'm going to grab another cup of coffee. Do you want anything?" she asked as she headed toward the door.

"Another soda would be great, thanks," Tokaido replied without looking up, already planning the next phase of their surveillance.

CHAPTER THIRTY-THREE

"What do you mean, the Mercedes-Benz people can't help you? They're supposed to be able to track their cars if they're stolen, right? Well, that's exactly what's happened to this one!...What do you mean, *they* can't find it?...Wait a minute, wait a minute, they're saying *they've* lost track of the car, as well? That is incredible... Of course I want you to keep on them about it! Call me if there is any update, anything at all...yes...all right, goodbye."

Disconnecting his phone, Fang resumed pacing back and forth outside the facility's main gate, resisting the urge to check his watch yet again. Other than the manufacturer's inexplicable lack of awareness of the location of one of their own vehicles, there had been no other updates for the past ten minutes and he was growing very concerned that the window to catch with the American and Liao was truly closing for good.

So far the organ transplant facility's surveillance system had been a complete failure in revealing any data on the intruder. Everything had been scrubbed—destroyed, to be blunt—from the time the car had first pulled into the parking lot to the time he left. If there hadn't been four eyewitnesses, they wouldn't have even had that sketchy description—and part of a license plate—to broadcast.

The blast of an air horn tore him out of his thoughts

and Fang looked up to see two army trucks approaching. The heavy-duty 6x6 troop carriers were long-haul vehicles meant to transport a dozen men and their equipment comfortably. The sight brought a long-lost smile to his face.

General Zhao leaned out of the passenger window of the first truck and waved him over just as Fang's phone vibrated. He pulled it out as he ran over to the APC, where the general opened the door for him to climb aboard.

Zhao had recovered from the Shanghai incident well and was now the epitome of the career military officer. He kept in scrupulous shape, running five kilometers every dawn, and his career record was impeccable. With a neat mustache, sharp brown eyes that missed nothing, and razor-cut hair—his one affection—he looked fresh and ready for action, the very opposite of Fang at the moment.

"Hang on!" the MSS agent said as he read the update. "Finally, some news!" He showed it to Zhao. "Take us to this address as fast as you can!"

With a belch of black smoke the lead truck pulled back out into traffic as Zhao extended his hand. "It is good to see you, Deshi. What's it been, three years now?"

"Something like that." He shook the other man's hand distractedly and finally had to tear his gaze away from the front windshield with an effort. "I apologize for my rudeness, my friend. This whole situation has spiraled more and more out of control with each passing hour. Thank you for coming to my aid."

"Of course. It is no more than what you have done for me," he replied. "Without jeopardizing any matters of national security, what can you tell me about the situation?"

Fang glanced at the driver before he spoke, eliciting a chuckle from the general. "Do not worry about him. Every one of these soldiers was handpicked for this mission. You can count on their discretion."

"All right." The MSS agent gave the description of the fugitives they were looking for, but told the general nothing about why they were wanted.

Zhao hadn't gotten to his current position by being dense, however. "Sounds like the Americans are up to no good again. This seems to be going to a lot of trouble for one person, even for them."

"I cannot comment on that," Fang replied, which was, of course, an answer in itself.

"It is not much of a description to go on," the general remarked. "Are you certain the US is behind this?"

Fang nodded. "Indeed, all I have to go on is the man's voice and his eyes, but that's enough. Besides, Liao hadn't gone to any other nations seeking asylum, so the idea that someone else just happened to stumble across him and tried to bring him out is ludicrous. Add in the idea that they would try to rescue his family as well, it's even more ludicrous. Can you imagine the Russians even considering such a thing?"

Zhao chuckled and shook his head. "All right, so the question now is where are they trying to get to? Of course, you have notified all transportation centers to be on the lookout for this man?"

Fang nodded. "Once I realized what I was dealing with, it went out immediately. Yet somehow he managed to sneak the rest of the family out, right under my nose. Either that, or he has them so far hidden underground that we cannot find any trace of them."

"First things first. He is the primary target, and the

family, although their loss is embarrassing, is secondary," Zhao said. "We know that he is in a car, the description of which is plastered all over the media. Surely it should not be that hard to find."

"One would think so, except it is also in a city of twenty-one million people," Fang replied. "There are many sedans similar to it here. Who's to say he hasn't ditched it already?"

"Simple, he wants to get out of the city as soon as possible—" Zhao said as Fang's phone vibrated once again in his pocket. Holding up a finger, he pulled it out and saw that HQ had sent him a video file, along with a curt message: Pulled from traffic cameras at 1143.

Playing the file, he watched as a car matching the description of the one they were looking for sped east on G110. The screens were all time-stamped and looked accurate, but something about it struck Fang as off. He watched it twice and then looked up at Zhao. "What were you saying just now?"

"I said now that he has acquired his target, he will want to leave the city as soon as possible."

"Right…" He handed over the phone. "Take a look at this while I check out what happened here."

By now they were at the pharmacy where the car had last been sighted by actual people. Three police cars were already there, with the damaged one off to one side. Everyone turned to look at the olive-drab military vehicles pulling into the parking lot.

"I guess we could have been a little more subtle in our approach to this, eh?" Zhao said with a smile.

Fang turned to him, his expression mirthless. "Forget subtle. I want this guy's head and balls on a plate when this is through. Stay here, I'll be back."

He got out and walked over to the police officer in charge. "Agent Fang, MSS. Give me every detail about what happened here."

After a hasty but unnecessary salute by the flustered police officer, he gave Fang a report cobbled together from several eyewitness accounts, including the officer whose car had been disabled. Once he'd gotten the particulars, including the fact they had taken antibiotics and water, Fang thanked the officer and ran back to the army vehicle.

"I may be staking everything on this, but my gut is telling me that traffic footage is faked somehow, and that they're headed west," he told Zhao as he climbed back inside.

"I agree. This just doesn't look quite right," Zhao said. "But if they are not going in that direction, then where are they headed? Once you leave Beijing on the western road, there's nothing out there but steppe and hills. Do you think they're actually going to try to drive to Tibet or Pakistan?"

"Maybe," Fang replied. "And we're going to follow them until we either find them or run out of country." He settled more comfortably into his hard-backed seat. "Let's go."

CHAPTER THIRTY-FOUR

"All right, Doc, you can take the blindfold off now."

They'd been driving for about an hour and before leaving the edge of the city Bolan had made the doctor blindfold himself so he couldn't see where they were headed. He wasn't going the kill the man, although a large part of his brain said he was crazy to leave a witness behind. He protected the innocent, no matter what regime they were under. Besides, enough people at the organ transplant facility had seen his face as it was, so more than one person could provide a description of him. With a philosophical shrug, he dropped the matter.

However, that certainly didn't prevent him from laying a false trail for Gao to provide to the MSS when he was brought in. Bolan used the navigation system in the Mercedes-Benz to figure out the best place to let the doctor go that was far enough from civilization but wasn't so far out that he would keel over and die before he was picked up. It would help if the fake trail also wasn't too far from the real road he was going to take to Mongolia.

Once he'd figured out his route, Bolan drove several miles past the one he planned to take, then pulled the sedan over to the side of the road at an intersection and made the doctor get out.

Gao pulled his tie off his eyes and looked around at the stark, rolling plains surrounding them in every direction. He stared back down the stark, desolate road they'd traveled to get there, and his shoulders slumped. "I don't exercise that much, you know. Can you at least tell me how far back it is to town?"

"You're a long way from Beijing, but we passed a small village about two miles back." Bolan pointed down the road. "If you keep up a steady pace, you'll be there in about two and a half hours."

"You sure are an optimist. Could I please get some water for the trip?"

"Sure." Bolan handed over two bottles. "And thanks for mixing up the solution for him." He nodded at Liao, who was still sitting in the backseat. Once Bolan had verified that the doctor had indeed gotten the right drugs, Gao had mixed up three bottles of antibiotic in water, and had been overseeing Liao's ingestion of it ever since.

"Just make sure he keeps drinking it—regardless of the taste," Gao said. "I don't suppose there's any way I could get my phone back, is there? Listening to music would make this forced walk you're putting me on go so much quicker."

Bolan smiled at the request. "Gao, you're lucky I'm letting you keep your shoes. Now get out of here, before I change my mind."

The doctor nodded. "I had to try." He stepped forward and extended his hand. "Thank you for the adventure, Mr. American."

Bolan shook it. "You're welcome. I'm surprised you enjoyed your kidnapping. Most people don't, you know."

"Indeed. But as I think you know, I am not like most people." With a smile, he waved goodbye and began trudging down the road, holding a bottle of water in each hand.

Bolan waited until he was a speck on the horizon before getting into the car and pulling back on the road. "The front seat is open if you want it."

"I might as well stay here," came the quiet reply.

"You know, far be it from me to tell someone how they should be feeling, but I'd think you'd be a bit more cheerful to have escaped that butcher's den back there," Bolan said. "But you are ill. Maybe that's what's got you down. By the way, the doc said you needed to keep on the fluid intake, so I want to see one of those bottles drained before the hour is up. That gives you about—" he checked the dashboard clock "—thirty-three minutes to drain it."

"It is not my illness that has made me sad, it is the fact that my family…my family…" Liao turned away, but not before Bolan saw the gleam of tears on his cheeks.

"What about them?" he asked.

"They're dead!" Liao cried.

"What are you talking about?"

"The MSS agent…" he said between sobs. "Before he began interrogating me…he told me that my family had been killed in a failed attempt to rescue them by the Americans."

"And you believed him?"

"Of course. Why would he lie?"

"To put you in a more fragile mental state, so the drugs he used on you would have a greater effect. It's a common interrogation trick." Bolan brought the car to a stop. "Liao, look up. Look at me."

The defector turned his tear-streaked face up to stare at Bolan.

"Your family is not dead. I put your wife, daughter and son on a private jet not more than twelve hours ago. In fact they're still on that jet, which is the same one we're heading to Mongolia to meet. If all goes well, you'll be seeing them in a few hours."

Bolan had rarely ever seen a man go from the utter depths of despair to transcendent joy so quickly. "They're alive?"

"Yes."

Liao bent over and, for a moment, Bolan thought the man was having a stomach cramp, but after a few seconds, he straightened and was laughing almost hysterically. *"They're alive!"*

"Yeah, so why don't you get up here in the front seat, and let's get you on the way to them, okay?"

"Yes…yes, I think I will come up there." Liao climbed over the back of the passenger seat, unable to keep the broad smile off his face. "Thank you, American, thank you so much for this news… You have no idea how grateful I am that you and your government considered my family as important as me."

"You're welcome, but you're the one who made the tough decision to go against the direction your own government is heading," Bolan replied. "There aren't a lot of people who'd be willing to toss everything they've earned away and risk their lives to throw in with a potential enemy to try to keep the peace, and we appreciate that even more. What I guess I'm saying is that if you have to leave everything you know and love behind to start over in a foreign country, you damn well better have your family with you."

Liao nodded. "Exactly. Again, your compassion is greatly appreciated."

"Hey, I'm just glad that this is almost over for both of us." Bolan grinned. "You wouldn't believe the trouble I had tracking you and your family down."

Liao nodded. "No, I imagine they did not make it easy for you."

Liao stared out the window at the featureless steppe around them for a minute then turned back to Bolan. "A quick question, if I may—my daughter, Zhou, was she able to bring her little portable console game with her?"

"Yeah," Bolan replied. "She kept a death-grip on it everywhere we went. The last I saw, she was playing it on the plane. Why?"

Liao smiled quickly. "It helps her handle difficult situations, that's all. I am glad she was able to take it with her."

"Yeah, it did seem to help," Bolan said. "Your son, on the other hand, is quite a heavy sleeper. I've never seen anyone sleep that hard." He caught himself before going into the dangerous details of the situation the child had slept through.

Liao apparently didn't notice, and laughed instead. "I swear that boy could sleep through a typhoon. Whenever there's a fire drill at night, we have to carry him out to the front of the building. I wish I slept half as good."

"You and me both," Bolan replied.

Liao was silent for a few seconds more. "And Baozhai...how is she?"

Bolan looked at him for a few seconds before replying. "She's fine. She handled herself extremely well during the extraction. You've got yourself one hell of a wife, Liao."

"Thank you, but I wouldn't have any of them now, if it wasn't for you, Mr.—" He frowned. "Okay, now that we are alone, I have to call you something else besides 'Mr. American.'"

Bolan nodded. "Edwards. Carter Edwards." There was a *thunk* from the engine, and the car lurched forward, then resumed running smoothly.

"That didn't sound very good," Liao said after he lowered his antibiotic drink.

"No, it didn't." Scanning the instrument panel, Bolan noticed a new light had come on. "Damn." As he said that, the car lurched again as the engine sputtered and died. Shifting it into Neutral, he wrestled the suddenly sluggish car to the side of the road before its forward momentum died completely. "What is the matter?" Liao asked.

"We appear to be out of gas," Bolan replied. "I think one of that cop's bullets might have hit the tank or a connection somewhere. I'm going to take a quick look."

He got out and looked underneath the vehicle in the fading light. Something was dripping from near the gas tank, and he smelled gas, as well. Getting up and dusting himself off, Bolan got back inside. "Yeah, the tank's leaking. It must be a pretty slow one, since we got this far before it conked out."

Again, Liao looked out at the barren countryside around them. "So now what?"

Bolan was already pulling out his cell phone. "I'm going to—damn." He tossed the cell phone aside. "I'm going to use that as a paperweight, because we're outside its coverage."

"The car!" Liao said. "Your people spoke to me from the car—a Hal Brognola?"

"Great!" Finding the concierge button, Bolan pressed it. "I hope this works. I think they run through a satellite, so—"

He was interrupted by a familiar voice. "Acme Roadside Assistance. This is Akira, how can I help you?"

"You have no idea how happy I am to hear your voice," Bolan said with a grin. "I've got a bit of a problem here, Akira. We're out of gas with more than a hundred miles to go to reach the LZ, and I have no real idea anymore how close we are to the nearest town. Is there anyplace nearby that might be able to provide us with some fuel?"

"Well…" The clack of keys could be heard in the background. "Wow, you really are in the ass end of nowhere, aren't you? But you may be in luck. There seems to be some kind of farm or something about half a mile north along the road you're on. Just head up there, it'll be on your right. That's about all the intel I have—the rest is up to you. How are you doing otherwise?"

"You mean other than being stranded in the middle of nowhere in northern China and probably being chased by—" Bolan glanced at his passenger and changed tack. "We're fine, Akira, although I'd give just about anything for a HELO extraction right about now."

"And I'd love to make that happen for you, too, but unfortunately, that isn't happening," Tokaido replied. "If you can scrounge enough gas to take you about another thirty miles, there's a tiny town that seems to have a gas station in it, and not much else. Fill up there and take extra with you, because where you're going is even more nothing than you're already going through."

"Thanks for the heads-up, Akira. We'll contact you if we need anything else," Bolan said.

"Good luck, guys. Acme out."

Bolan turned off the service to conserve the battery and glanced out the window at the setting sun. "All right, here's the plan. I'll head up to the place he told me about and hopefully return with some gas. You stay here and keep an eye out—for what, I don't exactly know." He reached into the backseat and took the police officer's revolver out of his bag and handed it to Liao butt first. "Have you ever fired a pistol before?"

The other man shook his head.

"It's simple." He showed him the manual safety—odd for a revolver but perfect for the Chinese police, who usually had little experience with guns—and how it operated. "If you get in any trouble, try to fire a warning shot so I'll know. I should be back in an hour at the latest, so with a bit of luck, we'll be back on our way in no time. Just keep sucking down your medicine, and I'll return before you know it."

"All right." Liao wrapped the doctor's coat around him and clutched the pistol close. "It's already getting colder."

"I know. I'll be back as soon as I can. Just keep thinking about seeing your family again, and you'll be fine."

Liao smiled and nodded as Bolan took his phone and his main weapon bag and got out of the car. Adjusting the strap tight so that the bag clung to his back, he set off at a ground-eating lope, estimating he'd be at the building Tokaido had mentioned in about ten minutes. Remaining alert to the environment around him, particularly the sound of any approaching cars, Bolan settled into his jog and let himself simply run.

The distance passed quickly and, almost before he knew it, Bolan had reached his destination. Tokaido was right. It was hard to tell exactly what purpose the cluster of gray, weathered buildings served out here. They might have been part of a farm; they might have been a storage warehouse; they might have been a drug smuggler's hideout. Either way, Bolan was going in to see what he could find.

Removing his submachine gun from the bag, he approached the nearest building, alert for any sort of security measure or sentries, but he reached it without incident. This one was a long, windowless structure with a large metal door that looked as though it might be some sort of vehicle garage.

There was a side door with a padlock and Bolan took out his picks and was through it in under a minute. Pushing the door open, he used the light on his phone to illuminate the interior.

As he had suspected, it was a garage, with space for vehicles up front and an old tractor and an even older motorcycle on flat tires sitting in the back. Various automotive and other tools were scattered along a workbench on one wall, and what looked like an engine hoist was in the back next to the cycle. Although a layer of dust covered everything, there were also recent tire tracks and footprints on the concrete floor. Spotting several new-looking fifty-gallon drums along the near wall, Bolan hurried to the closest one and shoved it. Finding it empty, he repeated the process until he found one that sloshed when he heaved on it. Grabbing a pry bar from the bench, he opened the top and smelled the sharp odor of gasoline inside.

Now he just had to figure out a way to get some back to the car. A few minutes' search came up with an empty, battered, red-metal container with Chinese lettering on it. It looked as if it would hold enough for him to get the car here, and then he could fill the tank and leave some cash for the fuel.

Unscrewing the container cap, Bolan carefully wrestled the drum over and filled the smaller container, splashing only a bit on the floor. Setting the drum upright, he screwed the cap on, put his submachine gun away, grabbed the container and headed for the door.

Once outside he closed it but left the lock open in the hasp and then started back to the car.

Weighed down by the heavy container of gas, Bolan couldn't move as quickly as he wanted, but wasn't too concerned about getting back before Liao got too cold. But as he crested a hill about halfway there, he heard a single, muffled gunshot.

Immediately he dropped the container and ducked into the nearby ditch, pulling the submachine gun out once he got to cover. He waited a few seconds for another shot but didn't hear one. Making sure the gas container was concealed in the grass of the ditch, he left the road, walking twenty paces out into the field on the same side as the car, and headed toward it.

He'd gone about five hundred yards when he heard a loud engine running and voices in the distance. Hitting the ground, he crawled through the dry grass until he could see the car, which now seemed to have smoke coming from the passenger compartment.

It was still there, as was Liao. He was standing outside the vehicle, his hands in the air, surrounded by a half dozen men dressed in dark green jackets, pants and combat boots, and all were pointing assault rifles at him.

CHAPTER THIRTY-FIVE

Liao was crestfallen, even though there really had been nothing he could do about his situation. On hearing the sound of an approaching vehicle, he had ducked, still clutching the pistol, hoping that whoever was passing by would simply keep going.

But the vehicle had pulled over behind the car, its bright headlights illuminating the interior. Gripping the revolver tightly in his sweating palm, he'd waited to see what would happen, vowing that they wouldn't take him alive.

The truck's lights were turned off, although its engine kept rumbling. A powerful flashlight shone through the car windows, and Liao had caught a glimpse of someone standing behind the spotlight. Panicking, he'd raised the pistol and pulled the trigger.

The report was deafeningly loud. The side window shattered and the light disappeared. He'd heard shouts from outside. Someone had said "Shot fired" and "One person inside" and then he'd heard ominous clicking noises before a louder voice told everyone to be quiet.

"Here's how we're going to handle this."

Straining his ears, Liao heard another click, followed by a pop, and then something fell into the backseat through the missing rear window. It had hissed as it bounced to the floor, spewing a stream of white smoke that had burned his eyes and throat the moment it touched him.

Tear gas! Liao actually had a bit of experience with this sort of thing, as he had gone through government-supplied training on what to do in the event he was ever caught in a mob where the police used tear gas to disperse them. He'd even experienced being exposed to the gas, which, while very unpleasant, had been nothing compared to what he was going through now with his eyes and skin feeling as though they were being pricked with thousands of hot, tiny needles.

His choices had been either to exit the vehicle or to try to remove the canister. Eyes stinging and tearing, he'd tried to find the grenade, but it has apparently rolled under the seat, for although he could feel the gas jetting out and burning his skin, he hadn't been able to reach it.

The entire compartment had filled with gas and even the broken window hadn't made it dissipate fast enough. Barely able to stand being in the cloud, and knowing the discomfort was only going to worsen, Liao had tossed the revolver out and shoved the door open, shouting between coughs, "Don't shoot! I surrender!"

"Hands up! Put your hands up!" They'd grabbed him immediately grabbed, shoved him onto the hood of the car and searched him, which hadn't taken long.

Liao now stared at the quartet of gas-masked individuals pointing short-barreled submachine guns at him.

"He's clean, sir!" the searcher shouted.

"Bring him over to the truck while the gas dissipates," a voice near the truck called out. Pulling him upright, they marched him over to the side of what looked like a military surplus truck, where a bald, potbellied man dressed in fatigues and looking as if he'd been cast from spring steel-eyed him while puffing on a cigar.

Through his swollen, tearing eyes, Liao made out a holstered pistol at the man's waist.

Seeing Liao's discomfort, the man put a sloshing canteen into his trembling hands. "Pour this over your face. It'll take most of the sting away."

Liao did so, the tepid water feeling better than any five-star spa treatment. He washed out his eyes and took three large mouthfuls, rinsing and spitting after each one. When he handed the canteen back, it was almost empty. "Thank you."

The man nodded at Liao's police revolver, which sat on the fender of the large truck. "As you can imagine, we have many questions for you. Let's start with your name."

"Chen… Li Chen." The alias had come out before Liao had realized he was going to reply in the first place. Now that he had committed, though, he needed to come up with some kind of plausible story as to how he had ended up out here.

The leader nodded. "And judging by how you're dressed, I'm going to take a wild guess that you have no papers to back that up, do you?"

A couple of the men chuckled, but the man turned his steely glare on them for a moment and the laughter died as quickly as it had begun.

Liao humbly nodded. "You are right. I do not have any papers. I am from the Anding hospital in Beijing. I was being transferred to another facility under guard, but managed to overpower my escort and take his gun. I stole the car and drove until I ran out of gas. I was not sure what I was going to do next, then you arrived."

"And the reason you fired on my men?" the man asked.

Liao spread his hands. "Well, I am a fugitive, and your man was shining a bright light inside the car. I thought he was with the police and I panicked."

As a story pulled right out of thin air, it wasn't half bad, Liao thought. And at least it might delay these men from finding out who I really am for the time being... Hopefully long enough for Mr. Edwards to figure out some way to rescue me.

The man nodded. "And there is no one else with you?"

Liao shook his head and even puffed his chest out a bit. "No, I did this all on my own."

"Well, you don't have to worry about what you're going to do next, Mr. Chen, because you're coming with us."

Liao nodded. "And where are we going?"

The man puffed on his cigar again. "Why, to the Cheng Dao reprimand center, of course."

He nodded to his men, two of whom came up behind Liao, pulled his arms behind his back and handcuffed him. "Once there, we'll make sure you're fed and clothed...and then we'll find out if you're really who you say you are."

CHAPTER THIRTY-SIX

As he watched Liao being led to the back of the large military truck, Bolan wasn't sure his day could get any worse.

He'd already come up with and discarded a few plans for trying to free the defector from his new captors while sitting there, but had discarded each one as being too risky, both for Liao and himself. Although this new group didn't read as military, despite their transportation, they appeared to have some training, including a well-disciplined chain of command.

There was a brief conversation between the men clustered at the front of the truck before they all broke up, the subordinates heading for the rear of the vehicle, the bald man who had been talking to Liao climbing back up into the cab. With a puff of black smoke, the truck pulled out onto the road again and drove off into the night.

Bolan waited a full minute, making sure the truck's lights had disappeared from sight before getting up and running to the car, which was still leaking a thin stream of tear gas. Holding his breath, he opened all of the doors, then reached in and found the still very hot canister. He grabbed it and tossed it onto the road, then got out and took a deep breath of fresh air. Filling his lungs again, he went back inside the car, opened a bottle of water and poured it under the seat, making sure nothing there was going to catch fire. The floorboard hissed as the stream flowed across it, confirming his suspicion that the grenade had left flammable chemicals behind.

Taking a small breath, Bolan tasted the lingering acrid harshness of the gas, but it was a minor irritant compared to what he had to do now. Climbing into the driver's seat, he hit the concierge button, raising Tokaido immediately.

"Listen carefully—Liao's been captured." Bolan gave him a brief rundown on what had happened. "I need you to track the truck they're in, which is probably about a mile away from my current."

"We're already on it, Striker," the young hacker replied. "Once I got a fix on your location, I patched into a satellite over the area, and I have it for another four minutes. Hopefully that should be enough time to figure out where they're going."

"Good. I'm going to retrieve my gas can, so I'll be back in a few minutes for an update. Striker out."

Bolan turned off the link and slid out of the car, grateful to be in the night air again. He drank some water to hydrate and rinse the acrid taste of the tear gas from his mouth, then jogged up the road to find his gas can. It took him a few minutes longer than he wanted, but at last he spied it in a clump of grass. Grabbing it, he double-timed it back to the car, where he realized the can didn't have a spout to pour it into the tank. Also, the car had the usual metal plate blocking access to the tank to prevent theft.

Looking around, he spotted one of the empty antibiotic medicine bottles lying on the floor of the car. Bolan scanned the area to make sure no one was nearby, then grabbed the bottle, stuck his pistol in the small end, pointed it away from the car and pulled the trigger twice. The oddly muffled report echoed out across the plain, but more importantly, the bullets had torn two ragged holes in the bottom of the bottle. Turning it over, he inserted the improvised funnel's small end into the tank and carefully began pouring the gas into the car.

When the container was empty, he popped the trunk and put both it and the funnel inside, then got into the car and called Tokaido again. "All right, the car's fueled again, try to start it."

The engine turned over but didn't catch. "Hang on, might take a couple times before it gets going," Tokaido said. True to his word, the engine caught on the third try.

"What's the word on the truck?" Bolan asked as he shifted into gear and pulled onto the road, stomping on the gas to reach the isolated garage as quickly as possible.

"Not great. Unless they're visiting, they're headed back to what used to be called a *laogai,* or forced labor camp. Now the sign says Cheng Dao Reprimand Center. Sounds like a new name for a really old method. Guess Liao was in the wrong place at the wrong time."

Bolan grunted. "The story of this mission so far. Well, the good news is that I wasn't with him. The bad news is I now have to figure out a way to get him back."

"Yeah, there is that," Tokaido replied. "Any ideas yet? By the way, you'll want to be careful approaching that fuel depot. They're there right now, loading some barrels."

"Thanks for the heads-up," Bolan replied, turning off the car's lights to avoid being spotted. "Regarding a breakout plan, that's kind of hard to construct when I don't know what I'm heading into."

He was close enough to the storage buildings to see the lit-up truck backed up to the end of the garage. "They better not be taking all the fuel," he muttered. "Are you going to be able to track them all the way to the camp, Akira?"

"Oh, don't worry about finding the place," the hacker replied. "It's a big open pit mine or quarry or something out there. Believe me, you can't miss it."

"This just gets better and better," Bolan replied as he watched. "Any intel on guard strength or security?"

"Working on it," Tokaido said. "Mainly it looks like they're counting on the desolate countryside to take care of any escapees. The place is ringed by a double chainlink fence topped with razor wire and there's one guard tower to cover the whole area, but other than that, the obstacles are all natural."

"Yeah, there's still the problem of getting in, finding Liao and getting out again," Bolan said. "Hang on, they're finally leaving." He watched the truck pull away from the gray storage building. It turned left onto the road and sped away into the distance. "It looks like they didn't find the open side door. I'm going to sign off for now, Akira. I'll report in when I reach the camp. Striker out."

"Good luck, Striker," Tokaido said. "Stony Man out."

Still keeping his lights off, Bolan slowly pulled up to the gray building. Pistol in hand, he got out, looking around warily as he walked to the trunk and got the container and funnel out. He was about to head inside when he caught the scent of cheap, harsh tobacco. He froze with his hand reaching toward the doorknob and took a slow, careful breath, catching it again, stronger this time.

Maybe they aren't as disciplined as I first thought. In fact, given that amazing lack of common sense, they might be less intelligent that I gave them credit for, Bolan thought.

However, he still had the problem of how to bypass

whoever was inside—without having them alert the main camp—and get his fuel.

Changing tacks on the fly, he raised his hand and knocked on the door. "Hello? Is anyone here? Hello?"

There was no reply from inside for a few seconds and then the door flew open. On the other side stood a man dressed in dark green fatigues, his hand on the butt of his holstered pistol, saying something in Cantonese.

"Oh, great, someone is here!" he exclaimed, talking over the man's speech, even as he took a step backward. "Look, I'm really, *really* lost and need directions," he said, speaking slowly and loudly, just like a typical American tourist.

As he'd hoped, the man stepped forward to follow him, his eyes widening as he saw the nearby car. The moment he took his eyes off Bolan, the big American exploded into action.

Stepping forward again, he pinned the man's gun hand against his side as he rocketed a short punch into his opponent's jaw. The guard's eyes glassed over and he sagged against the side of the door. Bolan followed up with another shot to the man's jaw, knocking him out.

He was about to ease the man to the ground when another shape appeared out of the darkness inside the garage, pointing a pistol and shouting at him. Instead of dropping the man, Bolan lifted him and shoved him at the second guard. The limp body fell to the floor, not coming close to the other man, but it did distract him for a crucial second.

Not wanting to risk a gunshot near the fuel drums, Bolan leaped at him, chopping his pistol aside as he lowered a shoulder and plowed into the man. This guy was more alert, however, and tried to spin out of the way. He was only partially successful, however, and Bolan was able to stay with him, taking the man down in a tangle of struggling limbs.

The guard tried to club Bolan, but the Executioner went for the guy's face, raking him across the eyes. The man grunted in pain and twisted his head away, exposing his throat. Stiffening his fingers, Bolan jabbed them into his adversary's Adam's apple, making him gag and choke. That worked so well that he did it again. The man's struggles were weakening; he was fighting to breathe more than anything.

Wrestling the pistol out of his grip, Bolan smacked him on the side of the head twice, the second blow collapsing him to the floor with a last wheeze. He turned and quickly dragged the first guard farther inside, then opened the large door, went to get the car and drove it inside the garage. He closed the door behind him. Unfortunately, besides the guards and the tractor, there was nothing else in the building—and certainly no drums of gasoline. Bolan double-checked everywhere, but the barrels were gone.

Stripping the guards of their pistols, radios and ammunition, he tied them both up and left them behind the tractor, figuring someone would eventually notice they were missing and come out to find them. By then, he hoped to have Liao back and be long gone.

For a moment he considered trying to pose as a guard and infiltrate the base, but one look at the uniforms put the kibosh on that idea. The fatigues were short for a six-foot-three man. Checking under the car again, he wasn't thrilled to find a small puddle of gas forming, either.

All right, if I can't get gas, I'll just have to get another vehicle, he thought. Time to get a look at where Liao's being held to see if I can figure out some kind of way in.

Collecting some tools he thought he might need before the night was over, he walked to the side door and checked for any lights on the road before pushing up the door and driving the car out. He went back and closed the door, knowing he should leave the place as close to the way he found it as possible. Once he was satisfied, he turned left onto the road and started driving. It wouldn't do to have the guards discovered too soon.

It didn't take long for his destination to become visible in the distance. Powerful arc-sodium floodlights illuminated a giant, gaping pit in the ground, easily several football fields in diameter and probably two hundred feet deep.

With the floods bathing everything in bright, white light for several hundred yards in every direction, Bolan stopped the car behind a hill just off the road and crawled to the top of it with his weapons bag and binoculars.

Surrounded by a double layer of ten-foot-high chain-link fence with razor wire, a large cluster of buildings stood about twenty yards from the lip of the pit. There were several long structures that looked like barracks and a larger hall where the prisoners most likely got their meals. Separated by yet another fence were buildings that looked more comfortable, with amenities such as screened windows and something resembling a small patch of meticulously kept grass bordered by white rocks. He didn't see any sign of the truck, although there was a large building that he marked as a probable motor pool.

The guard tower was manned by three people that he could see. He confirmed that when they changed shifts, with Bolan marking the time. The trio of off-duty guards immediately headed for their own quarters, entering one of the nearest buildings to their entrance. Other than that activity, he saw no sign of anyone around.

But as he kept watching, a whistle blew and a few minutes later a line of dusty, exhausted-looking prisoners in light gray uniforms began trudging up from the pit. They headed straight for the largest building, filing inside under the watchful eyes of another squad that had come out to supervise the transfer. Bolan counted at least one hundred and fifty men in the group. They'd be a great distraction, he thought, and most likely one of them had to speak English. But would it be worth the risk? After all, they didn't owe him anything, and even the promise of escape didn't mean much if they had nowhere to go once free of the camp. No, he decided, it would be best if he just slipped in, got Liao and slipped out.

And that was the next question: where the hell was he?

The sound of an engine echoing in the pit attracted his attention and he turned and focused his binoculars in time to see a small 4x4 truck drive up and out, with several men sitting in the back. It stopped in front of another building, not as large as either the mess hall or the barracks. The men in the back got out, removed another man lying on a stretcher from the cargo bed and carried him inside. The truck drove on to the building Bolan had thought was the motor pool and headed inside when a large, metal door opened.

Well, that was two facts confirmed, Bolan thought. He was pretty sure he knew where Liao was being held and he knew where to get a vehicle when they left. Now there was just the matter of figuring out everything else.

CHAPTER THIRTY-SEVEN

"And keep your tongue out... Say 'ahhhh.' Thank you."

Liao was getting really tired of doctors poking and prodding him every time he sat down.

He was in a simple examining room, sitting on a bare wooden chair, while what looked like one of the prisoners who had been made a trustee looked him over using equipment that looked as if it had seen better days in the last century. He had received a new hospital gown, but this one was made of paper, not cloth, and was a marked step down from his previous one.

However, the tiny, stooped man examined him with swift professionalism, assuring Liao that he was a physician with more than twenty-five years experience before he'd been arrested and sent here.

After shining a light down Liao's throat, he straightened and motioned for the man to close his mouth. "Well, you look to be in more or less good health, except your temperature is a bit high."

"That's because I'm ill," Liao replied. "I have the beginning of a sepsis infection."

"However did you get that?" the doctor asked.

"It's a long story, but without my medicine, it's probably only going to get worse."

The doctor frowned and jotted some notes on his onionskin-paper chart. "And you have antibiotics for it?"

"I did…" Liao's voice trailed off as he realized where it was. "It's back in the car."

"I see." The doctor made a few more notes then looked up. "The warden is making some inquiries into your background, but if you do have sepsis, then I can't let you out of—well, this room, actually. I'll have to keep you under quarantine until we figure out what we're going to do with you."

"Isn't there anything you can give me for it?" Liao asked.

The doctor shook his head. "Our supplies are carefully rationed by the government. If I treat you, then I have nothing left when my fellow prisoners fall ill. I'm sure you understand."

"Yes, Doctor, of course."

"All right." He flipped through his papers one more time and then turned toward the door. "As I said, you'll be staying here for the time being. Please do not try to leave, as the door is guarded."

"May I go to the bathroom?" Liao asked.

"I will see." The doctor opened the door and stepped out. Liao peered out to see another room, this one containing actual medical equipment and supplies, including medicines in a glass-paned cabinet.

The doctor spoke with the guard for a few seconds then turned back to him. "The guard will escort you to the restroom. Again, do not try to leave, for the consequences would be severe."

Liao frowned. "I'm sick and alone, dressed in a paper gown with no supplies and stuck in the middle of nowhere."

The doctor cocked his head. "What's your point?"

"Tell me, Doctor, if I were to escape, where in the hell would I go?"

Grinning at that, the doctor laid a finger beside his nose. "Exactly." He nodded at Liao to come to the door. "Come on, let's get you to that washroom and then maybe I can authorize something for you to eat."

As he left the examining room, Liao looked around—without being too obvious about it—at the prison camp, trying to locate some sort of weakness to exploit. Where before he had been willing to die before returning to government custody, he wanted to stay alive—and free, somehow—to see his family again.

He noticed the fence and the sharp, barbed wire coiled atop it. He saw the sharp-eyed guards tracking him as the guard escorted him to the squatting toilet, where he gratefully relieved himself. While returning to his room, he saw the long line of exhausted-looking prisoners trudging up from the quarry to the mess hall. Each one looked exactly alike: shaved head, gray, dirt-smudged uniform, cloth shoes, staring down at the dusty road. Well, it could be worse, he thought, I could be a true prisoner here.

The guard escorted him back to the holding room without a word. After testing the door, which was securely locked and earned him a harsh reprimand from the guard, and then looking out the high, wire-covered window for a few minutes, Liao sat to conserve his strength.

A half hour later, the door rattled open and the doctor walked in carrying a tin bucket on which was a cloth-wrapped bundle. He handed it to Liao with a wink. "Can't have any patients dying on me, now, can I?"

"Thank you, Doctor, your kindness is appreciated."

Liao opened the cloth to find two hunks of coarse cornbread inside. The hot bucket had a cover, as well. When he opened it, the smell of vegetable soup made his mouth water; his stomach rumbled as he realized he was ravenously hungry. Resisting the urge to lift the bucket to his mouth and guzzle the hot liquid, he began dipping the cornbread into the soup and eating slowly, forcing himself to chew and swallow each bite before taking another.

He didn't entertain any illusions that he could escape this place on his own. He certainly couldn't do what Mr. Edwards could do. Merely firing that pistol once had almost scared the hell out of him. He couldn't beat up anyone or shoot them. He'd done everything he could do at the moment—making sure he was somewhere that could be reached by the American.

Because the one thing he was sure of was that Mr. Edwards was coming for him. And Liao definitely wanted to be ready when he got here.

CHAPTER THIRTY-EIGHT

"There must be *something* we can do to help him," Brognola said, his arms tightly crossed on his chest. "These guys must use the internet for more than just emailing their wives."

"Yeah, but from what I can tell, the primary use is downloading amazingly shameful amounts of Asian pornography," Kurtzman replied. "It's just like at the other prison—not every system is wired to the internet, especially in these more rural areas."

"Okay, Bear, then what can we do to assist Striker?" Price asked.

"Well, I can jam their communications once he begins his operation. That will at least slow their response, since they won't be able to radio each other. But the electricity..." He spread his hands in the universal symbol for futility. "If I can't access it, there isn't much I can do with it."

"So, he's going to have to sneak into that base in full view of everybody?" Brognola asked.

"Not necessarily," Tokaido answered. "Lights like that take a lot of power. I'd be amazed if they kept them on all night. The fuel bill would be outrageous."

"But if they do, there's nothing we can do about it, right?" Brognola asked.

"Not unless you wanted to set off a low-yield nuclear device a few miles above them—the EMP would probably fry the electronics in the base." He shrugged. "However, that would include any vehicles in the area, meaning Striker and Liao would have to walk the remaining 125 miles to the airport. Also, that sort of thing would be kind of hard to miss."

Brognola sighed and rubbed his temples. "Days like this make me wish I took something stronger than antacids. All right, do we have any sort of plan that's based in reality?"

Kurtzman shrugged. "Like I said, once he starts the operation, the best we can do is jam their radio transmissions to impede communications. Other than that, the only thing we can really do is watch."

"Maybe not." Tokaido swung his chair around to face Price and Brognola. "Since we do have access to their communications, what if we sent them a fake message ordering them to conserve more power, perhaps giving them the excuse to shut the lights off early? It's near the end of the month, and it looked like they brought in a lot of fuel from that off-site storage facility. It may be a long shot, but worth taking, I think."

At an approving glance from Brognola, Price nodded. "Go for it. I don't see anything to lose."

Tokaido hacked into the state comptroller's files and pilfered the language from a previous exhortation to not waste precious resources of the state. He modified a few sentences here and there, and kept the same bureaucrat's signature on it. "How's this?"

Price leaned in to read over his shoulder. "Looks good to me," she said. "I think you might have a career in middle management if you ever leave here."

The young hacker shuddered. "What, are you *trying* to give me nightmares?"

"Send it," Brognola ordered.

Tokaido hacked into the government official's email account, backdated the email's time stamp so that it looked as though it was issued during office hours and sent it. "Now all we can do is wait," he said.

"When's the next satellite that we have access to due over the target area?" Price asked.

"An NSA satellite will be flying by in about ten minutes," Kurtzman replied. "But it won't be overhead long—something about the Chinese getting antsy over what they perceive as 'undue interest in certain areas,' and if Striker has to delay his infiltration for whatever reason, we might miss it altogether."

"What else is new?" Brognola groused. "We've been a day late and a dollar short on this op ever since it started—and no, I'm not talking about you guys," he continued after catching a warning frown from Price. "I know there's a certain amount of friction that goes with every op, but this one has just seemed...well, worse, somehow."

"No, you're right, Hal," Kurtzman said while still keeping an eye on his screens. "Whether it's faulty data or us getting rooked by the bad guys, there's been a string of issues on this op that would be considered just bad luck in any other profession, but for us, one too many of them—or one that's severe enough—can mean the death of our man in the field."

"And that's something we all take very seriously," Price said.

Hal shook his head. "No, I wasn't leading up to some corny, morale-boosting speech. I know everyone here knows the challenges and dangers all the guys face out in the field every day. And all of you will do everything you can to help them. Everyone who works here is willing to risk a lot—sometimes everything—to accomplish the mission. But when the mission itself seems to be resisting our efforts—I know that sounds crazy, but at the same time, I can't help thinking that it's…"

"Karma telling us to stay out of China?" Tokaido asked.

The joke broke the tension and everyone chuckled.

"Could be… I don't know." Brognola shook his head. "Maybe I'm just getting superstitious in my old age."

"Well, I know what I'm getting you for Christmas this year—a big ol' rabbit's foot," Tokaido said. "Wait a sec—the satellite is in place."

He brought up the view of the central northern plain, with the huge hole of an even blacker, stygian pit in the darkness.

"Well, for whatever reason, the lights are off," Price noted. "I hope Striker can make good use of it."

"He always does, Barbara," the big Fed said with a smile. "*That* is the one thing I am absolutely certain of."

CHAPTER THIRTY-NINE

When the huge floodlights winked off, Bolan didn't move for another two hours. He was acutely aware of the time passing, knowing that every minute gone was possibly bringing the MSS agent closer to finding Liao and him. As much as he wanted to keep moving, he knew that going after Liao too early exponentially increased the risk of getting caught.

Only after much of the general activity around the camp had died down did he prepare himself, and after the next time the guard tower finished its sentry rotation, he began his insertion.

Rising from his surveillance post, he crept to the corner of the fence nearest the medical building. Taking out the wire cutters he'd lifted from the storage room, he cut enough links to form a flap that he could push open enough to slip through. Inside the perimeter, he replaced the section of fence so that it looked as if it was still relatively unbroken. It wouldn't pass a close inspection, but he only needed it to pass muster for the next thirty minutes, an hour at most.

He had just started working on the interior fence when he caught a familiar-sounding noise—something was running toward him. Glancing in the direction of the sound, he saw two bull mastiffs charging toward him along the corridor formed by the two fences.

That explains why there weren't any guard patrols here, he thought as he rose and turned to face them. Once again, the use of guns was out, so he'd have to resort to more creative measures.

Both animals were sleek, brown-black death machines as they homed in on him. The only good thing was that neither dog was barking, their silent, fang-filled mouths open to rend and tear. While the Executioner never liked killing guard dogs, which were only doing what they were trained to do, in this case it was either them or him, and that was no choice at all.

The first dog reached him slightly ahead of the second. It leaped, teeth flashing, as Bolan launched his own counterattack the moment it left the ground. His combat boot whipped up in a powerful kick that slammed into the dog's jaw. The blow smashed the mandible up into the palate with an audible *click* as the dog's momentum was violently redirected into the air. Even so, absorbing all that force made Bolan hop back to avoid falling over. The guard dog flipped over onto its back and crashed to the ground, unmoving.

That defense worked well against one dog, however it left him unprepared for the second, which came in low and went for his leg still on the ground. It sank its teeth into his calf, hitting him with enough force to knock him over this time.

Sharp pain lanced through his leg, with the dog now growling as it hung on to him. Drawing his pistol, he swung it in a roundhouse shot to the side of the dog's head, hitting it hard enough to stun the animal and loosen its grip on his calf muscle. Drawing back again, Bolan smashed the dog's skull with the pistol, making the animal release him as it flopped over on the ground.

Panting from the exertion, Bolan sat up and examined his wound. The guard dog's teeth had sunk deep into the *triceps surae* muscle and moving his foot even a little hurt like hell. Bolan pulled a T-shirt from his bag and tied it around the wound, yanking it so tight he nearly saw stars at the pain it caused. If he could have scrubbed the mission, he might have, but there was no choice now. If he could free Liao and if they could make it to a vehicle, they'd be all right.

Keeping the pistol out in case there were more dogs, he turned back to the interior fence and finished making his cuts. Pulling the section open, he crawled through and closed it behind him, then tucked his legs under him, gritted his teeth and tried to stand.

The pain in his leg was intense, but he stayed upright. Putting any weight on it generated a sharp flare of agony, but he ignored it and began to move as quickly as he could toward the medical building.

The wire-covered window in the back was too high up and too small to get through. Bolan might have tried to contact Liao through it, but he was worried about making too much noise in doing so. Instead he limped around the side of the building, careful to not make a sound. Leaning against the dusty gray concrete, he took a moment to catch his breath and then slowly peeked around the corner.

The glow of a cigarette lit the darkness, pinpointing the sentry outside the door. Again, Bolan was surprised by the carelessness on the guard's part.

Normally one guard wouldn't have been a problem. However, with his injury, the lone man became a more formidable obstacle. He looked up at the roof a few feet overhead, noting that it was an A-frame, and that the pitch was such that he was mostly concealed from the view of the guards in the tower.

No sooner had he thought of the plan than Bolan began putting it into action. Heading back to the rear of the building, he carefully set his weapons bag on the ground and removed the shoulder strap. The gaps in the window wire were large enough to thread the ends of the nylon through and tie them off to form a sling.

Taking a deep breath, he leaped up and grabbed the windowsill with both hands. Slowly, carefully, he pulled himself up until his head was above the sill. Next, he drew his good leg up until he felt the boot slip into the strap. Praying it would hold, he straightened his leg, driving himself up. Halfway there, he felt the strap start to give and pushed off it while lunging up to grab the edge of the roof.

A high *twang* sounded as one of the wires snapped, but Bolan had gotten enough momentum to hoist himself onto the roof. He rolled over onto it as cautiously as he could. Although it appeared to be made of tin, it didn't flex or groan as he moved.

Once he was fully on top of the roof, Bolan made it to the side that hid him from the sentry tower and waited to see if any noise he'd made had alerted the door guard. After a slow sixty-count had passed, Bolan assumed the guard hadn't heard anything. In that time, he also realized how he could take out the guard with minimal risk to himself, assuming his primary plan didn't work.

Reaching down, he untied the strap from the window and wrapped it around his hand. Then he crawled over the roof to the front of the building. Still careful to avoid being spotted by the guards in the tower, he slowly, inch-by-inch, stuck his head over the edge to get a bearing on where the man was standing. Acrid smoke tickled his nose, and Bolan didn't make a sound as he waited for the man only a couple yards away from him to finish his cigarette.

When the smell of burning tobacco faded, Bolan knew it was time to move. Even more slowly, he adjusted his position until he had brought his legs around and under him. Tucking his good leg under his body, he raised himself to a crouch. Taking the strap, he uncurled it and held it between both hands as he waited for the right moment.

A minute passed. Then another. Stifling a yawn, the man stretched both arms above his head and took a step away from the building.

Like a nocturnal jungle cat, Bolan sprang from the roof, dropping onto the man. He landed perfectly, bearing the man to the ground with his weight. Before the guard could drag in a breath or recover enough to cry out, Bolan looped the bag strap around his prey's neck and pulled it tight while keeping the man pinned to the ground with his superior weight.

Already breathless from the surprise attack, the guard wheezed and clawed at the nylon strap, vainly trying to loosen it enough to suck in the smallest sip of air, which remained forever outside his purpling lips, constricted throat and straining lungs. With one last agonized heave, the man relaxed in death.

Bolan kept the stranglehold for another minute, listening for any sign that someone might have heard the brief scuffle while making sure the guard was truly dead. When the body underneath him remained still and no one came running, he got up and dragged the corpse to the door.

Limping to the rear, he grabbed his weapons bag and

walked back to the front again. The door was secured
with a simple bolt, which he carefully pulled back. Then
he opened the door, pistol ready in case someone was
inside waiting for him. The room beyond was empty.
After sweeping and clearing it, he dragged the dead guard
through the doorway and placed him in a corner, then
closed the front door. Taking his pistol and spare magazines, Bolan glanced around, aware that the trail of death
and destruction he was leaving meant he might have only
a few minutes left to get Liao, get a vehicle and get the
hell out of there.

The room was clean and sparsely furnished, with only
a small desk and a cabinet next to it. Another door stood
across from the entryway, but Bolan walked to the cabinet first. Seeing it was unlocked, he opened it to find a
variety of first-aid supplies.

Untying the improvised T-shirt bandage, he doused
the bloody rag in alcohol and pressed it to the injury, wel-
coming the antiseptic's stinging bite. Grabbing a sealed
bandage and some medical tape, he covered the wound
and then stuffed some more bandages, gauze and tape
into his bag.

Next, he headed to the interior door and slid back
the bolt. Easing it open, he saw Liao slumped in a chair
in the middle of the room, head down on his chest and
snoring softly.

Bolan walked over and clamped a hand over the sleeping man's mouth. He awakened at once, grabbing the
hand on his face and trying to wrench it away before
looking up and seeing the other man's face. Only then
did he relax, breathing hard through his nose.

Bolan bent to his ear. "We're leaving right now. Follow me, and do exactly what I say when I say. Do you understand?"

He pulled back to see Liao nod. Bolan jerked his chin at the open door and Liao got up and headed for it.

In the outer room, Liao gasped at the dark, still form of the guard crumpled in the corner. Bolan passed him and crossed to the exit, putting an ear to it to listen for any sounds of movement or conversation outside. Hearing nothing, he made sure Liao was ready before opening the door and heading for the motor pool.

CHAPTER FORTY

"Damn it, a luxury Mercedes-Benz doesn't simply disappear!" Fang shouted into his phone. "I already know its appearance heading east on the road was faked. Now, find me that car!"

Resisting the urge to smash his smartphone against the dashboard, he disconnected and put it away, then glanced at the general, riding across from him. "It is unseemly to show that sort of reaction to disappointing news, I know. I apologize for my behavior."

General Zhao waved his hand. "It is nothing I wouldn't do in your place. Indeed—" he looked around at the barren landscape they had been driving through for the past hour "—if something doesn't break soon, I think we're going to have to admit defeat."

Fang opened his mouth to protest, then closed it again. The simple truth was that the general was right. He couldn't keep going on this crusade, couldn't keep marshaling ministry resources and personnel to find this man, who somehow kept eluding him and the security dragnet around the city with ease. If they didn't come across a solid lead in the next few hours, it would be all over—and his career would be over, as well. There was no way to recover from such a monumental screwup. Most likely he would find himself back at the organ transplant facility, only as a donor this time not a Ministry of State Security agent.

He shook his head. "We aren't finished yet," he said, trying to keep his tone confident.

But he had to admit that the odds were growing longer with every passing minute. The two-truck convoy had been driving down the western highway for hours and was now far from the city. Yet there had been no sign of the sedan or the mysterious American. It was as if they had vanished from the face of the earth.

Fang knew that was not the case; it was simply impossible. What was possible, however, was that their quarry had gone to ground somewhere out here, found a bolt-hole in the thousands of hectares of trackless steppe to wait until the heat died down. Then, once he was off the case, they would slip over the border into Mongolia or Tibet, maybe even Russia, and disappear completely.

But he would keep looking for them for as long as he could.

Fang's musings were interrupted by his phone. He pulled it out and saw that he had a downloaded photo waiting for him. Opening it, he saw two pictures: the first one was of a car matching the one he was looking for by the side of a desolate road. The second was the map coordinates of where it had been spotted—more than 280 kilometers from their current position. "Son of a bitch! We've been going the wrong way!"

He showed the map to General Zhao, who grinned as he grabbed the truck's radio microphone. "I thought this might happen, so I've taken the liberty of enlisting some help. Forward those coordinates to me."

Fang did so and the general studied them for a moment before speaking again. "Turn the trucks around and start heading back to the city," he instructed the driver before talking rapidly into the microphone. Fang caught "Harbin" and "thirty minutes out" in the chatter back and forth.

"Did you just do what I think you did?" he asked.

"You're not the only one who has favors owed to him," the general replied.

About twenty minutes later their driver pointed into the air and said, "General Zhao, sir. It's here."

Fang gaped at the sleek, well-armed Harbin Z-9 military helicopter that was slowly landing in a nearby field. Able to carry up to ten armed soldiers, the twin-engine rotorcraft had a maximum speed of 190 miles per hour. It was also well armed, with a pair of 23 mm cannons, and pylons loaded with HJ-8 antitank missiles. It was the perfect equalizer for the hunt ahead.

"Nice, isn't she?" the general asked. "I thought we'd take a few men and catch a ride on this to go check out that car of yours."

"Th-thank you, my friend," Fang stammered, overwhelmed by what the general was doing for him. "After this, our slate is clean, I promise."

General Zhao nodded. "I know, but do not worry about that right now. Come on, we've got a flight—and a prisoner—to catch!"

CHAPTER FORTY-ONE

Submachine gun in his hands, Bolan limped toward the large building he'd seen the vehicle enter that afternoon. Liao followed on his heels, watching behind them for any guards.

Using the surrounding buildings as cover, they reached the large warehouse-like building with little difficulty. However, there was a problem with the structure itself. Light shone from under the main doors and Bolan could hear the sounds of someone working on something inside over the clatter of a gas generator, along with off-key singing.

"Great. A mechanic is working late," he said, standing beside the door.

"So, why can't you just shoot him?" Liao asked. "That generator's probably making enough noise to cover the sound."

It wasn't the plan Bolan had been about to go for, but the other man's logic did make sense.

Snugging the butt of the gun into his shoulder, Bolan reached for the handle of the door and was about to turn it when a loud voice directly on the other side abruptly stopped him.

"Back to the corner!" Bolan said, turning and hobbling as fast as his injured leg could carry him.

They rounded the corner just in time. The door opened

and a man stepped out, turning to call back once more to someone inside before loping off across the grounds.

"That was close," Bolan said as he pressed an ear to the wall. "The singer's still in there. We've got to get some eyes on what's all going on inside."

Liao pointed up. "There are some windows near the roof."

Bolan looked up and frowned. The small windows were about ten feet off the ground. There was only one way to do this...

"You'll have to climb onto my shoulders," he said to Liao. "Are you up to that?"

"I would crawl to the airport naked if it will get me out of here," he replied.

"Let's hope it doesn't come to that." Checking to make sure no one was around, Bolan laced his fingers together to form a stirrup. "Step into this, then up onto my shoulders. Go slow, don't get seen and don't fall."

Liao nodded, then braced his hands on Bolan's shoulders as he stepped into the improvised step. Pushing up, he clambered onto his shoulders, his left foot clouting the big American in the head as he tried to steady his footing. For his part Bolan tried to remain steady, although the man on his shoulders wasn't making it easy. "Calm down!" he whispered. "Stop moving around so much!"

"Sorry!" Liao whispered back.

"Just tell me what you see."

Now secure on his perch, Liao cautiously raised his head just enough to see inside the garage. As he did, the main door opened again, then closed with a bang, startling Liao and making him jump and shuffle his feet. Gritting his teeth, Bolan stayed put and braced himself against the wall, trying to ignore the throbbing pain in his calf.

"Okay...coming down." The Chinese defector climbed down almost more clumsily than he had gone up, kicking Bolan in the ribs as he went and stepping on his foot before hitting the ground.

Grimacing, he regarded the smaller man. "Well?"

"Besides the singing man, there are four others playing cards at a table," Liao reported, squatting in the dirt. "The layout is like so, more or less." He quickly sketched the interior of the motor pool and where the various people were, then looked up at Bolan. "What do you want to do?"

"We need some kind of distraction to take out some of them before I go in."

"Wouldn't the simplest way be to turn out the lights?" Liao jerked a thumb toward the rear of the building, where the generator clattered away.

"Isolated yet accessible. Liao, we might just make a special agent out of you yet," Bolan said. "Come on."

The two men walked to the back of the building where the generator was housed inside a small shed. "Better and better," Bolan said. "All right, you wait on the far side and keep a lookout while I go in and disable the generator and wait for the guard to show up. I doubt I'll need any help with him, but if there's any trouble—" he handed Liao another pistol "—hit him hard over the head with this. *Do not* shoot him."

"Got it." Liao nodded and took his position outside, while Bolan opened the door and slipped into the darkness inside. Once his eyes adjusted to the moonlight peeking through the thin gaps, he looked at the rattling generator—its racket even louder in the confined space—

found the choke and pushed it all the way over. The motor coughed and then died with a sputter. In the silence Bolan heard the loud cursing of the men inside. As he'd hoped, this was something that happened fairly often, so it didn't engender much attention.

There was a quick discussion—no doubt over whom was going to go out and fix it—then he heard the scuff of boots as someone approached the shed door. Bolan thought he heard movement near the door and tensed, pistol butt raised, but the door didn't open, and he stood there for a few seconds before it swung wide and a light shone inside.

Bolan shrank into the corner as the man walked in and headed straight for the silent generator. As he bent over the hot machine, Bolan stepped forward and brought the butt of his gun down on the back of the man's neck. He slumped over the motor and slid down it to the ground.

He retrieving the man's flashlight and dragged him into the corner. Leaving the door ajar and the flashlight on the floor as bait, Bolan reset his trap and waited. Sure enough, a few minutes later he heard the sound of another guard ambling out.

"Sun? Ni qu na'erle?" a slurred voice asked at the door. The man stumbled in and kicked the flashlight away from him. As he bent to pick it up, Bolan stepped out and gave him a swift blow to the head with his pistol, dropping him to the floor.

Bolan dragged him over to the corner, as well, wondering if he could actually repeat the maneuver a third time. He set it up again, complete with flashlight and open door, and waited. This time, he heard two voices talking as they approached the door.

An irritated voice posed a question as they stepped

up to the doorway. Bolan tensed, knowing he'd have to strike quickly to knock out both men.

The first man said something, shaking his head as he stepped inside the shed. He was more alert than the other two, however, and shone his own flashlight around as he advanced. Fortunately he swept it to the right first, toward the empty side of the shed. As he did, Bolan stepped forward and clocked him hard on the side of the head, felling him like a short tree.

He turned, pistol raised to nail the second man, only to see the sentry already falling forward, out cold. Behind him stood Liao, his pistol raised and a huge grin on his face.

"Nice work," Bolan said as he grabbed the first man's shoulders and dragged him inside. "Get that one."

Liao shoved the second unconscious guard inside the room. After stripping the men of their weapons, they secured the men's hands and feet with their bootlaces and gagged them with their belts. When Bolan realized Liao was taking longer than he expected, he looked up to see the other man changing into pants taken from one man, a shirt taken from another, and socks and boots from a third. When he was finished, he looked almost exactly like one of the guards they'd just subdued.

Nodding at the combined practicality and intelligence of the move, Bolan finished his look by setting him up with a belt and pistol combination on his waist, and used his hospital gown to gag the man whose belt he'd taken.

"If we keep this up, we might manage to get out of here without too much difficulty," he said as he finished tying the last man's feet. Turning one of his three flashlights toward the generator, he adjusted the choke to normal and hit the ignition button. The machine rumbled to life again, filling the small area with its noise and a bit of smoke. "Let's go."

After wedging the door closed with one of the guard's boots—even if they got their gags off, Bolan figured the generator would drown out any shouts they made—they headed toward the door of the motor pool building again.

After checking to see if the front of the building was clear, Bolan and Liao slipped to the main door and opened it, letting out the singer's voice as they slipped inside.

The interior of the large room was filled with vehicles in various states of disassembly, from a 6x6 truck on blocks to the frame of what looked like an old APC from the 1960s near the back. Bolan scanned the area for a usable vehicle—he had no wish to push his luck any further than he already had—and came up with one that was just about perfect.

The olive-drab 4x4 was an Iveco NJ2046, a light but sturdy Italian-built truck that could carry about ten men and their gear. Bolan had seen versions adapted to also mount the HJ-9A antitank missile, but this one, unfortunately, was not, although it seemed to have the mount for the weapon still attached. Still, it had a decent range, and for where they were going, would be the perfect vehicle to take them through the rough country that lay between them and safety in Mongolia.

"Come with me, but keep an eye on the door." Bolan walked over to the mechanic, who was singing some sort of love ballad, he guessed, as he worked underneath a large army-surplus vehicle from the 70s that had been driven onto ramps. Grabbing the man's feet, he yanked him out from under the vehicle and pointed his pistol into the mechanic's face.

Already startled by the movement, his song died off in a terrified squeak as he stared down the muzzle of the gun. His gaze flicked to Liao, staring at him sternly with folded arms, and his forehead wrinkled in puzzlement. Bolan adjusted his vision with a light tap of the pistol on his forehead, making the man refocus on him.

"Liao, translate," he ordered, nodding at the Iveco. "Does that truck run well?"

Liao asked the question and the man nodded, rattling off a rapid-fire Cantonese reply. "Yes, the work on it was just finished this evening, and it is supposed to go back out for duty tomorrow morning."

"Where is your fuel stored?" Bolan asked.

Liao translated and the man answered again. "The truck is fully fueled and carries a twenty-liter spare. The rest of the fuel is stored in a building two blocks behind this one," he told Bolan.

Although tempted to try to grab some more, Bolan knew that move would probably land them in trouble. "Tie him up and gag him," Bolan said. Liao scurried to comply while he walked over to check out the truck. Everything seemed okay. The tires were sound, the engine looked good and the spare full gas can was there as promised.

"You ready?" he asked Liao, who ran over to him and slid into the passenger's seat, only to get a shake of his head from Bolan. "What, you think *I'm* going to drive out of here? Get over here. If we can, we're going to head right out the front—"

A chorus of shouts made him look up and, moments later, an alarm went off.

"Damn it!" He got into the passenger seat and readied the submachine gun. "Let's go, right now."

The front door opened and he got a glimpse of guards rushing in. Leveling the weapon out the window, Bolan squeezed off two short bursts, catching one guard in the stomach and making him pitch over, and scattering the rest.

"Go, go, go!"

Liao had already started the truck and jammed it in gear while stomping on the gas pedal. The vehicle leaped forward—straight at the closed garage door.

"We stopping to open it?" he asked.

"Hell, no!" Bolan punctuated his answer by raking the middle of the door with his subgun, putting a neat line of bullets through the door. When they hit, the weakened section burst open and the lower half of the door was carried forward with the truck's momentum. Bolan saw one guard who had been bowled over by the breaking door roll to a stop in the middle of the compound. He fired another burst to keep the rest of the nearby guards' heads down. A few return shots whizzed by, but none came even close to them.

"We are still going out the main gate, right?" Liao asked as Bolan reloaded.

"Right!" He pulled back the cocking lever and stuck his head and shoulders out the window.

"What about the tower?"

"Leave them to me," Bolan replied. "Just go as fast as you can. We're going to have to ram it!"

Their makeshift armor flew off as Liao took another corner so fast the truck slewed around it on two wheels. "Easy there! Crash this thing and we aren't going anywhere!"

"We're coming up on the main road and the tower," Liao said. "It's just around this corner."

"All right, the second you get around it, step on it!" Bolan said.

They took the second corner almost as hard as the first, and the moment Bolan saw the gate and tower and guards in the distance, he opened fire. He put two bursts into the guard room between the gate and the bottom of the tower, then emptied the rest of his magazine into the sentry position itself as they got closer, starting near the bottom and letting the weapon's natural climb rate do the work for him. Splinters flew from the floor and sides as the slugs chewed into it. Bolan heard at least one scream of pain from inside.

The magazine ran dry while they were still thirty yards from the gate. Instead of reloading, Bolan drew two QSR pistols. Pointing one behind him and one in front of him, he pulled the triggers on both as fast as he could, laying down a barrage of 9 mm rounds intended to keep the guards under cover instead of intending to hit anything.

"We're about to hit it!" Liao yelled, making Bolan duck back inside after spraying the tower with the last of his bullets. He braced himself as the heavy-gauge wire and metal-framed gate loomed large in the windshield.

"Here we go!" Liao shouted as he hunched over the wheel, teeth bared in a maniac grin.

The truck slammed into the gate and punched through, smashing the left side open and tearing the right side completely off its hinges, sending it spinning into the dust. The truck swerved to the right upon impact, but Liao handled it as if he'd been breaking out of prison camps all his life. He got the truck back on the road and zooming away to the north in seconds.

Bolan had reloaded his submachine gun and now emptied the magazine at the guard tower as they sped away. He hoped to keep them under cover so they couldn't get a bead on the truck before it sped out of range. Someone up there did manage to get the machine gun on line, but all the person did was chew up a line of dirt behind the truck before it disappeared into the night.

"Holy shit—we did it!" Liao yelled as they rocketed down the narrow dirt road.

Bolan was less sanguine as he reloaded the submachine gun and both pistols, sticking both of the smaller weapons in his belt. "Yeah, but we're a long way from safe. And they're not going to just sit back and let us get out of here. In fact…" He caught the glare of headlights in the rearview mirror. "They're already coming after us."

"What's the plan?" Liao asked.

Bolan climbed into the back. "You just concentrate on getting us as far from that camp as possible. I'm going to do everything I can to get them off our ass."

CHAPTER FORTY-TWO

"There's the vehicle!"

His sweating fingers tightly gripping the butt and fore-stock of the QBZ-95 assault rifle loaned to him by General Zhao, Fang sighted along where the other man was pointing as they flew through the air at more than 173 miles per hour.

Although he wasn't a religious man, if asked, Fang would have said the helicopter was a godsend. It would have taken hours to drive back along the highway and over the narrow, twisting roads that cut through the steppe to reach their target. The Harbin, however, didn't even have to hit its top speed to bring them there in just under an hour.

Now they were approaching the Mercedes-Benz, which appeared to have been abandoned in the middle of a field, a short distance from a converted prison camp. It looked used and abused, with its back window missing, and was covered in dust and chaff from being driven on the roads and into the field.

"Let's take it!" he said into his headset.

"My men will clear the vehicle first, then we will inspect it—for your protection, of course," Zhao replied, the unmistakable ring of command clear in his voice. It was the first time Fang had heard it today.

"That's fine, but I want to see it for myself," he replied.

Zhao nodded. "Just give them sixty seconds. Then you can look at it all you like."

Grudgingly, Fang nodded, although he was pretty sure they had kept moving. There would be no point staying with the car if it had broken down or run out of gas.

Using hand signals, the general directed the six-man squad to surround the car and capture—alive—anyone they found inside. The helicopter hovered a few feet above the ground and the squad opened the side doors and jumped out, fanning out to cover the car while giving themselves intersecting fields of fire for protection and reinforcement.

They advanced on the forlorn vehicle in a line, the ends of which walked faster to encircle the car in a U-shaped formation. At a signal from the team leader, each man on the end approached the car from either side and covered the passenger area, careful not to catch each other in their field of fire. At the same time, two men approached the trunk. The leader signaled again and the soldier on the driver's side popped the trunk open, the pair of soldiers next to it covering the empty space with their weapons.

"Sir, this is Red Squad One, the target is clear. Repeat, the target is clear. There are no hostiles inside. Repeat, no hostiles inside."

"Take it down. I want to see for myself," the MSS agent said.

Zhao ordered the pilot to land the helicopter and the moment it was on the ground, Fang exited and ran to the car. The soldiers cleared a path for him as he sprinted over.

"Someone used tear gas to clear the vehicle," the sergeant shouted as he looked inside. "You can still smell it."

"Yes, Sergeant, thank you." Fang opened the glove box

and riffled through it, then looked underneath the seats. All he found was a bag holding several empty bottles. Two were water bottles that contained a few drops of a cloudy, off-white liquid. There were also several empty antibiotic medicine containers in the bag.

"This was their car," he said, holding up the bag as he emerged. "General, you said there was a prison camp nearby?"

"Yes, the Cheng Dao Reprimand Center," the general replied.

"And the tear gas…" Fang said. "That's where they are. With any luck, the prison guards have captured them." He started back to the helicopter. "This day might still have a happy ending yet."

Zhao recalled his men and within sixty seconds they were airborne and heading to the prison camp.

As they approached, Fang saw that the main gate had been smashed open, with one half hanging crookedly off its hinges. The nearby guard tower had also been chewed up, with bullet holes pockmarking its exterior. Armed men ran all over the place, shouting to one another as they formed a human perimeter. Cold dread iced over in the pit of Fang's stomach as they got closer—he knew what had caused this kind of chaos—and he feared that they had arrived too late yet again.

A spotlight was trained on the helicopter and a voice shouted at them through a bullhorn to identify themselves immediately or be fired upon.

Zhao got on the external loudspeakers, identified himself and Agent Fang, and let the prison know that they were touching down and to summon the warden immediately.

That put the fear of the state into the guards and one

took off, running toward a building in the back. By the time Fang and Zhao were out of the helicopter and approaching what was left of the main gate, a bald man with a small potbelly and a ground-churning stride was coming to greet them.

"General Zhao, Agent Fang." Despite the circumstances, he snapped off a crisp salute. "I am Warden Rong Yam. I appreciate your promptness, although confess to being surprised at your arrival, since we just sent out the alert about this escape attempt a few minutes ago—"

"We have been chasing these fugitives for the past twenty-four hours," Fang interrupted. "It's a pair. A local man and a tall American, right?"

The warden frowned at the description. "One was Chinese, yes, but I don't know about an American. We found the local in a car about five kilometers away, but he was alone. He said he was a fugitive from a Beijing mental hospital—"

"That man is a traitor to our nation, and his accomplice is an American trying to get him out of the country. It is imperative that they are captured as soon as possible," Fang said. "Where are they now?"

"That explains the shooter," the warden said. "They broke out of here about ten minutes ago. They stole one of our trucks and headed north. We're in pursuit right now."

"Mongolia…of course! Come on, General!" Fang said as he turned and ran for the helicopter. "Radio your men, Warden, and tell them the two must be captured alive!"

All the general's men boarded quickly and in a few seconds the helicopter took off, following the pursuit toward the border.

CHAPTER FORTY-THREE

Bolan kept an eye on the two vehicles as they approached the speeding truck. One was a much larger truck, a six-wheeled monster that took up almost the entire roadway. Ahead of it was another Iveco—only this one had a light machine gun sitting on the pintle mount that usually held the antitank weapon.

"Damn!" he said. No matter what kind of gun it was, it would have a far superior range to Bolan's submachine gun. Depending on the skill of the person manning it, the pursuers could chop the rear of their vehicle into pieces at their leisure, then take them when they were forced to stop.

As if confirming his prediction, the gunner let loose with a long burst, the bullets kicking up dirt to the left of the truck. Liao swerved right, almost running off the road, and then overcorrected, making them fishtail wildly. Bolan crouched to remain upright through the crazy gyrations.

"Settle down up there!" he shouted. "They didn't actually hit us!"

"This is only the second—no, the third time I've ever been shot at!" Liao yelled back. "Pardon me for not being used to it!"

"Well, you better get used to it quick because more's incoming!" Bolan said, hunching in the seat as another fusillade chopped up the road on their right. He returned fire, but as expected, they were far out of his weapon's range. The enemy would soon have their range. There had to be a way to even the odds… His gaze fell on the spare tank of gas attached to the rear of the vehicle, and he winced at having to sacrifice it, but knew if their pursuers hit it with a stray shot, the truck could become a speeding Molotov cocktail. It would be better to use it to their advantage than the enemy's.

"Tell me when we're coming up on a curve or a valley—any place where we'll be out of their sight, even for a few seconds," Bolan said while scrambling to grab the heavy container. He was lugging it back to the middle of the truck when the latest barrage drilled into the rear, shattering the window and punching a series of holes through the tailgate. Bolan checked the tank for damage. Fortunately, it hadn't been hit.

"Are you okay?" Liao shouted.

"Yeah, but that was too close," Bolan replied.

"We're coming up on a dip in the road in about 150 meters," Liao shouted.

"Perfect." Tearing off his shirtsleeve, Bolan unscrewed the cap and stuffed the cloth into the hole. He knew just shooting it would have no effect; the fuel wouldn't explode without an actual flame.

He rooted around in his pocket for the matches from the nightclub. They were still slightly soggy and smelled of sewage, but the word "waterproof" was plainly visible on the cardboard. "Stop at the bottom," he called back while ripping one out and dragging it across the ignition strip on the back of the book.

It didn't light. Bolan tried again as they slowed to a stop. "Now what?" Liao asked.

"Just a second..." Bolan dragged the match head across a third time. It sparked, smoked and lit brightly. "Got it!"

He touched it to the cloth, which flared sullenly to life. Bolan made sure it caught as he scrambled into the back of the truck again.

"They're coming!" Liao cried.

"I hear them. I'm just going to leave a little surprise..." Bolan could hear the rumble of the approaching larger truck, almost drowned out by with the roar of the smaller one. He set the gas can on its side in the middle of the road. "Floor it!"

Liao hit the gas and they shot forward. Bracing himself, Bolan snugged the butt of his submachine gun tight to his shoulder and aimed at the rapidly shrinking gas tank.

The lead truck roared into the depression. Seeing their quarry less than fifty yards away, the machine gunner scrambled to adjust his aim—just as Bolan fired.

The bullets punched into the gas can, sending fuel spurting out. For a second nothing happened and he feared the gas might have smothered the fire.

But as the pursuit truck roared straight at them, the improvised incendiary detonated with a dull *whomp*!

Unable to stop in time, the truck plowed straight through the huge fireball. The driver lost control and drove the flaming vehicle up the embankment before regaining control and stopping.

"Stop!" Bolan shouted. As his truck skidded to a halt, he jumped out and limped as fast as he could toward the burning vehicle. The machine gunner was trying to track toward him, but Bolan shot first, a long burst that knocked the man backward, making him slowly topple off the truck.

The panicked driver clawed at his door in an attempt to get away from the flames licking at the windshield. Bolan helped cure his fear permanently by putting a burst through the window and into his target. The driver slumped over the steering wheel, face and upper chest leaking blood.

A second guard got out of the passenger side and brought his gun around to aim at the big American.

Letting loose the last of his magazine, Bolan's bullets pulverized him, dropping him to the dirt.

Leaping onto the back of the truck, the Executioner yanked the locking pin loose from the pintle and lifted the light machine gun, a bullpup-model 5.8 mm QBB-95 with an 80-round drum magazine behind the butt. Glancing around, he saw another ammo drum lying on the bottom of the truck and grabbed it, too. Looking over his shoulder, he saw the bigger truck closing fast.

Leaping out, he carried both items to their truck and tossed them in, then started back to the burning vehicle.

"Where are you going?"

"Diversion!" Bolan yelled over his shoulder. "Hang on!" He ran to the other vehicle, where the flames were almost out. Opening the driver's door, he threw out the lifeless body and jumped in. The engine was still running and he jammed it into gear and floored the gas pedal.

The truck lurched forward along the side of the small hill and for a heart-stopping moment Bolan thought it was going to roll over. Then he got it straightened and drove down to the road again. Once there, he hit the gas, heading straight toward the larger truck.

Seeing the oncoming vehicle, the bigger vehicle honked its horn, but Bolan didn't stop. When the two vehicles were a hundred yards apart, he opened the door and dived onto the ground, rolling hard with the impact.

At that velocity, the big truck couldn't turn aside fast enough, although the driver tried. The front of the 6x6 crashed into the smaller truck on the passenger side, crumpling the hood and engine compartment and sending the Italian truck flying through the air.

The large cargo truck hit its air brakes immediately after the impact, shuddering to a stop. Bolan wasn't waiting around to find out what they were doing, however. The moment he stopped rolling, he got up and bolted back to the truck, ignoring the steady stabs of pain from his left leg every time it hit the ground. He reached the vehicle, which Liao had thoughtfully backed up for him, at the bottom of the dip. Diving into the back, he banged his knee painfully on the machine gun on the floor as he yelled, "Go, go, go!"

Liao hit it and the truck began speeding away. "They'll never catch us now!" he shouted, pounding the roof with his fist. "We did it!"

"We aren't in Mongolia yet!" Bolan, still in the back compartment, slumped against the tailgate, breathing heavily. His leg twitched, and he noticed his phone was vibrating.

He dug it out and answered. "We're—"

Akira Tokaido's voice screamed in his ear. "Missile! Evacuate the vehicle—they've locked-on an antitank missile!"

"Stop now! Right now!" Bolan yelled to Liao as he shoved the phone into his pocket and grabbed the machine gun with his other hand.

The truck skidded to a halt and as the other man turned to him, Bolan yelled, "Incoming missile. Get out now!"

Liao scrabbled at the door handle and got it open as Bolan hit the ground on the other side of the rear door. He made sure Liao was scrambling away from the truck before running himself.

As he did, he saw the bright flash of a missile launch about a mile away and shouted, "Hit the dirt!" as he dived to the ground.

Two seconds later the world exploded.

CHAPTER FORTY-FOUR

"Jesus H., tell me you got something!"

Brognola was nearly beside himself, sleeves rolled up, his latest cigar mangled into a wet, brown stub dangling from his lips.

Everybody around Tokaido had held their breath when he'd seen the antitank missile being set up. The big Fed had overridden all protocols and not only had him patched through, but turned the phone on so that Bolan would get the message. "If we fail, he's dead, and it won't matter anyway," he'd said at the time.

Tokaido said he thought he'd seen two people leave the truck before the massive explosion, but he wasn't sure. The truck had been obliterated, the antiarmor warhead blowing it into a twisted, charred sculpture of burning metal and rubber.

"I'm still trying to raise him," the young hacker said. "If he's stunned, there won't be much we can do over his phone."

As he said that, the view of the destroyed truck fuzzed with static, then vanished in a sea of black-and-white snow. "Satellite's out of range."

"When's the next one due?" Price asked.

"Not for thirty-four minutes," Kurtzman answered.

Tokaido established the call link again.

"Could there be some sort of interference messing with the signal?"

"Maybe, but doubtful." Kurtzman grunted. "Bouncing a signal directly off a satellite is pretty damn good for accuracy. If he isn't answering…there's probably only one of two reasons."

"Well, it could be that the phone was damaged in the blast, too," Tokaido pointed out.

"Okay, three reasons," Kurtzman said.

"I sure hope it's one of the first two," Brognola added quietly.

CHAPTER FORTY-FIVE

Mack Bolan clawed his way back to consciousness, which consisted of a roaring headache and a ringing in his ears that felt as though someone was rapping a hammer directly against his skull.

Where...explosion...warning...

He felt a wave of heat coming from something nearby and heard a faint crackling under the bell tone reverberating through his head. Swallowing through a parched throat, he opened his eyes. The world swirled crazily around him for a moment and he squeezed them shut for a moment.

Liao! Have to get up. Keep moving...

Forcing his eyes open again, Bolan blinked until the landscape around him calmed down. He took a deep breath, than another, then felt around him until his fingers closed on the comforting stock of the machine gun he'd liberated from the truck as he'd escaped.

Pulling it close, he checked it out, finding it in perfect working order. With the weapon charged and ready, he sat up, pointing it at any potential enemies. His head spun and he gritted his teeth, keeping his eyes open until the sensation passed. The ringing in his ears was fading, although he was sure it would stay with him for some time.

Feeling something flex and crack in his hip pocket, he pulled out his last smartphone to find the screen shattered. It was useless to him now, but he shoved it back in his pocket, still aware he couldn't leave any evidence of his presence behind.

There was no one around them—yet. Bolan was sure the guards would arrive any minute now, if only to confirm their kill.

"Liao?"

A low groan was the only answer he heard. Looking around, he saw a sprawled form a few yards away. Keeping an eye on the road, Bolan got to his feet and walked over to the other man.

The defector had definitely looked better. Unaware of the shock wave accompanying an explosion, he had apparently still been upright when the truck had blown up and the force had knocked him off his feet. He moaned softly and then shuddered, and Bolan saw why.

A jagged shard of shrapnel was embedded in his right thigh. It wasn't bleeding much, which Bolan took as a good sign. If the metal had sliced through the femoral artery, he would have been dead already.

"I can't take it out now," Bolan muttered. He knelt by the other man, rolled him over onto his back and patted his cheek. "Liao? Liao! Wake up!"

"It is Monday already? Just five more minutes…" Liao's eyes fluttered open. "Where am I…and why does my leg hurt so much?"

"You're hurt, so just lie still," Bolan began, but Liao lifted his head and gasped when he saw the metal dart sticking out of his leg.

"What is that?"

"Shrapnel from the exploding truck. Listen to me," Bolan said. "We're getting a new ride, but I'm going to need your help, all right?"

"What can I do like this?"

Bolan pulled a pistol from his belt. "Act as bait."

TWO MINUTES AND twenty-eight seconds later Bolan watched down the barrel of the machine gun as the 6x6 lumbered off the side of the road about two hundred yards away. Once again he wished he had a sniper rifle, but this weapon would have to do.

Four men spilled from the vehicle and approached the now smoldering wreckage of the truck. On seeing Liao's crumpled form, a shout went up and two of the men advanced to investigate him, while two others stayed back.

Bolan took a rough sighting on the pair in back, then on the approaching two, knowing he was going to have to make some of the best shots of his life in the next few seconds.

I hope Liao remembers to stay down, he thought as he dropped the sights on the nearest of his targets.

One of the lead pair stretched out a boot and nudged Liao's motionless body. Making sure the second man was covering him, he slung his rifle and bent to turn him over. This was the part where everything depended on Liao.

"Don't shoot the man right next to you. I'll take care of him," Bolan had told him. "You have to kill the guy who's going to be covering you, understand? If you don't, we're both dead. So get your sights on him and don't stop firing until you're empty, got it?"

It was an incredibly risky plan, and Bolan hated putting the man in this position, but they needed an element of surprise for their trap to work. Liao had nodded at the time, but now was when they were going to find out whether he could really do it. His first shot was the signal for the slaughter to begin. The moment his body rolled over, he raised his pistol and squeezed the trigger at the man standing less than five yards away.

Anticipating that first shot, Bolan squeezed the machine gun's trigger. The QBB-95 roared and several rounds tore into the body of the man checking on Liao. Before he fell—conveniently on top of Liao—Bolan quickly adjusted his aim and sprayed the rear guard pair with a short burst. At that range, there were more than enough bullets flying to knock both men down.

Now came the tricky part. Sighting in on the driver's side of the truck cab, Bolan sent a burst into it, shattering the side window and stopping the engine from turning over.

Two men jumped from the back and sprayed fire wildly into the darkness as they ran for the front cab. Bolan cut them both down with short bursts, then realized that he might have the same problem on the other side. Rising, he limped to the truck's far side in time to see a man climb into the passenger seat. Throwing the heavy gun to his shoulder, Bolan put a burst through the front windshield, smashing the heavy glass and spraying blood across the interior.

Finally, everything was silent. Even so, he headed to Liao first and made sure he was okay. The man was still lying under the motionless body of the guard who'd been checking on him. The front of his stolen uniform was soaked in blood. Bolan shoved the body off and eased the empty pistol out of his hand.

"Did I get him?" the former politician asked.

Bolan glanced back at the very dead body of the second guard, his chest covered with blood from several bullet holes. "Yeah, you did good. Stay here. I just need to clear the truck and then we're getting out of here."

"Don't worry. I'm not going anywhere fast," Liao replied.

Grabbing an assault rifle from the dead man, the Executioner headed for the truck and cleared the cab first, pulling out the two bodies and tossing them to the ground. Once that was done, he walked to the back, clearing each area underneath around the tires in case someone was hiding beneath the truck, then whipped around the corner to check the cargo area.

It was empty, save for a still smoking HJ-8 antitank launcher tube lying on the cargo bed next to a box of missiles. Bolan checked the four-pack of warheads and found one missing.

"Time to go," he muttered as he carefully jumped down and limped back to Liao.

"Okay, new transportation has been secured," he said as he hauled the other man up and slung his arm around his shoulder. "We've got a long way to go, so let's get moving."

"Fine by me," Liao replied, exhausted by the flight and his injury.

"Just a few more hours and we'll be safe," Bolan stated.

"Should we remove the metal in my leg?"

Bolan looked at it. "It's not bleeding now, and if we take it out, it might start to. It's best to leave it right now. Besides, it'll leave a hell of a scar for you to impress your kids with."

"Yes, but my wife will probably kill me for getting hurt in the first place..." Still, Liao smiled as the two weary, battered men trudged over to the large truck and Bolan helped him climb aboard. The Chinese man only cried out once as he got himself settled. Bolan worked his way up and into the driver's seat, then started the truck, which roared to life, and put it in gear.

"Now let's get the hell out of China."

FOUR MINUTES AFTER leaving the prison camp the Harbin helicopter came upon the wreckage of the small truck and several bodies lying on the ground.

Fang's fingers tightened on his assault rifle as they landed nearby, and this time he was the first to jump out, running straight to the smoking debris. The truck had been utterly destroyed, but he saw no evidence of any bodies inside.

Turning, he saw General Zhao and the rest of the squad policing the area, paying special attention to the various bodies scattered around. The MSS agent rejoined Zhao as his sergeant reported what they'd found.

"All were killed with small arms fire. From the burst patterns, it was most likely the machine gun taken from the other truck, except this one—" he pointed at one body with a chest full of red "—who was killed by pistol fire at relatively close range."

"So, where'd they go?" Fang asked. "They couldn't have just disappeared out here."

"No, judging from the tire marks, they killed the prison guards and stole their truck," the sergeant replied. "We can't be more than two to three minutes behind them."

"Then let's go!" Fang ran back to the helicopter, the bitter tang of defeat turning to the sweet taste of victory.

Oh, yes, I will have you both, he thought as the rest of the men climbed aboard and the helicopter took off. And then you both shall pay.

CHAPTER FORTY-SIX

The military truck was never built for speed. Bolan was finding that out the hard way as he wrestled the 6x6 vehicle down the rough dirt road at a bone-rattling 53 miles per hour. Every bump caused a jolt of pain to shoot up his injured leg, and he could only imagine how Liao, who had soon turned white-faced as they'd torn down the road, had to have felt.

Still, every mile they put between them and the prison was one more closer to Mongolia and escape. Despite the close calls and near-death experiences they'd both had in the past hour, Bolan was starting to feel good about the possibility of making it to the border and through the arid wastelands of southern Mongolia to the airport.

Those hopes were dashed by two gouts of flame that bracketed the road ahead of the truck, sending up huge fireballs and shooting dirt several dozen yards into the air.

Bolan slammed on the brakes, sending Liao crashing into the dashboard of the truck with a scream of pain. Both men stared as a military helicopter, its missile launch tubes still smoking, dropped into the road in front of them.

"Zhang Liao and unidentified American, you are hereby ordered to turn off the engine of your vehicle and come out with your hands up!"

Bolan looked over at Liao, who stared back at him with bright eyes out of a dirt-and-smoke-smudged face. "Feel like surrendering?"

Liao grabbed a loaded and charged assault rifle from the floor beside him. "Hell, no!"

The Executioner slammed the vehicle into gear and hit the gas. They shot straight at the helicopter, with Liao spraying the front canopy with bullets. It barely managed to rise into the air before the cab of the truck would have hit it, and Bolan and Liao raced underneath, gaining speed as they roared down the road again.

In the rearview mirror Bolan saw the helicopter turning in midair to give chase. "Can you drive?" he shouted over the wind rushing into the cab.

"Yes, but where are you going?" Liao asked, taking the wheel as Bolan headed into the cargo area.

"I have one last present for them," he replied. "Try to give me at least two minutes, then stop when you don't have any other choice."

"All right!" Zhang wrestled the truck into a higher gear and mashed the gas pedal to the floor, making the truck leap ahead as bullets chewed into the road on either side of it. "But whatever you're going to do, do it fast, okay?"

CHAPTER FORTY-SEVEN

"Careful, damn it!" Fang said as he watched the stream of bullets from the Harbin's two 23 mm cannons kick up dirt on either side of fleeing vehicle. "The truck is to be disabled, not shot to pieces!"

"Yes, sir!" the pilot replied tightly. After they had almost killed the helicopter pilot and nearly rammed the aircraft, the general's man had tried shooting the truck's tires out, but that was proving nearly impossible.

"Deshi, the pilot cannot perform miracles," General Zhao said. "He's doing the best he can."

"And if either of those two men are killed by his actions, he will have to answer to the ministry as to why," Fang said, glaring at his friend.

"I am sure it won't come to that," the general replied, then hit his headset. "Fire for effect again, but directly in front of them this time." He turned to Fang. "Sometimes, more direct measures are called for."

Within seconds the missiles were armed and ready, and at the general's signal, the pilot launched them directly into the road not more than fifty meters ahead of the truck. This second pair of explosions almost knocked the vehicle off the road and it slewed wildly to the left before skidding to a stop.

"Drop us right in front of them, and do not move, even if he drives straight at us!" Fang shouted.

On the general's nod, the pilot made the helicopter descend until they were less than ten meters off the ground, about thirty meters away from the truck. A huge cloud of dust rose in the downdraft from the rotors and Fang squinted to make out the truck as he requested the loudspeakers be activated again.

"Zhang Liao and unidentified American, you are…" He paused as a blurry form appeared on the top of the truck, holding a long tube. Even at that distance, Fang swore he saw the man's cold blue eyes bore into his as he adjusted the thing he was carrying. "What's—"

The general recognized what the American was holding sooner. "Antitank missile! Climb! Climb!"

Those were the last words Fang ever heard. The long tube spewed forth something that raced straight at his face and then the world erupted in a millisecond-long burst of fire before going completely and utterly black.

EPILOGUE

Jack Grimaldi paced back and forth on the tarmac outside the Gulfstream jet in the early morning light, worry knitting his features into a mask of concern.

It had been several hours since anyone had had contact with Bolan and repeated attempts to raise him had all gone unanswered. With the Liao family here, neither Grimaldi nor Charlie Mott could mount any sort of exploratory trip to see if they could find the two men—not that they had any inkling about where to look in the first place.

The Stony Man pilot was determined to stick it out here as long as he could, but Price's inquiries about the status of the Gulfstream airplane were getting more difficult to put off.

Gonna be hell to pay when I get back, he thought. Even so, it was worth it—especially if he brought Sarge back with him. *When* he brought him back with him.

"Hey, Jack."

He looked up to see Mott standing in the jet's doorway, pointing down the tarmac. "Someone's coming this way."

Grimaldi squinted in the dim light from the rising sun, his furrowed brow relaxing as the figure of two men became visible in the distance. "Get the preflight done and the engines warmed up, Charlie," he called over his shoulder as he broke into a run. "We're getting the hell out of here the second those two are aboard."

He ran toward the pair, who were limping slowly toward him. He slowed as he got closer, then finally stopped as they approached.

Both men looked as if they had both gone through hell. Covered in dust, two pairs of steely, determined eyes—one brown, one blue—stared back at him from faces covered in blood, dirt and smoke. Their clothes were the same: torn, stinking and covered in a dark mess of blood and dirt.

"Jesus, Sarge, what happened to you?" he asked as he helped take the Chinese man's weight.

"There was a bit of disagreement about our leaving the country," Bolan said through dry, cracked lips. "In the end, we had to make a forceful diplomatic point."

"Well, I assume they listened," Grimaldi said as they headed toward the Gulfstream, its jet engines already turning over.

"Didn't…have…much choice," the Chinese man said, sharing a weary yet triumphant smile with Bolan.

"All right, then, let's get both of you aboard and get into the air," Grimaldi said. "We'll get you both cleaned up and your wounds looked at, and get some food into you both, as well. And, Mr. Liao, there are some people aboard who are very anxious to see you."

THIRTY MINUTES LATER BOLAN, showered, shaved and wearing a clean flight suit from the jet's stores, looked in on the reunited Liao family with Grimaldi.

The reunion had been earsplitting, with screams and sobs of joy echoing through the cabin. Bolan had watched it all from the end of the room, after making sure Liao had gotten treatment for his injuries before getting any help for himself.

Now he stared at the family, all of whom were sleeping on the huge bed in the master bedroom—father, mother and children all snuggled up together, happy, peaceful smiles on their faces.

"Warms the heart, doesn't it, Sarge?" Grimaldi asked.

Bolan turned to him and nodded. "Sure does."

He held out an odd device to the pilot. "Make sure Bear and Akira get this when we touch down, will you?"

Grimaldi stared at the small game console in his hands. "Um, okay. I assume it's important, right?"

"Along with that family in there, it's the reason I almost got killed a half dozen times over the past forty-eight hours," Bolan replied. "Now, if you'll excuse me, I have a quick call to make, then I'm going to sack out in one of these fine chairs and sleep until we get to the States."

The Executioner walked into a tiny office space and sank into the soft leather chair there. Picking up the satellite phone, he dialed a number that would be rerouted through several cutouts until it reached its true destination. When the person on the other end picked up, he smiled.

"This is Striker reporting in... How are you, Barbara?"

* * * * *

COMING SOON FROM

GOLD EAGLE®

Available October 6, 2015

GOLD EAGLE EXECUTIONER®
UNCUT TERROR – *Don Pendleton*

Mack Bolan sets out to even the score when a legendary Kremlin assassin slaughters an American defector before he can be repatriated. His first target leads him to discover a Russian scheme to crash the Western economy and kill hundreds of innocent people. Only one man can stop it—the Executioner.

GOLD EAGLE STONY MAN®
DEATH MINUS ZERO – *Don Pendleton*

Washington goes on full alert when Chinese operatives kidnap the creator of a vital US defense system. While Phoenix Force tracks the missing scientist, Able Team uncovers a plot to take over the system's mission control. Now both teams must stop America's enemies from holding the country hostage.

GOLD EAGLE SUPERBOLAN™
DEAD RECKONING – *Don Pendleton*

A US consulate is bombed, its staff mercilessly killed. The terrorists scatter to hideouts around the globe, but Mack Bolan hunts them down three by three. When the last one vanishes, the world's leaders are caught in the crosshairs and the Executioner must stop the terrorists' global deathblow.

They'd almost made it to the river, with roughly another block or two to go. Bolan had swiveled in his seat, bringing up his AKMS carbine, thankful that the Audi's right-hand drive gave him a better angle firing backward than the shooter in the Mercedes-Benz Vaneo had.

That wouldn't matter in the least to Bolan if his opposition scored a lucky hit.

Behind the Mercedes-Benz, he glimpsed a motorcycle, keeping pace. Bolan had seen a bike outside Alek Nimeiry's shop, but they were everywhere around Kassala, nothing remarkable about them until they turned up in the middle of a running firefight through downtown.

So, make it *five* shooters whom he and Grimaldi might have to deal with, if the biker weighed in on the other side.

"I see the river, Sarge."

It lay in front of them, maybe two hundred fifty yards across to reach the other side, with waste ground stretching out another couple hundred yards between a road that paralleled the river and its eastern bank. The soil looked solid.

"Can you drive on that?" Bolan asked.

"It's worth a try," Grimaldi replied.